THE
HOUSEBOAT
DETECTIVE

A Jake Sommers Mystery

Jay Allan Storey

Jay Allan Storey/Non-Sequitur Publishing
566 - 1771 Robson Street
Vancouver, BC V6G 1C9

Website: www.jayallanstorey.com
Email: jayallanstorey@shaw.ca

- 4 -

Houseboat Detective/Jay Allan Storey. -- 1st ed.
ISBN: 978-1-7382817-5-6

BOOKS BY JAY ALLAN STOREY

Eldorado (2014)
The Arx (2015)
The Black Heart of the Station (2017)
Vita Aeterna (2018)
Black Heart : Arrival (2020)
Black Heart : Origin (2020)
Vita Aeterna : Outliers (2022)
Tucker vs. the Apocalypse (2023)
The Houseboat Detective (2024)

DEDICATION

Dedicated to the beautiful city of Victoria, BC, Canada.

CONTENTS

I

MORNING

Rule #4: A good detective has an analytic mind. He loves to solve puzzles, and is driven to know the answers.
- Shadow Mac's Comprehensive Guide to Private Investigation

When Jake Sommers emerged from his slumber and opened his eyes, he was immediately sorry.

A pile-driver-like throb was hammering the inside of his skull, each pulse accompanied by searing pain. His mouth tasted like a used gym sock, and the light from a gap in the curtains across the room drilled into his left eyeball like a laser beam. Something unholy was lurking in the depths of his gut waiting to find its way out, and he wasn't sure which exit it was planning to use.

Disjointed images of last night swam through his crippled brain: throwing back lines of shots amid a cheering crowd at the Lame Duck tavern a few blocks away; stumbling like a hunted animal through darkened and suddenly unfamiliar streets searching for home; staggering along a swaying dock; tripping on the sill of his front door and falling on his face; then struggling out of his clothes, climbing into bed and passing out.

As he fought desperately to return to unconsciousness, he realized that something outside had woken him, and was likely to continue keeping him awake. A series of deep thuds were echoing from the direction of his front door. He lay still, praying that the percussive booms weaving in and out of sync with his own jolts of pain would fade away—but they just kept coming.

Worse still, as if to announce the event, each new bout of hammering was preceded by the world tilting sideways, while Jake's brain and the contents of his stomach inconveniently remained stationary.

It was at that moment that he became aware of three vital facts simultaneously. First, he remembered that he lived on a houseboat (hence the tilting). Second, he realized that a person was pounding on his front door (he gathered this from the thuds and muffled shouts outside). Third, he understood that every time that person stepped from the dock to his doorstep for another cycle of pounding, his home was going to sway like an overweight hula dancer. If the situation continued, he was definitely going to lose whatever he'd eaten for dinner last night.

Admiring his success at keeping that dinner in its place long enough to drag himself out of bed, he staggered down the ladder from the loft where he slept, across his living area, and up a small set of stairs to his front door.

He peered through the peep-hole.

"Shit," he said, seeing the fish-eye-distorted image of a head with a ruddy red face, a wispy beard, and a sparse growth of ginger hair. The body it was attached to was dressed in its familiar plaid jacket, baggy jeans, and gumboots.

The pounder was Jake's neighbour, Bert McCluskey. The vessel tilted forward, Jake's view expanding so that McCluskey's nose filled the entire bulb, as McCluskey stepped aboard for a new torrent of blows. Jake's body twitched as each thud, now centimeters away, resonated in his frontal lobes. The world then tilted back, the image receding, as his neighbour stepped to the dock.

Jake unlatched the door and swung it open.

"Christ!" McCluskey said, shielding his eyes with his right arm.

Jake felt a draft, and looked down... As proud as he'd been of his observational skills moments earlier, one fact had failed to register—he was completely naked.

"Jeez, Sommers," McCluskey said. "What if I was a Jehovah's Witness or somethin'?"

Jake shrugged, still half asleep. "Then you'd get an education."

"You look like shit."

"You woke me up to tell me that?" Jake finally thought to grab a baseball cap from a hook by the door and cover as much as he could of his lower regions.

"No," McCluskey said; "I woke you up to tell you to come and get Gordon in line." He nodded to his right. "He's sleeping on Maggie's deck patio again. He dumped a half-eaten fish on there too—icing on the cake. She's waving her shotgun around. I wouldn't care, but she might shoot me."

Jake fought to ignore the evil stew bubbling somewhere deep in his gut, waiting to burst forth like the Antichrist from the bowels of the earth.

"Since when is Gordon my responsibility."

"Since you're the only one around here who doesn't want to wring his slimy neck. Come and get him before Maggie shoots him or something."

Jake lost his balance and staggered sideways, momentarily dropping the hat. He continued to sway as he peered over at Maggie's houseboat on the other side of the dock. The middle-aged, curly-haired woman came to the front door, glanced at his naked form, gasped, and ran back inside.

Thirteen minutes later, dressed and pumped full of ibuprofen, Jake stepped aboard Maggie's vessel and knocked on her door. She scowled as she pointed toward the aft section. In his hand was the object he generally used to entice Gordon back to his place—a dead fish. He breathed through his mouth, hoping to keep the stench of it from accomplishing what the swaying of his vessel had so far failed to do.

Gordon was lying on his side in his usual spot—the patch of morning sun on Maggie's aft patio. The two hundred fifty kilogram California sea lion casually waved a flipper to ward off a bothersome fly. Gordon lazily opened one eye as he heard Jake approaching, contemplating whether it was an event worth moving for. The eye lazily closed again.

A patch of slime and scales stained the deck in front of Gordon's head. Jake wasn't sure how long it had been since the sea lion had eaten, and whether the tactic he had in mind would work.

He approached and waved the fish in front of Gordon's nose. Gordon opened his eyes and sniffed once at it, but didn't seem interested. Cautiously, Jake edged the head a few centimeters closer. So quickly that Jake had no chance to react, the sea lion's head shot up and snatched it from his hand.

"Shit!" Jake yelled.

Still fighting to breathe through his mouth to avoid the fish's, and now Gordon's, smell, he grabbed the tail of the slimy delicacy and began a tug-of-war with his giant nemesis.

Gordon grunted and moaned, tugging on the head, still hoping not to have to go to the trouble of changing position. Jake put his full body weight into the fight, his fingers slipping on the slimy scales. Something gave way and Jake fell back, landing on his ass on the patio deck. He looked down at his hands and found he was holding the tail half of the fish—the head was in Gordon's mouth. The sea lion munched contentedly, still showing no interest in going anywhere.

Jake waited several agonizing minutes for Gordon to swallow his prize, then approached again, farther back this time, holding the remainder of the fish as close as he dared to Gordon's nose. The sea lion honked and blew out a breath, spraying Jake with foul air and fish guts.

Through a heroic application of will power, Jake successfully kept down last night's dinner and held firm. Gordon finally rolled over onto his stomach, and began to crawl in his direction.

Jake backed away, still holding the precious remnant. He put his left foot back and down. There was nothing there. He glanced behind him. He was at the edge of the deck. Panicked, he brought his foot back and waved his arms in the air, fighting to keep from falling into the water, with Gordon still lumbering toward him.

He finally righted himself and jumped down to the dock. To his relief, Gordon followed, waddling down the gangplank. The giant beast had finally achieved some kind of momentum. Jake considered just leading the sea lion out to the end of the pier; he didn't want Gordon around his place either. But he knew that, if left on the dock, Gordon would just head back to Maggie's as soon as he finished his breakfast. Jake resigned himself to leading him onto his own vessel, where he would likely hang out for the rest of the day.

Gordon clumsily followed as Jake staggered onto the forward deck of his own houseboat and backed toward the aft section, waving the half-shredded carcass in front of him. After what seemed like an eternity he was finally within throwing distance. He tossed the disgusting remnant on the deck and watched as Gordon crawled the last few meters, flopped down, and began to devour it.

Jake waited until the sea lion had vacuumed up most of his prize and put his head down for an extended stay. Finally, he straightened up and smiled, dusting his hands together and congratulating himself for keeping it together through the entire ordeal.

He was about to turn away when a loud 'bbrrraapp!' issued from under his guest's backside. Jake's eyes bugged out of his head. He spun around and took a giant step, preparing to run for it, but he was too late—it was Armageddon.

Gordon had farted.

Before Jake could take another step the evil stench had begun wafting into his nasal passages.

Why had he been fighting it, Jake considered?

It was as inevitable as the sun rising or the tide ebbing in the harbour. As certain as day following night, winter following autumn. He dropped to his knees and studied the patch of oil lapping against a tar-stained pylon as he hung his head over the swirling waters and emptied his guts once and for all.

During a momentary break from his exertions, he felt the deck under him move, and heard the tap of a footstep. He lifted his head.

"Is this a bad time?" a female voice said behind him.

II

A CLIENT

Rule #16: Study the subject's clothing and accessories, walk, gait, and stride, posture, and idiosyncratic movements.
- Shadow Mac's Comprehensive Guide to Private Investigation

Jake froze. He watched the disjointed fragments of his reflection bob in the rippling water and the ring formed by the former contents of his gut slowly drift out into the harbour. Reflected above his broken image was a blinding, curving splash of red. He wiped his mouth on his sleeve, and turned to look behind him.

A woman stood on the deck a meter or so away. She was young, probably in her early twenties, and exceedingly beautiful. Long ash-blond hair tumbled in waves over her bare shoulders. She was wearing a tight, knitted, candy-apple-red dress that barely reached her thighs. The lipstick on her full lips matched her dress, as did the polish on her fingernails and the spiked heels she was wearing.

He'd meant to answer her, but all that came out was "Uhgggh". A pair of seagulls swooped toward the ring he'd left in the water, looking for a meal.

He staggered to his feet, tucked in his shirt, which somehow had come out, smoothed it down with both hands, wiped off the remnants of dead fish guts courtesy of Gordon, and hoisted up his jeans.

"You're Jake Sommers?" the woman asked, smiling.

"Unfortunately," he managed to croak.

"Shall I come back later?" she said. "I'm sorry to bother you, but I really need your help."

If it were anyone else he would have brushed them off and staggered inside to pursue further unconsciousness.

"Sure," he said, squinting in the bright sunlight, his head still throbbing. Gordon grunted and waved a flipper at him. He considered inviting her to sit at the table on the deck, but he didn't think he could survive another emission from Gordon's interior. He guided her toward the door of his living area.

"I like your friend," the woman smiled as they walked, nodding at the sea lion.

"Gordon? He's no friend of mine," Jake said. He put an arm out and stopped her as they reached the door. "Could you wait here for just a second?"

He stumbled through it and down the stairs into the living room. Stabbing jolts of pain continued to pulse through his skull as he gathered up the dirty clothes that were strewn around the floor and the furniture. He tossed the paper plate with the half-eaten pizza slice in the garbage, quickly washed the fish stench from his face and hands, and threw a dish cloth over the dirty dishes piled in the sink.

He turned to survey his work. The place still looked like the aftermath of a hurricane, but he'd managed to mitigate the impression from that of a Category Five to something closer to a Category Three.

Resigned that it wasn't going to look much better without the aid of an explosive device, he returned to the doorway, half expecting the woman to be gone. To his surprise she was still standing there, her beauty that much more stunning in contrast with the pigsty that was his home.

"We can talk here," he called up to her, gesturing with one hand along the stairs. "Watch your step."

The spiked heel of her right foot moved down to rest on the first step. Her incredible thighs appeared below the top of the doorway, and she reached down a hand. He swallowed hard as he took it and led her downward into his home.

He laid a clean towel on one of the bench seats of his dining nook, stood back, and swept a hand toward it. She sat, putting her small red clutch purse on her lap. He sat across from her.

"I like your place," she said, turning her head to scan the crooked pictures, dusty knick-knacks and miscellaneous garbage crowding the room.

"I know it's a mess," he said, "I've been meaning to clean it up—"

"It's charming," she interrupted him. "I wouldn't change a thing."

He cringed, aware of how distant any description of this place was from 'charming'. He put it out of his mind.

"W...what can I do for you?" he asked, still not convinced he was actually awake.

"I saw your ad in Kijiji," she said.

"Ad?" That confirmed it. He was definitely still asleep, and having another one of his twisted dreams.

"For detective work," she said.

"What?"

She opened her purse and fished around for a few seconds. Her hand emerged with a folded up printed page.

"Here," she said, unfolding it and handing it to him.

He blinked a few times, trying to jump-start both his brain and his blurred vision. His hand shook as he held up the printout.

'Professional & Discrete', read the title. 'Jake Sommers—Private Investigator—available immediately. Many years' experience. Former intelligence operative. Reasonable rates. No job too small.'

Underneath was a blurry picture of Jake. In the picture, his eyes were partially closed, his hair stuck out in every direction, and he looked half asleep. In fact, it occurred to him that in the picture, he looked pretty much the way he looked and felt right now. At the bottom was a phone number and Jake's address.

"What?" he said again as he read the page.

"Is something wrong?" she asked. "That *is* you, right?"

"Yeah, that's me," he said. He stood up, holding the paper. "Sorry—could you excuse me for a minute."

She nodded.

The paper in hand, he climbed the steps to the outer deck, glancing back to confirm that Gordon hadn't moved, jumped down to the dock, and strode toward the houseboat on the other side.

The curtain in his neighbour's window fluttered as Jake approached. He stepped onto the gunwale and pounded on the door. A few seconds later McCluskey's door opened and he stepped outside.

Jake held up the paper. "You did this?"

McCluskey said nothing.

Jake held it flat in front of him and read out the copy. McCluskey remained silent.

Jake shook the page at him. "What the hell is wrong with you?"

McCluskey finally shrugged. "Somebody had to do something. You're pissing your life away playing piano in that bar. Anyway, does that mean you got a client already?"

Jake crushed the paper in his fist. "How can I have a client when I don't have a business? And where the hell did you get that repulsive picture."

McCluskey smiled. "You didn't object at the time. Mind you, I think you were about to pass out. I told you to smile—I can't help it if you never listen to me."

"What I do with my life is my affair," Jake said. "Just keep your big ugly nose out of it."

McCluskey shrugged again. "You don't have to thank me. Anything to help a friend."

"I could get sued or something—for false advertising."

"Haven't you looked around you lately?" McCluskey asked, nodding toward the city. "We live in a pretend world. Pop-stars on the radio pretend they can sing. The musicians pretend they can play, the politicians pretend they can govern... Hell, the goddamned doctors pretend they can heal. Why shouldn't you pretend you're a detective? Anyway, you were some kind of cop in the army, weren't you? Basically the same thing."

"I was in training to be an Intelligence Operator. I sat behind a desk most of the time. I didn't even graduate."

"There you go."

Jake turned and checked behind him. The woman was standing outside his open door. He waved to her and smiled. She waved back. He gestured dismissively at his neighbour, and turned to head back to his vessel. As he climbed aboard, the woman descended the stairs into his living room. He returned and again sat across from her. A rumble deep in his gut told him that there was more internal disturbance to come.

"Look," he said to her, "Somebody's just playing a joke on me. I'm not really a detective."

"But your ad..." she said, confused.

"Maybe in a parallel universe," he answered, "not in this one—sorry."

She pouted her lips. "You're just trying to brush me off."

"What? No," he said. "What are you talking about? It's the truth. It's my neighbour—" he nodded his head toward McCluskey's houseboat. "He's just messing with me."

She pouted again, and her hands twisted the purse they were holding. "Please—I really need your help." She was achingly beautiful.

"I just told you," he said, annoyed. "I'm not a detective. There's lots of *real* private detectives out there. Google them, or check the Better Business Bureau, or whatever people do nowadays."

"What made you pick me, anyway?" he asked, partially unfolding the slip with the ad in his hand and cringing once more at the ridiculous photograph.

"I didn't choose you," she answered, suddenly animated. She raised her hands up to the heavens. "The universe declared that we should work together."

Jake was in no shape for this conversation.

She removed another folded sheet of paper from her purse. "It's all here in black and white." She opened it and pointed at a list of scribbled notes on the page. "Our physical, intellectual, and spiritual planes mesh perfectly."

"Huh?" he said.

She slid the page across the table and rotated it for him to analyze. "The numbers don't lie."

There were several diagrams drawn on the page, sets of intersecting lines that looked like Tic-Tac-Toe games. Instead of the expected X's and O's, the gaps between the lines contained sets of numbers. His vision was still blurred as he scanned the diagrams. He could make out his first and last name, and his address, followed by multiple rows of numerical calculations.

Below what he assumed was 'his' diagram, was a list of written comments. He shook his head to clear it, wincing at the pulse of pain that followed, and finally grasped what she was saying.

"What—Astrology or something?" Confused enough by the events of the past half-hour, this was one more wrinkle his muddled psyche couldn't process.

"Numerology," she said. "The ancient art of divination. I'll need your birth date to complete the calculations, but it's clear that you and I are nearly a perfect match."

Jake blinked and sat with his mouth open. If he was still asleep, he should have woken up by now.

"According to this," she said, pointing at the diagram, "your Soul Urge is a six, meaning you are creative and resourceful. You also possess innate intuition and strength—just the qualities I believe will be necessary for the task I have in mind."

She looked up at him and smiled. "Your Outer Expression Number is three. The bearer of that number has need for attention, and self-expression. You are obviously a very creative person—a musician or an artist—an entertainer."

Jake raised his eyebrows.

She continued. "All of which reinforces my view that you are the ideal candidate. Your Home Number is also a three, which is very auspicious, particularly when combined with your other attributes."

Her finger moved down excitedly to more words and numbers on the page. "See, your Destiny Number is a one. That means you're ruled by the sun. You're a leader, you're independent, and think outside the box..." She gave him a chastising look. "On the other hand, you're stubborn, and get angry when things don't go your way."

She took back the page and eyed it with satisfaction. "And, most importantly, your attributes are in perfect sync with my own."

"Anyway," she smiled, folding it up and returning it to her purse, "the others all looked so stodgy. And your expression in the picture is so intense."

"I was half passed-out."

"Your manager said you had a lot of life experience. He said you were very deep."

Jake opened the page with the ad. It finally occurred to him that the contact number written there was McCluskey's.

"Manager?" he said. "Private detectives don't have managers."

She laughed. It was a little-girl laugh, completely out of character for her composed, refined bearing. It was like there was another person in there, one that only came out rarely, and usually by accident.

Jake was blessed, or was it cursed, with a little voice that woke from some deep fissure inside his brain and made itself known at critical points in his life. In one way, the voice was a blessing because, in his experience, its advice had unfailingly been correct. In another, it was a curse because, at least up until now, he'd never paid any attention to it.

The voice arose now, accompanied by the image of a flashing red warning sign saying: Danger! Danger! As usual, he ignored it.

"You've got some kind of accent," he said, changing the subject to give his grey matter a chance to shift into gear. It wasn't so much an accent as a fine pronunciation of every word. And almost imperceptibly, she sometimes placed emphasis on the wrong syllable.

"You're very observant," she said, clearly flattered. "Yes, I grew up in France, near Lyon."

The whole idea was ridiculous. What was he was doing here, sitting across from this woman he didn't know, contemplating a task he wasn't even remotely qualified to perform—and generally allowing the swirling winds of chance to bat him around like an errant beach ball?

McCluskey, he thought again, clenching his fist.

He studied the woman's face: mid-twenties, hooded eyes that implied haughtiness, full lips. A smattering of freckles around her slightly turned-up nose lent an almost adolescent cuteness that was at odds with her aristocratic features. The light from a hanging stained glass ornament outside the window bathed her face in a moving rainbow of colours.

"Evangeline Sirkants," she said, reaching an impeccably manicured hand across the table and shaking his. Her touch was soft and warm.

"Can I call you Jake?" she said.

"Sure," he said, envisioning himself circling the event horizon of some massive black hole before plunging headlong into the void, powerless to stop the descent.

"You must help me," she said. "The numbers have chosen you above all the others."

He shut his eyes for a few seconds. He imagined himself looking back on this moment in some distant future and cursing the decision he was about to make.

"Well, you took the trouble to come here," he said. "And you did all those calculations. I guess the least I can do is hear your story."

III

EVANGELINE'S STORY

Rule #28: A good detective makes the effort to understand the reality of a contact's work life, empathizes with them, and uses that knowledge to develop a rapport and maintain contact.
- Shadow Mac's Comprehensive Guide to Private Investigation

Evangeline tossed her head back and her shining hair tumbled around her shoulders. "Our family moved to Canada when I was a young girl. I was an only child. At first, we lived quietly in Quebec City, where my father worked as an importer, specializing in jewelry from Europe. He worked hard, and over the years I was growing up he built the tiny shop into a multi-million dollar business.

"We eventually moved from our dingy apartment to a fabulous mansion in Haute-Ville, in one of the best parts of town. I had everything: jewels, designer fashions, exotic cars, the best schools. But as our fortunes improved, my father spent less and less of his time at home. My mother began to accuse him of having an affair, which he always denied. Still, he was obsessed with his business, and for the limited amount of time that he spent at home, he and my mother fought constantly."

She removed a tissue from her purse and wiped away a tear.

"Occasionally they would attempt to make up, for my sake and for the sake of their marriage, but the good times never seemed to last. One night, when I was nineteen, they arranged to have dinner together. My mother took me aside to explain that they were going to review their relationship and perhaps reconcile. I was overjoyed at the prospect of no longer having to deal with the constant stress of their accusations and bad feelings."

Her features hardened as she spoke. "That night, neither of them came home, and I learned the next day that their car had driven over an embankment and into a nearby river. Both were killed."

"I'm sorry," Jake said.

Her hands pulled and twisted the tissue she was still holding. "My father had been driving. There was an investigation and the crash was deemed an accident, but I was left always wondering whether it could have been something else—maybe a murder-suicide.

"With my parents both gone I was alone. When I looked into my father's business dealings I found he had over-extended himself and was actually massively in debt. I was forced to sell the business, then the mansion, to pay it all off. For several years I was lost in a downward cycle of drugs and depression."

She straightened in her chair, and her features brightened. "But then something happened that changed my life. I don't remember when or how I first hit on the idea, but a few months ago I decided to submit my DNA to an ancestry site called *MyNewFamily.com*.

"We'd moved to a new country, and my parents had never been forthcoming about whatever relatives we had left behind. I wasn't really expecting anything, but to my surprise and shock, the site said it found one sibling, a sister, and that she lived here in Victoria. I'm not sure why, but that knowledge gave me a new strength—I wasn't alone after all. The idea that I might have an extended family somewhere was comforting."

Jake straitened up, struck by the similarities to his own background. He too was an only child, and both his parents were gone. He'd never considered doing the ancestry thing, but he could imagine how it would feel to find you weren't alone.

She continued. "There's a feature on the site that allows you to send messages to people that have come up as matches, but they have no obligation to reply."

"And your sister didn't?"

She shook her head. "It was strange, but it made me even more determined. At the time I was still living in Quebec City. I gathered together what money I had left and headed out here."

Jake sensed that this moment was a turning point—his last chance to brush her off and continue his uncomplicated life.

"Would you like some coffee?" he said, squelching down his inner voice screaming in the background.

He glanced back at her several times as he set up the coffee maker, double-checking first that she was really sitting there, then that she wasn't scared off and getting ready to leave. She stared back at him, smiling.

As the machine burbled in the background he sat back down, confident that a major injection of caffeine would jump-start his brain. In fact, it occurred to him that if he'd had a shot of coffee earlier this morning, he probably wouldn't be traveling along this road in the first place. But he felt like he was committed now.

Resigned to being drawn into her story, he pushed on. "Did the site provide any more information, other than her living here?"

"They let you choose what information to disclose," she answered. "The only other thing I remember was her age. She's a bit younger than me—eighteen. And the name on the account didn't look like a real name. I wrote it down, but the next time I checked the entire account was gone."

"You can do that? Remove an account?"

She shrugged. "Apparently."

"Even if it's a bogus name, at least it might be a place to start."

He stood and quickly washed a pair of cups in the sink, then set one down for each of them. The coffee maker began to gulp as it completed its cycle, and the heady aroma wafted through the cabin. She took it black—like him. He shuddered, thinking back on her comment about their spiritual planes meshing perfectly. He got up and grabbed a notepad and pencil from a drawer by the sink.

Back at the table he took a sip. "Not that I'm agreeing to do this, but if I *was* to take it on, I'd need to start somewhere. Do you have other information? Was there a picture of your sister?"

She shook her head. "She hadn't submitted a picture. It just showed the generic head-and-shoulders icon. If she's really my half-sister, maybe she looks something like me?"

Jake tried to imagine two Evangelines walking around this city. He wondered again why he was having this conversation, considering taking on a task that was probably impossible, and that he wasn't even remotely qualified to do, for someone he barely knew—a task requiring a license he didn't have, and wasn't ever likely to get.

She stretched out both her hands and placed them on his. "Can you help me?"

He looked into her eyes, so pleading, so helpless, so innocent.

"I'll see what I can do," he said.

She flopped her purse on the table, opened it, and withdrew a stack of bills.

"I'll give you this to start," she said, peeling off several and sliding them across to him.

He glanced at it—it was five hundred dollars. His eyes widened.

"Much of our family fortune is gone," she said, answering his look. She smiled. "But not all."

"What about the name from your sister's DNA entry?"

She dug through her purse, removed a folded piece of paper with the pseudonym her sister had registered on the MyNewFamily.com site, and handed it to him. He unfolded it, read it, and closed his eyes momentarily.

"WIFRUN2345?" he said, holding it up to her. "Really?"

"Well, yes, I suppose it's not a real name..." she said defensively.

He shook his head. "You suppose? Well, in a way I guess it's good. At least we know absolutely for sure it's not a real name, so we don't have to waste our time looking for it in phone records or anything."

The bogus 'name' brought him back down to Earth. He realized that he'd been ridiculously optimistic to think he could locate this girl. He reflected again that he wasn't even a detective. In reality, he had no idea how to go about finding someone given the pathetic amount of information he had available.

She closed her purse and set it in her lap. "We can arrange to meet again in a day or so, and I'll see if I can come up with anything else that might help your investigation."

She rose to leave. It was a crucial moment—his absolute final chance to bail out of this bizarre scheme. He opened his mouth to speak.

She turned back. "Oh, and I need your date of birth."

"Date of birth?"

She smiled. "For my calculations—I need to refine our relative positions in the astral plane. It's critically important."

Jake stood at his door and waved, smiling, as Evangeline stepped down to the dock.

Across the way, his neighbour Maggie stood mopping the aft deck of her vessel, the location of Jake's battle with Gordon over the fish. She glanced at Evangeline, then at the wad of bills Jake was holding, and gave him a suspicious look. He quickly hid the hand with the money behind his back.

He watched, hypnotized, as Evangeline's incredible form strolled along the wooden dock and headed up the long ramp to the parking lot. His fist tightened on the bills in his hand.

What have I gotten myself into? He thought.

IV

THE SALTY DOG

Rule #10 : Always be prepared for a surveillance session to last much longer, and possibly take you much farther, than you expected.

- Shadow Mac's Comprehensive Guide to Private Investigation

That night, in a far corner of the Salty Dog tavern, a half-empty glass of beer on top of the piano bounced and vibrated as Jake pounded out another round of Fats Waller's *Lulu's Back in Town*. The piano playing gig was the closest thing Jake had to a job, and the stipend he earned from the bar was one of the sources of income that provided enough for him to survive.

The tavern was on Kingston Street, a few blocks from the Wharf. It catered mostly to tourists, though the occasional bored local would show up for a drink. It was only mid-March—the tourist season wouldn't ramp up for at least a month. Most of the tiny crowd tonight were locals.

In keeping with its location, within walking distance of the harbour and Fisherman's Wharf, the bar's decor featured a nautical theme. The walls were adorned with glass fishing floats, nets, boat anchors and wheelhouse wheels, and paintings of sailboats with their spinnakers billowing in the wind.

A colourful but beaten-up stuffed parrot watched over the action from a swinging perch above the bar. Max, the manager, even resembled an aging sea captain, with rolled-up sleeves, tattooed arms, a shock of grey hair, and a scruffy grey beard.

Tonight, even though it was Saturday, fewer than half the tables were full, and the crowd was more subdued than usual. Occasionally a loud voice or a shout would erupt at a table, but most of the patrons were quietly drinking and talking. A big-screen TV on one wall was showing a European soccer match, one of an endless string of sports shows, mercifully with the sound turned off.

The music, and the largely free booze, were a great way to help Jake forget about his problems—like the fact that he'd agreed to conduct an investigation as a private detective when he didn't have the credentials, a license, or the slightest idea how to fulfill that function.

Most of the crowd tonight weren't even listening, but Jake didn't particularly care. For the moment he was lost in his own music—Stride jazz from the 1920s and '30s—his favourite. *Jelly Roll Morton*, *Willie 'The Lion' Smith*, *James P. Johnson*, and the king, *Fats Waller*. The music they pioneered more than one hundred years ago—Stride, was what kept him alive.

He loved the walking bass notes bouncing against the upbeat chords. He loved the driving rhythm that almost commanded you to dance. He loved the complex lattice of sound knitted together by the syncopated melody, weaving in and out of the tune like the turning points of a piece of fine crystal.

But most of all, he loved the joy and the abandon that flowed through every note, and permeated every chord. Stride made you believe, at least for a short time, that the world was a beautiful place, and for Jake, music was the one unmoving anchor in a life that, in every other way, seemed to drift aimlessly.

In fact, for the moment, he'd actually forgotten that there was anybody else in the room. So he was surprised when a hand pushed his shoulder from behind.

"You deaf or somethin'," said the extremely drunk male voice attached to the hand.

Jake glanced over the shoulder in question. A guy in a baseball cap, a tee-shirt advertising Expo '86, and rumpled jeans was standing beside him. Jake was almost at the end anyway. He wound up the final chorus and turned to face the guy.

"What?" Jake asked.

"I said—can you play 'Piano Man'," the guy said, staggering backwards and almost falling over.

"I don't do requests," Jake answered. He turned back to the piano.

"You know," the guy persisted to his back, trying to sing now, "Sing us a song, you're the...—Billy Joel—everybody does it."

"Not me," Jake said without turning around. He put his hands on the keys, trying to ignore the guy, hoping he'd go away.

"What is this shit you're playin', anyway," the guy persisted. "Nothin' I ever heard of."

Jake turned back around. "Fats Waller," he answered, not sure why he was bothering.

"What?" his visitor asked. "The 'Blueberry Hill' guy?"

"That's Fats Domino," Jake corrected him. "Different Guy."

"Anyway," the man said, "they both suck. Play somethin' good, for fuck's sake."

Jake turned back to the piano, and started to pound out the intro to *Piano Man*.

"That's more like it," his guest said, smiling and tapping along with his foot.

Jake played a few bars, then started to change things up. He modified the left hand to be Stride style, sped up the tempo, and began to improvise on the tune, which soon became unrecognizable.

"Fuck this," he heard behind him.

Jake plunged into the improvisation, surprised at how well it was going. Once again he forgot where he was, and played for himself alone.

Five minutes later he took a break, and reached for his beer. He thought about Evangeline's numerological assessment: *You are obviously a very creative person—a musician or an artist—an entertainer*. He didn't believe in all that stuff; still, it gave him the shivers.

He turned back to see the Piano Man guy standing at the bar, holding on, to keep himself from falling over. He was talking to the bartender, arguing, and pointing at Jake.

At closing time, after the last few drunk patrons had staggered out, Jake was still sitting at the piano. Several beer glasses sat on top—all empty. Max, the bar manager, strolled toward him, as a kid in the back swept the floors and hauled out a black bag with the night's garbage.

"Hey, piano man, I need to talk to you," Max called as he approached.

Jake ignored him and continued noodling around on the keyboard. Max arrived, stepped forward, and grabbed the lid of the piano as if to slam it down on the keys. Jake just got his fingers out in time. He finally turned back and stared up at his boss.

"Personally, I kind of like that 1920s and '30s crap," Max said. He paused, seemingly for effect, and crossed his tattooed arms. "But it's not about what I like, or what you like. It's about what the audience want. Why can't you throw in some hip-hop or something—"

Jake cringed.

"Or rap," Max said.

Jake looked up at him, his eyes narrowed. "What? You want me to blast somebody else's ripped-off music on a boom-box while I stand at a microphone mumbling entries out of the phone book?"

Max shook his head. "I don't think they've got phone books anymore—yet more proof that you're out of touch. Could you at least play something written since the last half of the twentieth century?"

Jake was drunk—again. He wasn't feeling accommodating. The message wasn't really getting through.

"You're good, Sommers," Max said. "You're real talented, and you're a great showman, when you want to be. The crowd like you. But they don't want to hear any more of that old time boogie-woogie shit."

"Stride," Jake drawled, barely paying attention. He opened the piano lid and resumed noodling.

"Whatever," Max said. "You know, I don't want to have to let you go."

Jake looked up and stifled a laugh. Other than drinks, tips, and a minimum wage for a few hours on weekends, he wasn't costing the bar anything.

"Work with me here," Max smiled, and put a hand on Jake's shoulder. "Play mostly modern stuff. Keep the audience happy. I won't complain if you throw in an old clunker once in a while."

Back at his vessel, Jake stumbled down into his living area, tripping, and almost landing on his portable piano wedged into the back corner. He righted himself, and gazed up at the dog-eared picture taped to the wall above it. It was Fats himself, his fingers poised over the keyboard of an upright in a low-rent bar, mugging for the camera in the middle of striking the keys.

Fats' trademark bowler hat was tilted back on his head, and a half-smoked cigarette hung from the left side of his mouth, which was curled up in something between a smile and a snarl.

Jake had never noticed it before, but somewhere behind Fats' hammy expression was a hint of what Jake would have sworn was fear. Fats had died at the age of forty-two, from a combination of overwork, booze, and a lifetime of hard-partying. Maybe he'd known what was coming, had known what his lifestyle was going to buy him. Jake glanced at his own image in a nearby mirror. Was there a trace of that same fear?

V

THE HONEYSUCKLE ROSE

Rule #12: *When evaluating a crime scene, a good detective looks for 3 things: What's there, what's there that shouldn't be there, and what isn't there but should be.*
- **Shadow Mac's Comprehensive Guide to Private Investigation**

Jake's houseboat, the *Honeysuckle Rose*, consisted of a box-like living area with a peaked roof, perched on an ungainly, wooden, boat-like structure that made it look like a miniature version of Noah's Ark. Its cedar siding and roof gave it an almost lifelike quality, as if it had been magically assembled by elves, or had somehow sprouted from the ocean and grown in place.

Jake didn't know whether the vessel had been built near its current location or moved in the past from somewhere else, but judging from its design, he didn't think it would last long if it ever actually had to put out to sea.

The 'Rose' was about fifteen meters long, and had a beam (width, in nautical talk) of nine meters. The living area was seven meters by six meters, around the size of a studio apartment. Inside was a small galley (kitchen), a gas heater, a small table in a nook with a bench on either side, and a tiny head (bathroom), with a tiny shower. At the back, a 'loft', accessed by a ladder, was occupied by Jake's single bed and an office with a small desk.

Outside, a narrow section of deck ran along either side of the living area. Both sides were littered with enough curios and knick-knacks to fill a leprechaun's warehouse: glass balls from fishing nets, chunks of driftwood shaped like dragons and butterflies, a 1928 British Columbia license plate, a hanging stained-glass sculpture shaped like a mermaid. The portion of the deck facing the dock was crowded with potted plants and concrete garden ornaments.

The *Rose's* best feature was the massive planked section of deck that extended at the aft end, facing the harbour. One of Jake's greatest simple pleasures was to sit at the tiny table in the center and watch the boats go by.

Spinner, Jake's seven-meter sailboat, bobbed in the water at the back, its sail presently stowed and hatches sealed. Jake was a fair-weather sailor, and the weather hadn't been good lately. As the spring progressed he might have the chance to get out and race with the wind.

The plants, ornaments, and most of the knick-knacks were holdouts from Jake's great-aunt Deirdre, from whom he'd inherited the vessel. Most of the plants were still alive, though not through any action by Jake. Being outside, they got regular watering and sunlight. They survived in spite of him, not because of him.

Over the years, Jake had been beaten down by his share of tragedy. During one of his armed forces training assignments in the high arctic, his mother, Millie, had been diagnosed with stage IV cancer. He'd put in to return to Victoria on compassionate grounds, but by the time he made it back, his mother was gone.

He'd eventually resigned from the forces, and returned to Victoria to look after his father, Graham, who'd developed early onset Alzheimer's soon after his wife's death. Jake took care of him until his condition made that impossible. Then he sold his parents' home for money to place the old man in private care, while Jake drove cab to make ends meet. His father had held on for another seven years. By the time he'd finally died of pneumonia at the age of sixty-five, the house money was almost gone.

And Jake was on his own.

Deirdre, his mother's aunt, had been an artist, successful enough to pay for the houseboat and provide herself with a reasonable income. She'd had no children, and had no significant other or next of kin. Growing up, Jake had spent a lot of his spare time with Deirdre, and they'd developed a special rapport.

So when lung cancer took her tragically at the age of seventy-five, she'd left him the *Honeysuckle Rose*, along with a six-figure nest egg that generated just enough interest to pay for moorage, and to keep him clothed and fed.

Displaying a sensible bent that would normally be completely contrary to his nature, Jake had managed to avoid blowing the principal, and had been able to live a meager but tolerable life for the two years since receiving his inheritance.

A photograph of Jake's benefactor still hung in a prominent spot on the wall of his living room. Deirdre had grown up in the sixties, and had been the quintessential flower child. In the picture, her long, arrow-straight blond hair, parted in the middle, was draped around the shawl she wore over her ankle-length dress. A few other photographs from Deirdre's travels hid in the limited number of available spaces: Deirdre praying at a Hindu temple in Katmandu; strolling the gardens surrounding the Taj Mahal; exploring the ruins at Machu Picchu.

The interior of the *Rose* was as crowded as the outside. There were samples of Deirdre's paintings, potted plants, hanging macramé planters, a menagerie of wood and clay animals, a statue of the Buddha, and one of a bronze wheel encircling a dancing Shiva. Jake had managed to keep the indoor plants alive, though he typically forgot to water them until he noticed the leaves wilting. A tiny TV, which Jake almost never used, was mounted on the wall above the nook. An Internet radio, which he used all the time, sat on the table.

Since moving in Jake had largely left the place unchanged. The only major addition he'd made was his electric piano keyboard, jammed into a cubbyhole at one end of the living room under the loft.

None of his string of girlfriends had stayed long enough to make an impact. As with pretty much all other aspects of his life, none of his relationships had lasted long.

Fisherman's Wharf, the interconnected set of docks where Jake's vessel was moored, occupied a part of the southernmost shore of the *Inner Harbour*—a small, picturesque body of water that took a substantial bite out of the south-western corner of the city of Victoria. The city itself covered the southernmost tip of Vancouver Island, a massive island in the northeastern Pacific, off the west coast of the Canadian province of British Columbia.

Victoria was a slow-moving town with two main industries. The first was government, since it was the capital city of the province.

The second was tourism.

Victoria was only a few hours away from the huge and lucrative US tourist market. Float planes regularly skimmed along the Inner Harbour on their way to and from the mainland, and horn blasts routinely announced the appearance of the 'Victoria Clipper' from Seattle, or the 'Coho' ferry from the smaller town of Port Angeles. The cruise ship terminal brought millions of visitors every year.

One of the city's most important attractions was the iconic Empress Hotel, which first unveiled its old-world opulence to the public in 1908.

The hotel's imposing facade loomed over a usually crowded esplanade bounding the harbour's eastern shore.

On the southern side stood another impressive landmark—the B.C. Parliament Buildings. Their ornate stone walls and green copper domes towered majestically over the surrounding lawns and gardens. Designed by architect Francis Rattenbury, who was famous for being brutally murdered back in England a few years later, the buildings were completed in 1897 and were the home of the province's Legislative Assembly.

The Wharf itself was a major tourist attraction, and was well positioned to welcome visitors. It was only a few blocks from the Empress and the Parliament Buildings, at the end of a strip of harbourfront property containing a half-dozen tourist hotels, a few blocks from the landings for US tourist boats, and within walking distance of the cruise ship terminal.

The farthest reach of the Wharf lived up to its name—hosting a marina with fishing boats and a sprinkling of pleasure craft. The section closest to shore catered mainly to tourists. The expansive main wharf was lined with cafés, tour outlets, and whale-watching operations. A long metal ramp extended from a parking lot above down to the wharf complex.

Extending northward from the main dock and the shopping area were a series of smaller docks housing thirty or so houseboats, or 'Floating Homes', as the residents insisted they be called, one of which was Jake's. The homes were all different shapes and sizes, and all different colours. From above, the assembly looked like a box of chocolates, or a multicoloured carnival ground.

The docks where the houseboats were moored were open to the public during the day, and the residents had to put up with noise, litter, and the constant prying eyes of tourists, who were free to explore at will.

But their view of the harbour was spectacular, a gate kept out all but the locals after nine PM, and the tourist activity tapered off sharply when the cooler fall weather set in.

The Wharf wasn't a lifestyle everyone would embrace, but Jake had taken to it ever since he first visited his great-aunt with his parents when he was a kid.

VI

COGITATION

Rule #34: To truly understand the intricacies of a case and uncover the truth, a private investigator must be skilled in the art of research and analysis.
- Shadow Mac's Comprehensive Guide to Private Investigation

The day after Jake's meeting with Evangeline, he woke and hauled his uncooperative body out of bed, his decision of the previous morning still swirling ominously through his psyche.

It didn't seem any more logical in the cold light of a new day, especially filtered through his now more or less lucid brain and clearing vision. After a shower and several buckets of coffee, he was ready to consider, or maybe reconsider, what he was doing.

During his two years in military college he'd been training to be an Intelligence Operator. On graduation, his duties would include: monitoring communications traffic, analyzing intelligence information, categorizing threats, and compiling reports, all while sitting behind a desk.

If you threw out a wide enough net you could call it law enforcement; but it didn't really prepare him for detective work. And he had zero experience with any of the activities normally associated with PIs: tailing suspects, interviewing witnesses, taking pictures, gathering evidence, and tracking down leads.

Anyway, he'd resigned from the forces before he graduated. You needed a license to be a private investigator, something Jake didn't have, and wasn't sure how to get even if he wanted one. Once more he cursed McCluskey. Why couldn't the bastard keep his nose out of other people's business?

A mental image of Evangeline surfaced, the sun lighting up her golden hair, the red dress clinging to her spectacular body. Then again, Jake thought, at the moment she was his only client. If she didn't blab to the authorities, who would know?

And the investigation didn't have to be strictly defined as detective work. In the unlikely event that anyone was to question what he was doing, he could say he was just helping out a friend with a problem. He poured himself another cup of coffee, and sat down at the nook table.

How *could* you find somebody with just a name? As the additional caffeine gradually kicked in, his mind seemed to sharpen. It wasn't entirely true to say he would only have a name.

Evangeline had said the girl she'd found was her younger half-sister. According to her, before the account was taken down, the *MyNewFamily* website had said the sister was living here, in this city. So he was looking for a woman a few years younger than Evangeline, who probably resembled her to some extent, and who was living here in Victoria. Each of these pieces of the puzzle would narrow down the search. Still, it would take a lot of digging.

And of course, he had the name, such as it was. It might not relate to her in any way, or at least not in any way he could understand, and it might not connect with anything else on the web. But it was common for people to reuse names and passwords. If he could cross-reference the name with other sites, he might be able to pinpoint the user.

Since the *MyNewFamily* account had been taken down, there wasn't likely to be much else Evangeline could provide him, but she'd wanted to meet again tomorrow in person.

The thought made his pulse quicken.

A few hours later, Jake stood up and rubbed the knot in his back, having spent ten minutes scrubbing at what might turn out to be a permanent stain on the galley counter. He surveyed the train-wreck that was the interior of the *Honeysuckle Rose*. If he and Evangeline were going to meet again, chances were that they would return here. If that happened, he wanted 'here' to be at least somewhat presentable.

After taking a step and tripping over a pair of gumboots lying on the floor, he picked the boots up, wondering where he could put them. No ideas presented themselves. He returned them to the floor in the spot where he'd gotten them in the first place.

In the end, he decided on an organized plan of attack: the galley-related items, then dirty clothes, then miscellaneous junk he either didn't really want, or had never gotten around to finding a place for.

But first, before anything else, there was the garbage.

Pulling a large black garbage bag out of the box he'd bought yesterday, he tossed in the used paper plates, disposable coffee cups, beer cans, empty booze bottles, and pizza boxes that littered the table, galley counter, and even places on the floor. He smiled. Progress was being made.

Deirdre's ornate sign saying: 'The Earth is Our Mother—Be Kind to Her' mounted on the wall above his head seemed to glow brightly as he hauled several overstuffed bags up the stairs and out of his home.

The air outside was warm—the radio had said thirteen degrees, typical for this late March day. Jake was comfortable in his jeans and tee-shirt. Victoria and a few of the nearby Gulf Islands were the only areas of Western Canada that lay south of the 49th parallel. Since the mid-1990s parts of the city were mild enough to grow Mediterranean crops like olives and lemons.

He tossed the bags into the blue metal bin at the end of the dock, turned back and gazed out at the world around him, then up at the sky, where maybe Deirdre somehow now resided.

"I promise I'll do better next time, Auntie."

Of course, he'd made that promise many times before.

By late afternoon, he could actually walk around in his living space without kicking anything. The vessel's interior had been transformed from that of a full-on Category Three hurricane to a mild tropical storm. The dining table was almost completely clear, the dirty dishes were washed and put away, and another garbage bag, this one full of dirty clothes, waited to be hauled to the laundromat.

"It *is* possible," he said proudly, as he examined his handiwork.

There were still things he hadn't found a proper place for, and even more that he'd have to throw out, "Or recycle," he said, smiling up again at Deirdre's sign; but the place was slowly coming to resemble the cozy, homey space he remembered from his childhood visits so many years ago.

He explained the sudden burst of organization by telling himself that he'd been meaning to get to this for weeks (months? years?). Still, he couldn't help but imagine Evangeline demurely setting herself down, smoothing out her amazing red dress on the now-spotless bench seat, and marveling at the transformation.

Jake understood that as beautiful as Evangeline might be, she was only his client. Still, the prospect was out there, and it was hard to ignore.

As the entertainment, in the spotlight, he'd been hit on by his share of women at the Salty Dog. Many had been from out of town, tourists looking for a holiday romance.

A lot of his liaisons were a blur, one-night, or several-night, stands. But there were a few that had gotten more serious. There was Julie, whom he'd gone out with for more than a year. She was pretty, and fun, but, as with many of the women in his life, she'd expected too much of him.

He'd felt like she was constantly testing him, presenting him with some challenge: buying exactly the right present on her birthday, or complimenting lavishly enough on her latest hairstyle or what she was wearing. And, of course, he would never actually be told what the challenge was, or how to achieve it. Most of the time, he didn't even realize he was being tested. He'd only find out after the fact—after he'd failed. Even then he'd have to guess his transgression from her subtle signals of displeasure.

Julie believed that if their psychic connection was strong enough Jake would somehow simply know what to do. Maybe she'd read too many web articles on 'soul mates', or seen too many fairy tale movies where the prince scaled castle towers or fought fire-breathing dragons to win the woman he loved. The relationship had him constantly on edge, always wondering what proof of the psychic mismatch would come next.

Julie would judge him on how well he met, or didn't meet, each challenge. When he inevitably failed, she would make a mental note in an internal black book to which he had no access, and no right of appeal. Apparently one day some tipping point of the scale had been reached. He'd exceeded his allotment of black marks—he simply hadn't measured up, and she was gone.

He still saw her around town once in a while. She'd married a low-level government official, whom Jake assumed had achieved the psychic connection he had lacked, or had somehow worked out a way to steer clear of the black book.

Then there was Kate, his most recent. She had actually moved into the *Rose* with him, and for a few months their relationship had been a dream. But he guessed that she'd begun picturing their future together, and hadn't been too happy with what she saw.

She started asking him how long he was planning to live 'like this', gesturing around the interior of the vessel. It was something he'd never actually considered. She said she wanted more, like a nice house somewhere, and maybe kids... Jake never really looked that far ahead. He was happy where they were.

Then one day she too had simply disappeared from his life.

VII

DIERDRE

Rule #42: As a private detective, you need to know exactly what answers
your client's needs. Have specific questions for the client,
witnesses, and possibly suspects or subjects.
- **Shadow Mac's Comprehensive Guide to Private Investigation**

That night, after staggering home from another gig at the Salty Dog,
Jake unlocked the gate at the top of the walkway leading to the Wharf,
and stood for a moment staring down the length of the dock. As always,
he felt a sense of joy and amazement at the sight of the *Honeysuckle Rose*.

Joy, because he truly loved his floating home. He loved the gentle
sway of the vessel with the movement of the water, the lapping waves
lulling him to sleep at night, the mournful cries of the gulls waking him
in the morning, the spectacular view of the harbour from every window.

Amazement, because he still hadn't completely processed the fact
that the *Rose* actually belonged to him. When he was a kid, he'd spent
many days hanging out at Deirdre's houseboat, which was then called
'*Gaia Dream*'. His home life back then had been tense and cold, his
parents' relationship strained. And he didn't feel like he had much in
common with either of them. It was almost as if he wasn't really their
child, like he'd been left on their doorstep or something.

They had paid for his piano lessons as part of his overall education,
believing it would make him a more 'well-rounded' human being. It had
never occurred to them that he might turn out to have a lot of talent,
and would become captivated by music.

Growing up, there had always been an undercurrent of tension in the Sommers household. Jake would sit in his room upstairs playing his keyboard with the headphones on, the angry shouts, and even the occasional heavy object being thrown, still filtering through.

From what he could gather, most of his parents' fights had been trivial—basically about nothing. But he knew at least some them were about him. His father, a Chief Petty Officer in the Canadian navy, wanted him join the military. His mother, an accountant, thought he should do a business degree. And Jake? He just wanted to play piano.

In his teens, he'd kicked around with a succession of bands: heavy metal, a Bowie tribute band, jazz-rock fusion. None of them had gone anywhere, and in the end he decided he'd rather be a solo act.

The whole time, his parents had proclaimed that music was a frivolous pastime, and that he was wasting his life even considering pursuing it as a career.

So he spent a lot of time elsewhere; much of it with his great-aunt Deirdre.

"They say I've got a 'fanciful' view of life," Jake complained to Deirdre one day, when he was a kid, as they sat on the aft deck.

"I know your parents love you," Deirdre answered him. "They just have a different way of looking at the world. The things they think are important are different than the ones you value."

"Well, what am I supposed to do?"

"Do? Accept it, Jake. That's part of what growing up and becoming an adult means—accepting things not being the way you want. I don't think your parents will ever really understand you."

Jake laughed. "They still don't understand *you*."

"That's right," she laughed with him.

Deirdre's world had always seemed so much larger than his own— her interests ranged from organic farming practices in Ecuador to the teachings of mystical gurus in India, from the latest in modern astrophysics to the most ancient and esoteric philosophies. Her mind was always everywhere, always learning, always changing, always growing.

In Deirdre Jake found a kindred spirit, and she took him under her wing, gave him a taste of her world. He had kept, and still listened to, a lot of her eclectic collection of old records: Joni Mitchell, Leonard Cohen, Ravi Shankar, but also Miles Davis, Charlie Parker, Bach, Beethoven, Debussy, Stravinsky, Rachmaninoff. Dierdre's was a magical world of perpetual awe and wonder—one that was gone now, and probably would never return.

"You're taking some time to find out who you really are," she'd told him once not long before her death, when he worried about his future. "What's wrong with that?" She smiled at him. "You're blessed with something everybody else in the world just dreams of—don't ever forget it.

"You've got the makings of a first-class musician, and I know that music will always be a major part of your life." She laid a hand on his. "But there's something more to you, something you haven't found yet. I'm not sure what that is. You're going to have to discover it for yourself."

Deirdre's influence was part of his fixation on music of the past, music from the heart, that wasn't stamped out by the corporate money machine. Music that echoed from churches and bars, even basements, brothels and public squares. Music from before even her own time. He knew she wouldn't mind that upon inheriting his new home, he'd re-christened it the *Honeysuckle Rose*, after one of Fats Waller's most famous tunes.

As devastating as his great-aunt's death had been, her legacy was the one truly miraculous thing that had ever happened to him. He thanked her for it every day.

And though every day he vowed to do more to deserve it, so far, every day he had failed.

VIII

THE SISTER

Rule #5: A good detective is cautious of obvious statements and wary of persons quick to provide alibis and identification. He demands verification whenever possible.
- **Shadow Mac's Comprehensive Guide to Private Investigation**

One of the things Jake liked about the *Honeysuckle Rose*, apart from its proximity to numerous local bars, was its proximity to the set of restaurants lining Fisherman's Wharf, all of which served crappy, unhealthy food that he knew he shouldn't eat, but regularly did anyway.

After all the trouble he'd taken cleaning up his vessel's interior, in the end he decided he'd feel more comfortable if he met with Evangeline somewhere less confined. That is, where he wasn't too close to her and her immensely desirable form.

They'd agreed to meet for lunch in the retail section of the Wharf, at Barb's Fish and Chip shop. As he shaved, carefully combed his hair, and put on his best shirt and pants, he used the same argument to himself that he'd used the day before, as he'd lugged all his dirty clothes to the laundromat for the first time in weeks—that it was a good sign—that he was finally getting his act together—that he would have done all of it anyway, Evangeline or no Evangeline.

Yesterday afternoon, he'd dug out his long-expired library card and hit up the library for books on detective work. If he was going to travel down this path, he was determined to do it right. So far he'd only glanced through them. He still had a lot to learn, but he hoped he could at least convey the impression that he knew what he was doing.

He locked up the Rose, and turned to find a guy standing on the dock. He was in his mid-thirties, wearing a backwards-facing baseball cap and dressed in shorts and a gaudy Hawaiian shirt.

Guessing why the stranger was there, Jake glanced again at the door of McCluskey's vessel, shaking his head.

"Jake Sommers?" the guy asked.

"I'm not actually a detective," Jake said. He stepped to the dock and turned toward the commercial section, hoping the visitor would take the hint.

"Well, how come you put the ad on the web?"

Jake sighed inwardly, turning back. "It's all a misunderstanding. I applied to have it removed. Maybe you saw it before that happened. Anyway, I'm already working on a case."

"I thought you said you weren't a detective."

"Look," Jake said, "the bottom line is, whatever you want me to do, I can't take it on right now."

"Just hear me out," the guy said. "It should be simple—easy money. All you gotta do is follow her and find out where she buried it all."

Jake's eyebrows came together. "Buried it all?"

"Name's Bobby," the guy said, holding out his hand.

Jake leaned forward and shook it. "Hi, Bobby—so, who buried what?"

"Daenerys," Bobby hauled out his wallet and withdrew and held up a badly-angled picture of a long-haired grey cat with a set of keys in its mouth. "Every day I go to work at the planer mill, and she's got the house to herself. There's a cat-door at the front—she can basically come and go whenever she wants."

Jake nodded, beginning to wish he'd brushed the guy off while he had the chance.

"I noticed lately that stuff was missing," Bobby continued. "Little things. I thought maybe somebody was breaking in somehow. I installed a camera in the living room. It caught Daenerys carrying a memory stick from my computer in her mouth, then going out the cat door. Several times after that it's shown her carrying stuff off.

"I tried hiding things, but she keeps carrying off new stuff I didn't think of. I know she's burying it all somewhere outside, but I don't know where. The last feed showed her with one of my credit cards. This has got to stop."

"So, how do I fit in?" Jake asked.

Bobby looked at him as if the connection was obvious. "I want you to follow Daenerys," he made a gliding gesture with one hand, "figure out where she's hiding everything, and get it back before somebody else finds it. I'm really busy with work—I don't have time..."

Jake imagined passers-by pointing and staring at him, or even videoing him on their cell phones or calling the cops, as he stalked the felonious cat through yards, flowerbeds and alleyways.

"I'd pay you good," Bobby said. "I really need my stuff back."

"But even if I got your stuff," Jake said, "wouldn't Daenerys just carry it off again?"

Ten minutes later, Jake sat at an empty table on the open patio waiting for Evangeline. He'd finally succeeded in brushing off Bobby, the cat guy, though he couldn't help reflecting that the gig Bobby had proposed would probably be a lot easier than the one Jake had already agreed to.

He wasn't entirely sure Evangeline would show, and was almost afraid to imagine what she might be wearing if she did. It was late morning on a weekday—only a few people wandered the dock, exploring, or searching for an early snack. All the restaurant's tables were outside, spaced around the dock, and most were unoccupied. He'd selected one at the farthest extent, away from any other patrons.

"You're looking especially cute today," a dainty hand rested on his shoulder from behind.

Evangeline moved around and stood in front of him. This time, she wore a tee-shirt and faded jeans with the knees torn out. But she was just as striking, just as gorgeous as the first time he'd seen her. He swallowed. His little voice bubbled up from somewhere in the depths of his psyche, but it didn't even have a chance to surface before it was hammered back down with extreme prejudice.

"Sit," he said, nodding at the chair across from him.

Ordinarily at this time of the day, he would have ordered a beer, and he congratulated himself for his restraint as he stood at the counter and asked for a coffee. Evangeline had ordered the same.

"There's not much to go on, but we have a few clues," he said on his return, trying to sound confident, and faking that he knew anything about what he was doing. He hauled a pen and notebook from his jacket pocket. "There's the pseudonym, WIFRUN2345. I haven't had a chance yet to research it, but I guess *Wifrun could* actually be someone's name. Anyway, whatever it is, it probably means something to whoever created the account.

"And I might be able to find other references on the web—she might have used the same pseudonym on other sites. Can I get the email and password you used, so I can check out your *MyNewFamily* account?"

Evangeline hesitated for a moment. "I deleted it," she finally said.

"You deleted your own account?"

"I did it not long after I talked to you. My sister's account was gone. What was the point?"

"But you never know—she might get back online and try to contact you."

She shrugged.

He shook his head. "Well, one thing that might help me is the time line for your connection with her. When did all these events first happen? When did you submit your DNA?"

She looked away as if she was thinking. "I think it was four months ago."

"Can you remember if there was any kind of date on your sister's *MyNewFamily* entry? Is there any way to tell when she put hers up?"

She shook her head.

"Did the site say which side of the family she was from?"

"Not that I noticed."

He looked down at his open notebook. At the moment, the new page he'd opened was blank.

"And you said she was younger than you?"

"Yes that's right—eighteen."

"Eighteen..." he said, half to himself, as he wrote it down, even though he'd written it once already. "And the website entry definitely said she was living here in Victoria."

She nodded with confidence. "Yes, definitely."

He looked up from the almost empty page. "You know, you're not giving me much to go on. Is there anything else you can think of that could help me find her?"

She looked away again momentarily, thinking.

Finally, she shook her head. "I'm sorry..."

He sat staring at the notebook in front of him. A fake name, an indeterminate appearance, a questionable location.

She smiled at him. "I have one piece of good news..."

"You brought me your sister's address and phone number?"

She laughed as she shook her head. "I checked the birth date you gave me. The numerology is crystal clear."

She unfolded another sheet of paper from her purse, with several drawings of the now familiar Tic-Tac-Toe pattern, and spread it in front of Jake.

"This is a birth chart," she said, pointing at the first one. Each of its nine squares contained a single number, from one to nine. She ran her finger across the top row. "This row represents the *Mind Plane*—it embraces memory, thought, analysis." She pointed at the second row. "This is the *Soul Plane*—it governs sensitivity, intuition, and positive emotions." Finally, she moved her finger down to the bottom row. "The *Physical Plane*—it concerns verbal expression, motivation, and organization."

Jake nodded in agreement, though he had no idea what she was talking about. Beside the first grid was another similar one, but with the numbers arranged differently. A few grid locations were empty, others had one or two numbers.

She pointed at it. "This is *your* chart—divined from your birth date."

In the lower left corner were two ones.

"See," she said, beaming, "you have two ones—you're very fortunate."

"I am?" Jake answered.

"Of course. That means you have the gift of balanced self-expression."

She pointed at another location on the chart. "See, you also have two twos—better and better!"

"Two twos?"

She drew her finger diagonally across the intersecting lines. "And you have the 'Arrow of Determination'. Determination and persistence underlie everything you do. That's the kind of person I need—one who's stubborn, who won't quit. And it all reinforces the analysis from your name and address charts.

"Not only that, but your charts continue to mesh beautifully with my own."

"And all that's good because...?"

"Because it means we're a natural fit. There is absolutely no doubt that we were meant to be together."

He looked up. "Meant to be together?"

She laughed again. "Working, I mean."

IX

JAKE & EVANGELINE

Rule #32: *When preparing for surveillance, scout the area*
beforehand, wear appropriate clothing, and bring the
proper equipment.
- Shadow Mac's Comprehensive Guide to Private Investigation

Jake took a deep breath, savouring the aroma of the greasy, salty fish and chips dinner wafting from the takeout box in his hands, as he and Evangeline strolled away from the shop. The patio tables had quickly filled up, and Evangeline suggested that they have their lunch at Jake's houseboat after all.

"I was afraid that maybe you were a health nut," he said as they walked.

"I am," she laughed. "But even health nuts can fall off the wagon sometimes."

Jake nodded to their left. "This way—I want to show you something first."

At the western-most end of the commercial area, they joined a small group crowding around the edge and looking down into the water. To Evangeline's surprise, two or three seals were swimming below them, weaving in and out of the wharf pylons, and surfacing occasionally, looking for a handout.

"They like to hang out, hoping for scraps from the tourists," Jake said.

He held her lunch, and Evangeline's wonderful form was imprinted under her tight-fitting jeans as she leaned over and smiled broadly, clapping her hands together.

"They're adorable!"

"You used to be able to buy fish to feed them," Jake said. "They discontinued that. They didn't want to encourage them to get their food here. But the seals still show up. So now they get fed crap—French fries and stuff like that."

Jake snuck a few chips out of his box, broke them into pieces, and handed the pieces to Evangeline. She tossed them into the water, and giggled like a young girl as the seals swirled around, nosing each other out of the way trying to get them. One stuck its nose right out of the water. She tossed it a chip and giggled again as it leapt up and grabbed it out of the air.

"Beautiful!" she said, rising to her feet.

They turned and headed for the *Rose*. "It's a nice day," Jake said. "We can eat on the aft deck, in the sun."

Gulls wheeled over their heads, squawking, eyeing the boxes in their hands.

"Will Gordon be there?" Evangeline asked as they walked.

"That freeloader is off somewhere sponging off some other poor sucker," he answered, glad that he'd taken the time to scrub the stench of the giant sea lion from the deck, "and good riddance."

"I think he's cute," she said, laughing.

"I've never thought of a quarter-tonne pile of blubber that smells like rotten fish as cute—especially that one, but to each his own."

The curtains of McCluskey's window fluttered as they reached the *Rose*. Jake stepped up to the deck, offered Evangeline his hand, and watched in awe as she stepped aboard.

It occurred to him that if they stayed outside, he wouldn't be able to show off the incredible cleaning job he'd performed on the interior. Of course, if she had to use the head she would notice. And if not, maybe he could contrive some other way to show her.

They made their way to the aft deck. He invited her to sit at the small table there, as he set down his dinner and headed inside for the drinks.

"Keep an eye on them," he nodded at the boxes of food. "The gulls will carry them off, box and all, given half a chance."

He grabbed a couple of cans of beer from the fridge, two plates, cutlery, and two amazingly clean glasses, happier than he'd felt in months. Maybe his luck was really changing. She smiled as he approached and set the plates, glasses and beers down in front of her.

He sat and poured them each a drink. "To success," he said, holding up his glass of golden liquid for a toast.

She raised hers and clinked it.

The gulls continued to circle at a respectful distance as Jake and Evangeline opened their boxes and scraped their take-out meals onto the plates. Again, the mouth-watering combination of grease and salt wafted into his olfactories.

Probably drawn by that odour, a white cat with a black patch covering the left half of its face jumped up from the dock and came sniffing around the deck, ending up near Evangeline's feet. Again Jake was thankful he'd scrubbed down Gordon's sunning area. Still, the cat sniffed with interest at the remnants of the sea lion's presence.

"Is this yours?" Evangeline asked. She teased a piece of fish from the slab lying on her plate, and presented it to the cat, who quickly snapped it up.

Jake shook his head. "The animals in this place tend to be kind of communal. Technically, Kong belongs to my 'manager', McCluskey." Jake nodded with distaste at McCluskey's vessel. "That's his place across the dock."

"Kong?" Evangeline wrinkled up her nose as she stared at the cat, which was now licking itself.

Jake smiled. "It's a long story." He nodded at the cat. "His original name was 'Catta non Gratta'—he showed up at McCluskey's one day and McCluskey didn't want him around."

The cat finished cleaning itself and padded to the gunwale nearest them. Evangeline tossed him another morsel of fish, then reached out and petted Kong's head. He plopped down and lay on his side, purring.

"McCluskey got tired of saying all that," Jake continued, "So he shortened it to the initials, 'CNG'. Eventually he got tired of saying all that, too. You could pronounce 'CNG' like 'Kong', and that word's only one syllable, so that's how he left it."

Evangeline switched to scratching under Kong's chin. "Sounds pretty convoluted just for naming a cat."

"Hey, that's the way McCluskey's mind works. Believe me, you don't want to go there, it's a scary place."

Kong rolled over, got to his feet, and jumped up on Evangeline's lap, purring loudly as he drove his nose into her belly.

"Looks like he likes you," Jake said, smiling.

Kong curled up and continued to purr, as Evangeline stroked his head. One of the gulls glided in and perched itself on the back of an empty chair nearby. Jake clapped his hands together and it lifted into the sky, hovering in the breeze with its hungry brothers.

"Well, what's next?" Evangeline asked, stabbing into a greasy chip with her fork.

"In the investigation?" Jake shrugged. "There's not much to go on. I'll do a search for WIFRUN2345, and see if I get any hits. With luck maybe your sister's posted somewhere else using that pseudonym. If not, I'm not sure exactly what to do." He cut off a piece of fish and stuffed it into his mouth. "Like I've been trying to tell you, I'm not actually a detective."

"The numbers don't lie," she said. "I have faith in them—and in you."

"Well, that makes one of us," he said.

The same gull glided in and took up its former position on the back of the chair. It glared at Jake as he cut off another chunk of his fish. He noticed, but didn't bother doing anything this time—it was far enough away. Maybe he'd save a little morsel for it when he was finished.

He put down his knife and fork and picked up his beer. It happened so fast he had no time to react. A flurry of white flashed past his face, and he looked down to find what was left of his fish was gone.

He looked up. The gull sat on a pylon nearby, a large lump in its neck that hadn't been there before. Evangeline laughed until the tears rolled down her cheeks.

"I hope you choke on it," Jake called to the gull.

"Keep an eye on what's left," he said to her as he rose to grab them two more beers.

"You're sure there's nothing else you can tell me about your sister?" Jake asked when he returned. He scanned quickly for any seagulls nearby, then briefly left his chips exposed as he refilled his glass.

"All I know is what I got from the website," she answered.

Jake stared at the water lapping at the pier, contemplating how impossible finding this girl was going to be.

They talked for another half hour. Against every one of his instincts, Jake found himself more and more drawn to her: her smile, the texture of her skin, her shining ash-blond hair, and her breezy and exuberant personality. As they talked, she continued to stroke Kong, who was content to remain on her lap.

Oh, to be that cat, Jake thought as he took his last swig of beer.

"Well," he finally said. "If I'm ever going to find her, I better get at it."

"Come on," she said, nudging him with her elbow. "I'm not ready to quit yet. Let's celebrate."

"Celebrate what?"

She shrugged. "I don't know—the start of our relationship, the beginning of your investigation, being alive, or something. What does it matter? Why don't you take me out somewhere for another drink?"

His inner voice, joined enthusiastically by a queasiness in his gut, warned him in the most emphatic terms to say no.

"Where do you suggest?" he said.

X

A NIGHT OUT

Rule #13: *When conducting surveillance, a detective must train himself to be both separate and involved simultaneously.*
- Shadow Mac's Comprehensive Guide to Private Investigation

Jake knew he had a drinking problem. Part of it went with working at the bar and having the manager and patrons regularly buy him drinks. But there was more to it than that. Some people were susceptible to addictive behaviour—he was pretty sure he was one of them.

Though it would have been convenient if he could say he'd come from a broken home, or had a tough life, or suffered major trauma as a child, he'd actually had a pretty ordinary childhood. His home had been bent, but not broken, and in spite of their personality differences, and their inability to understand him, he knew his parents had loved him.

One factor behind his problem was his general feeling of isolation from the rest of humanity. He couldn't remember exactly when he'd first begun to feel that sense of distance. He'd certainly felt it even before he'd entered the army, but even though his time as a soldier had been limited, it had split him even further from the 'civilian' population, even his oldest friends—especially his oldest friends.

It seemed fitting that he lived in a floating home. Like the *Rose*, he himself was afloat, a lost soul, drifting through life—like most people, he guessed. He had no clear path, and other than music there was nothing that lit up his world. Events in his life drifted in and out like inscrutable ghosts. They would happen if and when they happened—he had no control over them, and felt no compulsion to plan for them.

Still, for some reason he felt apprehensive as he and Evangeline walked from the Wharf to the center of town. They sat for a while in the 'Docker's Bistro' sidewalk café, near the water. It was a brilliantly sunny, warm late afternoon, unusual for March. Every pair of male eyes in the place darted regularly toward Evangeline.

"Neither of your parents ever said anything about you having a little sister?" Jake asked.

"I had no idea," she said absently, twirling a martini glass between two fingers. "I guess I was pretty naive."

"You always lived at home with your parents?"

She nodded.

He straightened in his chair. "If your sister is only a few years younger than you, she must have been born while you were still pretty young. There's no way your mother could hide being pregnant or giving birth, so she must have been right—your father *was* having an affair."

Evangeline looked up, shocked. "What? Oh—yes, I see what you mean. Oh, God—I knew they were having problems, but..."

"Did your father take a lot of business trips? Do you know if he ever went to Victoria?"

She hesitated, then shrugged. "A few—maybe one or twice a year. I don't remember where he went."

"If this girl is really your half-sister and the web search route doesn't work out, we might be able to find her by digging into your father's past."

She shot him a look. "I really don't want to talk about it." She tossed back her drink, smiling. "Let's go someplace else. Someplace that's fun."

The sun was sinking low in the sky as they entered a night club that Evangeline seemed to know well, but that Jake had never seen before, in a giant stone edifice that looked like it had once been a bank. They danced, they drank, they danced some more, they drank even more.

A DJ was up on stage, wearing a backwards baseball cap and heavy-duty headphones. The volume of the music rose to a deafening level, and a rainbow of colours lit up the DJ's face as he gyrated along with the throbbing beat, his hands flying frantically over the console. Multi-coloured laser lights flashed around the room, sweeping up to the ten-meter ceiling and down again.

Jake pushed through the crowd of dancers to the bar for another round of drinks. When he got back to their table, Evangeline was gone. He surveyed the dance floor, and saw her dancing with a guy with fluorescent green hair and a ring through his nose. The sparkling light from a mirror-ball switched to a slow strobe, and at every flash Jake could just catch her image, robot-like, smiling and spinning with her partner. The room went black, and she disappeared for a time. When the light returned, she was dancing with a huge black man, then she disappeared again.

Eventually she rejoined him at their table, and the waitress brought yet another round of drinks. Long after Jake had wished he could be home in bed, Evangeline wanted to keep going, flirting with every guy who came within a couple of arm's lengths, scoring unnumbered free drinks: beer, wine, whiskey, shots.

Jake's drinking problem had usually been confined to the Salty Dog, and only occasionally to his home. As he and Evangeline spent the next few hours hopping from bar to bar, it became clear that along with her numerological expertise, she was on another plane in terms of alcohol consumption. In a rare lucid moment, he wondered whether the strange geometric diagrams she'd shown him said anything about that.

Jake figured he'd been around Victoria, but Evangeline knew places in town he'd never heard of. She was clearly as hammered as he was, but seemed to be powered by an internal battery that kept her on her feet and moving forward. They drank, and drank, and drank some more. Somehow they ended up at Big Bad John's, 'The Original Hillbilly Hideout', a well-known nightclub in the Strathcona hotel. Jake was grateful when, shortly after they entered, the bartender announced that it was closing.

They left and staggered along Douglas Street. Jake envisioned being gently rocked to an alcohol-fueled sleep, maybe with Evangeline in his arms, in his little loft in the *Honeysuckle Rose*, which was where he assumed they were heading.

It took a few minutes for him to grasp that they weren't headed in that direction at all.

"Where the hell are we going?" he finally drunkenly slurred.

"It's a surprise," she said.

"Don't you think maybe it's time to go home?" he asked hopefully.

They stumbled along a narrow alley. "Life will always disappoint you in the end," she said, laughing. She jabbed him with her elbow. "You might as well live it to the max while you can."

Jake was pretty sure he'd lived enough for one night. Evangeline grabbed his hand and swung it back and forth as they turned down another alley and made a quick right turn into a tiny back door.

They stepped through the door into intense light. It took a few seconds for Jake's eyes to adjust. To his shock, the place wasn't a bar, but a Chinese restaurant. A sign on the far wall said 'The Screaming Dragon'. It was crowded, even though his phone said four in the morning. They sat down. A waiter brought a dragon-decorated porcelain teapot and two small Chinese cups, and plopped a menu in front of each of them. Evangeline nodded at Jake to pour the tea.

"Don't you want to wait until it's steeped?" he said.

"Silly boy," she smiled.

He picked up the teapot and sniffed at it—vodka.

"Oh," he said, feeling warmth rush to his cheeks.

He scanned around the room. Almost no one had ordered food. All were drinking their 'tea'.

After only one drink Jake felt his eyelids getting heavy, and his chin began to sink to his chest. He was wakened by the sound of laughter close by. He opened his eyes to find a set of blurry shapes standing around them. He drifted off again, then woke to the clatter of dishes. The blurry shapes had moved to their table.

Once more he felt his eyelids drooping. When he finally opened them, a hand was shaking his right shoulder. At first he forgot where he was. He wasn't sure how long he'd been out.

"Time to go," an Asian waiter in a white coat said, shaking him again. "We close soon."

He looked up. The clock now said five AM. There were only a few people left in the place, and Evangeline wasn't one of them. There was no one at Jake's table. The waiter began clearing away several empty pots and cups scattered around it.

"What about the girl?" Jake asked him.

"Girl gone," the waiter answered. "Long time ago."

Jake scrunched his eyes shut, opened them again, and staggered to his feet, angry and confused.

He turned to the waiter. "You're lying! Where is she!"

The teacup on the table in front of him had fallen over, a dribble of vodka leaving a puddle on the plastic tablecloth. He wrapped his fist around the cup and threw it, smashing it on the floor.

"You get out!" the waiter shouted at him. "Get out or I call the cops!"

XI

THE AFTERMATH

Rule #24: Some individuals are just unpleasant. A detective doesn't let such things cloud his judgment.
- Shadow Mac's Comprehensive Guide to Private Investigation

The next time Jake opened his eyes, it was to blinding sunlight. He was sprawled in a lounger on the side deck of the *Rose*, still fully dressed, though his shirt was out and half-unbuttoned, his fly was open, and at some point he'd kicked off his shoes. His jacket lay on the deck beside him. The wooden slats of the lounger were digging into his side.

He was in the grip of the cruel, satanic god of hangovers, the one all the others bowed down and prayed to regularly. Between the prolonged, excruciating thuds in his skull that accompanied each of his heartbeats, his addled brain remembered flagging down a cab, and half staggering, half crawling to his vessel.

He heard voices to his right, and turned his head. A set of tourists—father, mother, and two kids, had been strolling along the dock a few meters away. One of the kids, a girl of eight or nine, was stopped, and was pointing at him. She said something to her mother. Jake didn't catch what it was.

Jake had no idea what had happened to Evangeline, and at this point, tried to pretend he didn't care. He fought to stamp down the painful jealousy he was feeling, telling himself that, after all, Evangeline was just a client, and he had no claim on her.

All of that was true, but it didn't erase the anger he felt thinking back to her laughing and flirting at the bar and restaurant, and leaving him passed out alone while she pursued God-knew-what depraved activity—with someone other than him.

He heard a hoarse honking sound and an exhaled breath in the direction of the aft deck, and suddenly became aware of a foul odour he hadn't noticed earlier. He twisted his head around to look. Extending beyond the far corner of the living space were Gordon's massive tail flippers. The sea lion's stench was overpowering, even from this distance.

Jake tried to push himself up and out of the lounger, but put too much weight on one side, and it toppled over, spilling him onto the deck. He glanced back at the dock. The mother had put a hand on her child's shoulder and was quickly guiding her away.

Rising to his knees, Jake fumbled the keys out of his jacket pocket, then staggered inside and to the head. As he emptied his gut, he tried to remember whether he'd eaten anything since the fish and chips of yesterday afternoon. He desperately rooted through the medicine cabinet looking for pain pills, eventually found a bottle, and downed several, then staggered up to the loft and flopped down on his bed.

"Lord, please kill me now," he whispered.

"France? Jewelry Empire? Murder-suicide? Searching for her long-lost sister?" McCluskey said that afternoon, as they sat at a table on McCluskey's rooftop patio. "Maybe. No offense, kid, but I think if that woman told you she was from Mars, you'd believe her."

Jake hadn't heard from Evangeline since the events at the Screaming Dragon. Numerous pills, coffee, buckets of water, breakfast, and lunch had transformed what had originally felt like a sledge-hammer pounding a samurai sword through his skull to a barely-tolerable dull throb.

He was doing what he knew was the last thing he *should* be doing, lifting the beer in his hand up to his lips. In the other hand he held a sandwich, hidden partly under the table. He set the beer down and lifted the sandwich, glancing quickly around to check for seagulls. He took a quick bite, then returned it to his lap and picked up the beer.

"It doesn't seem that far-fetched," he answered McCluskey. "Anyway, why would she lie? I don't even know her—she doesn't have to impress me."

"Who knows why anyone does anything," McCluskey said, shaking his head. "But the needle on my bullshit meter is moving toward the red line, and it's not wrong very often."

"Well, you're the one who got me into all this," Jake said. "If it wasn't for that ad..."

"You could've turned it down any time. You're a grown-up—at least you should be by now."

Jake took a sip of his beer. "Anyway, if I can't find this girl, which is a distinct possibility considering how little I've got to work with, I'll just give back her money. Other than that it should be a pretty innocuous gig, and you never know, maybe I'll get lucky."

"Get lucky?" McCluskey said, raising an eyebrow.

Jake felt warmth flow to his cheeks. "I didn't mean..."

McCluskey suddenly clapped his hands together, and Jake nearly dropped his glass as the sound reverberated painfully through his skull. A nearby seagull flapped its wings, lifted up, and hovered for a few seconds, then returned and perched on a railing not far away.

"Well, at least she's paying you," McCluskey said, hefting his own beer. "Are you actually making any progress with this investigation?"

Jake shrugged. "I've got a couple of leads. Nothing concrete. I researched the name 'Wifrun', the first part of the pseudonym, for an hour or so this morning.

"Apparently the name's of old English origin. It means 'secretive woman'. I guess that's appropriate. Whoever set up the DNA site account probably just looked it up on the Internet. I tried combinations with other search terms, but so far nothing's come up."

"And you haven't heard from this woman?"

Jake shook his head. "It was only yesterday—last night actually. If she was as hungover as me, I'm not that surprised. Anyway, she's just a client.

She's paying me to do a job, and I'm pursuing it to the best of my ability."

"Is that right," McCluskey said, as he took another swig of his beer.

Though it was a Tuesday, Max had called him in for a gig at the Salty Dog. Luckily, by the time he had to work he was beginning to feel close to his old self. And that was a good thing, because tonight the bar was livelier than usual. Spring was finally in full bloom, the first cruise ship had arrived, and tourists were starting to pop up at the various venues in town.

Since he'd started his first set at eight, Jake had been doing his duty, playing bland renditions of modern pop tunes he didn't really like. He'd managed to make them a bit more palatable by throwing in some improvisations and occasionally adding some old-time swing, even when the piece didn't call for it.

Already a few patrons had stuffed bills in the jar on his piano, and a couple more had bought him beers. He was feeling relaxed, and enjoying the groove.

He decided to reward himself by throwing in a Fats tune, *This Joint is Jumpin'*. It was upbeat, fast, rude and exciting, and his intuition told him the already boisterous crowd might actually enjoy it, if they could drag themselves away from the football game on the big-screen TV long enough to listen.

He waited for a break in the conversation, slammed the bass keys in a growling intro to get the audience's attention, then launched into the song, the driving Stride chords moving the beat, the top end working in a frantic cross-rhythm.

He glanced over and noticed a couple from a nearby table get up and start dancing on the little postage-stamp dance floor. They were good, maybe professionals, doing turns, throwaways, and arm-breakers, the tap of their feet blending in with the rhythm of the song.

Soon all background talk faded away, as the crowd turned and listened, and a couple more pairs of dancers moved onto the tiny space of available floor. Jake was lost in the music now, energized by the dancers' movements, which were now a part of his supporting orchestra.

Cheers and applause began to echo from the crowd. Jake glanced over. Even Max and the waiters had stopped what they were doing to witness the incredible spectacle.

If only every night could be like this, he thought.

"Good gig, Jake," Max said smiling at the end of the night, as Jake left the bar. "I knew there was a reason I was keeping you."

Back at home, Jake stepped through the front door and smiled, still electrified from the excitement of tonight's gig. He glanced up at the picture of his great-aunt on the wall. She had championed his music, while his own parents continued pressuring him to get a 'proper' job. In fact, it had been Deirdre who'd originally turned him on to Fats, and Stride piano music, one of many of her eclectic tastes.

But he and his great-aunt had had a major falling out when Jake enlisted in the armed forces. He'd insisted to her, and to himself, that it had been his own decision, but in truth it had been largely to appease his parents, who were determined that he 'make something of himself'.

To make things worse, Deirdre had confronted them about the decision, widening the rift that already existed between them. In fact, it wasn't until a year after he'd resigned and come back home that his relationship with his great-aunt had resumed; and even then, they never spoke of his time there.

He knew Deirdre would be happy he was continuing with his music, but he imagined the look of disappointment on her face if she could see the aimless, directionless routine his life had somehow become.

Still soothed by the evening's good vibes and a mild buzz from the beer, he expected to drift off as soon as he put down his head, but instead he lay there staring at the ceiling, every nerve alive.

XII

INTELLIGENCE

Rule #29: With the proper knowledge and equipment, the physical location of any computer online can be found.
- Shadow Mac's Comprehensive Guide to Private Investigation

"Detective, I'm absolutely at my wit's end," the old woman with unnaturally blond and curly hair snapped, as she stood on the dock beside the *Honeysuckle Rose* the next morning. She'd ambushed Jake as he returned from shopping. He stood, a bag of groceries cradled in his elbow, enticingly close to escape, only a few meters from a door that could be locked and bolted.

"I already told you," he said to the woman, "I'm not a detective, it's—"

"Don't be silly, young man," the woman said. "Of course you're a detective. Your ad on social media said so."

Jake took a step toward his vessel. Ten more like that and he'd be free.

The woman put a hand on his sleeve and pulled. "It's imperative that I know where he's going."

Jake turned to her, resignedly. "Where who's going?"

"Why, my husband, Gerald, of course," she answered. "Haven't you been listening? It happens almost every night. I can hardly get a moment's rest."

"From your husband?"

"I have no idea what he wants. At first I thought he was coming to say goodbye, but it's been dragging on for weeks now..."

"Goodbye? Where's he going?"

"Not going, detective—gone—gone before."

Jake's eyebrows came together. "You mean he's—"

"Of course he is," the woman answered. "Why can't you young people pay attention?"

"Gerald's ghost is visiting you..."

"It's very irritating."

"And—what does he do when he visits?"

She waved a dismissive hand. "Just stands there, staring at me accusingly—as if I could have done anything."

"And you want me to do what?"

"Follow him. Find out where he goes after he leaves. Maybe that will provide some clue about what he wants, and how I can make him leave me alone."

Jake gently tugged his sleeve out of her grip and moved his arm out from under her hand. "Look, I sympathize with your predicament, but like I said, I'm not an actual detective. The ad in Kijiji was a practical joke. I'm sorry."

He turned and strode purposefully toward his vessel.

"Well, could you recommend someone?" the woman's voice echoed behind him.

That afternoon, Jake finally heard from Evangeline—a text saying: *Please continue your investigation—it's vitally important. I'll be in touch soon.*

With a renewed sense of anger and disappointment he fought to squelch down, he reminded himself yet again that she was just a client. Despite her outrageous behaviour of two nights ago, his 'investigation' really seemed to matter to her, and she had given him a substantial retainer. He set his anger and jealousy aside and set out to make a deep dive into the convoluted bowels of the Internet, assuming he'd hear more from her eventually.

The process brought back memories of his days in military college, sifting through intelligence data in a room crowded with computers, monitors, big screen displays, and other soldiers, the walls echoing with clicking keyboards and hushed background conversations.

Despite his violent resistance to the idea while growing up, Jake had finally decided that joining the military was the career path that would generate the least conflict.

He'd deliberately avoided the Navy, picturing being assigned to some unit connected to his father. Instead he chose the army. He'd lost track of where he'd gotten the Intelligence Operator idea—it must have been something his father had suggested long ago. He enlisted, finished basic training, and attended the Canadian Forces School of Military Intelligence, in Kingston, Ontario.

He had no issues with the actual work: collecting, processing, analyzing and disseminating intelligence. The identification and assessment of information was interesting, and applying the results to military operations was challenging. Though he wasn't in the program long enough to venture into the deep analysis of all the data they were accumulating, he could see it would be a fascinating process, like solving some complex real-life puzzle.

But it only took a few months to figure out that military service was a bad fit for his personality and temperament. He couldn't breathe within the structured, stratified life the army demanded. Still, he stuck it out for two years, hoping maybe it would somehow grow on him. It didn't. When his mother died, he used that as an excuse to drop out and come home.

If his training in Military Intelligence had taught him anything, it was the importance of security. There was no reason to think that there was anything sinister about the taking down of the *MyNewFamily* account, but it didn't hurt to be careful. The investigation itself might be harmless, but the mere act of deep-diving through the murky depths of the Internet was hazardous, regardless of what he was looking for.

Jake knew that someone with the right skill set would be able to trace his web searches, both through the address of whatever computer he was using, and through the identity he was assuming on the web. Just in case, he found a working used computer at a flea market in town, and paid for it in cash, using some of Evangeline's retainer. It was fairly new, and the operating system was fully functional. The original owner would have no idea who they'd sold the machine to, and there would be no paper trail.

He performed a system reset on the computer, erasing all but the essential files. He then created an anonymous email account that he would use for all his searches and communication, and used his new account to install the latest security software (bought anonymously with cash) and perform a full scan of all the programs that were left.

Finally, he set up a VPN, to add another layer of security. If a hacker was clever enough to trace the computer, they might learn what city it was in. But Victoria was a big enough place. He wasn't particularly worried about that.

The precautions should allow him to safely perform the searches and probes deep into lesser known parts of the web that he guessed would be necessary in the daunting task of finding Evangeline's sister.

By the time he was finished setting it all up and staggered up to his bed, it was late in the evening. With spring, the air was gradually heating up, and tonight was the first one in the year where the heat was oppressive. His loft was at the highest point of the *Rose's* living area, and there was only one small window, which only opened halfway.

Tonight, thankfully, a cool breeze finally moved in off the water, drying the sweat on his skin, and for once he drifted off to blissful sleep, listening to the gulls crying in the distance.

For better or worse, he was ready to begin.

XIII

SAILING

Rule #2: *It is crucial to establish rapport with the person you are interviewing. Building a connection and gaining their trust will encourage them to open up and share information more freely.*
- Shadow Mac's Comprehensive Guide to Private Investigation

Initially Jake had considered broadcasting a request on the web for information on WIFRUN2345, but in the end, he'd decided against it. The girl's entry on the DNA site had been deleted shortly after she was contacted—why? Had the timing just been a coincidence? Had she herself done it, after reconsidering her actions? Had Evangeline's attempt to contact her spooked her? Had some third party, maybe her parents or somebody else in authority, forced her to shut it down?

Whatever the reason, if he broadcast to the world that he wanted to contact her, and whoever had taken down the account got wind of his interest, they might go deeper underground.

He would have to do it the hard way, sifting through masses of irrelevant information to tease out the important facts. There were times when Jake found the plunge down the rabbit hole of web searches and data analysis interesting. Clues twisted in and out of search sites, popping up like the intertwining melodies of a Bach fugue. The thrill of getting an unexpected 'hit' on a search, or of finding a clue or a connection between two sets of data could be exciting.

But the process could also be tedious—taking one result, cross-referencing it with countless others, sifting through the outcome, and repeating the exercise using the results of that process. Rinse and repeat. He could only maintain his concentration for so long. And the incidents of a few nights ago, culminating in Evangeline leaving him passed out at the Screaming Dragon, were still playing on his mind.

He came up with a task to distract him from the tedium and from his own thoughts. He hadn't taken out his sailboat, *Spinner*, since last September. The weather was improving—becoming more favourable for sailing. Before he took the vessel out, it would need a lot of prep work. The deck, canopy, and cabin would all have to be cleaned and inspected, and the lines checked. The sail and jib, currently stowed in a chest on the forward deck, would have to be washed and rigged. The outboard, also stowed for the winter, would have to be oiled, mounted and tested.

For a break, over the next few days he alternated between hunching over his flea-market computer in his tiny loft office, drilling down into the darkest underbelly of the Internet, and working outside on the boat, glad for anything to take his mind off her...

Over the days that had passed since the events at the Screaming Dragon, Evangeline had contacted him twice, asking about his progress. Her tone had been annoyingly businesslike, but she did seem impatient for word of her sister. He'd reassured her that he was working on it, and that progress was being made.

Unexpectedly, on the way back from buying some supplies for *Spinner* on Sunday morning, he spotted her as he descended the ramp to Fisherman's Wharf and walked along the slip.

She was sitting on a wooden bench on the dock, not far from his vessel, wearing a tight pair of jeans and a sleeveless top that showed off her navel. To Jake's shock, when she looked up and saw him, her face lit up with pure joy, like a child holding a dreamed-of gift.

He froze on the spot. He tried to call up his earlier anger over the other night, but somehow her innocent, ecstatic expression had instantly melted it away.

She stood as he arrived, and gave him a quick hug.

Jake made them coffee, and they sat in the nook in his living area. She said nothing about the events at the bar, and about leaving him passed-out alone in the restaurant like yesterday's trash.

He wasn't sure why, but he didn't ask. He pushed down his anger and annoyance. In spite of her expression on seeing him today, he was determined to pivot their relationship to one of strictly business.

"At first, I thought it would be impossible to find someone with nothing but a pseudonym," he said as they sipped their coffee. "But it turns out there's lots of online tutorials explaining how to cross-reference pseudonyms found on one account with other accounts containing the same name."

"Aren't you clever," she said, smiling.

"Yes, I am," he agreed. "I found a handful that matched. It occurred to me that since the DNA site account had been removed, maybe other social media accounts using that pseudonym had been removed as well. Have you ever heard of the 'Deep Web'?"

"You mean the 'Dark Web'? I've heard of that."

Jake shook his head. "No, this is different. The Dark Web has stuff on it that's illegal or immoral—stuff the average person wouldn't, and probably shouldn't, be interested in.

"The Deep Web is just web sites that don't appear on most search engines. You can find things there that don't appear to regular web users. Anyway, it turned out I was right. I found some tutorials there that showed how to access those deleted accounts.

"I ended up with a half-dozen actual names with links to the pseudonym. I'm in the process of sifting through them."

She tensed and her eyes widened. "You can see what's in the deleted accounts?"

"Not the actual contents, but some of the account settings—names, sometimes emails and addresses. Of course, that raises the question—why were the accounts deleted, and who deleted them?"

She eyed him strangely, almost as if she didn't believe what he was saying.

"Are you sure you've told me everything about your contact with this girl?" he asked.

"Of course," she said indignantly, her hands curling around her coffee cup.

"Well," she finally said. "The wheels are in motion. I knew I could count on you." She reached out and placed a hand on his. "I know sometimes I may not show it, but finding my sister is really important to me..."

Then, like the throwing of a switch, she was smiling, with that little-girl smile that drew him in like a moth to a flame.

"It's a beautiful day," she said. "Let's do something fun."

An hour later, the afternoon sun lit Evangeline's face with a golden glow as she leaned back on the starboard side of *Spinner*, the vessel skimming effortlessly through the placid waters of the Inner Harbour. She tilted her head back and closed her eyes, letting the wind blow through her hair. *Spinner* heeled over in the breeze as Jake, standing at the tiller, reefed in the mainsail and headed upwind.

At first he'd worried that her idea of fun would be another binge downtown, but when he suggested going sailing, she'd clapped her hands with excitement. It was a perfect day, warm, with steady winds, and only a few puffy clouds dotting the sky. Squawking gulls circled overhead, and tiny waves lapped at the vessel's hull as they sailed out of Victoria harbour past incoming sailboats, power yachts, and fishing vessels, the multi-coloured jumble of Fisherman's Wharf slowly shrinking away into the distance.

Jake smiled, truly happy for the first time for as long as he could remember. Evangeline claimed she knew nothing about sailing, so before they left port he patiently explained the basics, the points of sail, tacking, gybing, and the need to get out of the way when the boom swung across. He didn't intend to go far. He wasn't an expert sailor—he knew enough to get them somewhere close and back again, provided the weather was good.

"A lot of people I've taken out like this have been scared of the water," he called up to her. "Or maybe it's my sailing ability."

Evangeline opened her eyes. "A lot of *people?*—as in *women?*"

"Get ready!" he shouted. "We're going to come about."

He pushed a hand down, warning her. She remembered, and ducked down. Jake hauled on the tiller. The bow turned through the wind and the boom swung over her head. He reefed on the sail, and they continued on a new tack.

"If they've got no sense of adventure," she called back, "maybe you're better off without them."

"You think so?

She straightened in her seat. "You never know what's going to happen, do you?" she called up to him. "An asteroid could fall out of the sky and smash you to bits any moment. Why not take a chance?"

They sailed in a straight northwest line, past McLoughlin Point, the cruise ship docks, and the iconic breakwater with its red and white lighthouse. In the distance, the monstrous white shape of an incoming cruise ship slowly expanded as it sailed toward them.

They made a few more tacks, enjoying the sun and the steady breeze. Jake even let Evangeline take the tiller for a while, and stood with his arm around her waist as she practiced controlling the vessel. She caught on quickly, and laughed as *Spinner* heeled strongly, the spray shooting over the gunwales each time she ventured close to the wind.

Technically they had now entered the Salish Sea. A jog northwest around the tip of the island and they would be in the open Pacific. After that, they could sail over four thousand nautical miles west without encountering land, eventually reaching Japan. The concept never failed to give Jake the shivers, imagining the incredible immensity of the planet they lived on.

In reality, they wouldn't go more than a few kilometers west before turning around and coming home.

"What's that?" Evangeline's voice brought him out of his daydream.

He followed her pointing finger to the north. A large, curving black shape was periodically breaching the waves, then disappearing again.

"We're going to come about!" he shouted excitedly.

"What?" Evangeline stepped aside as he took the tiller. She stood with her hands on a back stay, staring at the spectacle.

"Orcas," Jake shouted. "We're incredibly lucky today. Hang on!"

She instinctively ducked again as he tacked and they headed north, directly for the giant sea creatures. The massive black and white shapes with their towering dorsal fins continued to emerge in an arc from the waves, then plunge back in, heading west. The winds had strengthened, and the stays hummed as *Spinner* approached the shapes quickly.

They reached the four-hundred-meter legal approach distance. Jake let the sails slack and maintained a slow drift along with the path of the animals. Evangeline moved back and sat beside him. The whales dove and disappeared for a few minutes. *Spinner* bobbed on the rolling sea, and there was total silence as Jake and Evangeline wondered where and when they would reappear.

A few other vessels approached in the distance, heading their way or pointing toward the spot the amazing creatures had been seen. Suddenly, a shiny, bulbous, black nose breached the waves, only a few meters away. The orca exploded from the water in a massive arc, then dove with a thundering splash into the foam, soaking *Spinner's* bow. Evangeline reached out and squeezed Jake's hand. Another orca appeared, then a group of three, all rising and arcing above the waves in unison, then diving in and disappearing into the depths.

The spectacle continued for more than ten minutes, the magnificent creatures gradually making their way west, toward the open ocean. Both Jake and Evangeline were frozen in place, until once more *Spinner* was rolling alone in the open ocean, surrounded by silence.

The light was beginning to fade by the time they made it back to the *Honeysuckle Rose*, still stunned by the spectacle they'd witnessed. Jake opened a bottle of wine he'd been saving for a special occasion. He poured them each a glass, and they sat on the aft deck.

"That was wonderful," Evangeline said, moving her chair closer to his. "Magical—one of the best days of my life."

"Wow," Jake said. "That's some compliment. The night's cooling off—I'll be right back."

He was gone a few minutes, returning with a light sweater and draping it around her shoulders. She nestled down into her chair. As if to crown what had already been a magnificent day, the sun turned brilliant crimson as it slowly descended behind the clouds, and the sky turned a wash of yellows, oranges, and pinks. They sat so close Jake could feel the heat of her body beside him. He reminded himself of her behaviour the last time they'd been together, and of his admittedly crumbling intention to confine their relationship to business.

They watched the sunset, sipping the wine. Evangeline's hand moved into his, and she leaned over and laid her head on his shoulder. Jake glanced at the sky. For some reason, her description, 'magical' resonated in his mind. Something *was* different. The night sky was awash with light and colour, magical, as she'd said. The colours swirled together like a Van Gough painting, glowing as they slowly melted into the night.

Jettisoning his vow not to get involved, he leaned over, lifted her chin with one finger, and kissed her on the lips. A jolt of electricity seemed to pass through his body. She leaned in closer and wrapped her arms around his shoulders. Darkness was falling, and the burning stars were gathering in the sky. He and Evangeline kissed again, more passionately. He pulled her closer and they explored each other's bodies.

The lights of the city swept through the sky like flaming fireworks as they rose together and headed down to the cabin. It had somehow transformed as well—as if they'd entered a primordial cave, and were surrounded by ancient symbols and magical charms.

He found the radio and switched it on, and they made their way up into the loft and to his bed. The lines of the cabin were lit up from outside like shimmering neon lights. Every sight and sound was intensified, as if all his senses had been cranked up an extra notch.

A sensuous, languorous tune began on the radio and echoed through the room, its throbbing bass line like pumping blood, the thudding bass drum like a beating heart, and sliding strings like his heightened nerve endings. The image slid through his brain of a steaming jungle, of vines spiraling to the ground from above, and water dripping from the deep green leaves of tropical plants, moistening the rich earth below. They were like the first man and woman on a shining new Earth.

Jake didn't know why, but his perception was energized, and his sense of excitement heightened. She touched him and it was as if an electric charge rippled through his body. The vibrations resonated through the room and the light danced across Evangeline's skin as they undressed each other and Jake took her in his arms. Their naked bodies moved together, the rhythm of those movements interwoven with the music.

And the *Rose* responded, swaying and pulsing, the answering motion amplifying their pleasure.

XIV

A DEEP DIVE

Rule #36: It's vital for a detective to maintain a professional, dispassionate distance from the cases in which he's involved.
- Shadow Mac's Comprehensive Guide to Private Investigation

It was a beautiful spring day, and Jake was jogging happily along a tree-lined city sidewalk in the sun. Every few steps he would take an extra-long stride, launching himself momentarily into the air. With each jump the height gradually increased, until he finally pushed off and lifted completely from the ground, now flying, sailing over trees and grass, the wind blowing through his hair.

Jake awoke with a start. He blinked his eyes, and memories of last night gradually drifted back into his psyche. He rolled over in bed. Evangeline was gone. It was still dark, and the whole experience felt like a dream.

For a few seconds he questioned whether it had actually happened, whether she'd really been here. He sat up and looked around. There were no tokens of her presence: no note, no text or voice mail. But a hint of her fragrance still infused the air. Their two wine glasses still sat on the counter by the sink, and the radio was still playing, now blaring some bland news story.

He thought back on the surreal ecstasy of their lovemaking. Had she drugged him somehow, maybe in the time he'd gotten the sweater, or were the events and his perceptions for real—had her presence induced some kind of hypnotic effect?

Since meeting this woman he'd felt constantly off-balance, pushed or pulled just as he was finding his feet—as if he was waist-deep in the ocean, trying to stay upright under a constant barrage of pounding breakers.

It was frustrating and infuriating, but right now, all he could do was try to roll with it, and treasure the exquisite experiences like last night. Part of his imbalance came from the fact that he never knew when he would see Evangeline next, or how she would behave when it happened.

Determined to put the experience behind him and return to his role as pseudo-PI and contractor, he showered, got dressed, made himself a coffee, and got back on his flea-market computer to continue with the investigation.

But it felt like last night he'd crossed a boundary—one he had always vowed to avoid. He was in deep now, against all of his intentions. In what he recognized might be his last expression of disinterest, since he was checking out people on the web, he decided to check out his client— Evangeline Sirkants. Strangely, after more than half an hour of searching he'd found absolutely nothing, not on Facebook, Instagram, TikTok, or any of the other social media platforms.

Did that mean anything? There *were* people out there who wanted nothing to do with social media—maybe she was one of them. But he guessed that you could find traces of almost anyone on the Internet if you looked hard enough, even if they didn't have an intentional presence.

Taken as a whole, the web contained a large fraction of the sum total of human knowledge. It probably included data on virtually every person who'd spent any significant amount of time on a computer. And though she admitted she'd deleted her account, Evangeline *had* spent time on the *MyNewFamily* site.

What his finding almost certainly meant, and what he did his best to put out of his mind, was that the name she had given him was false—it wasn't her real name. And if she'd lied about that...

It was yet another mystery to investigate, but later, in the future. He put her web presence aside for the moment, and concentrated on his actual investigation. Three of the half-dozen names he'd extracted from sites linked to the sister's pseudonym looked like dead ends—either they were the wrong age or gender, or they were so far removed in time or geography that they could be eliminated.

He smiled as he scanned the remaining three—maybe the task wasn't as impossible as he'd originally thought. And anyway, it was kind of fun. It was a painstaking process, cross-referencing the names with websites, current and deleted, sifting through the results, and repeating the process, like refining a tiny nugget of pure gold from a truckload of ore. Eventually he managed to glean email addresses from two of the remaining entries.

He came up with a cover story—that he was trying to locate a girl he used to go to school with, and emailed both those addresses. One of them didn't exist anymore, and he wasn't surprised that the other simply didn't respond. Neither of those outcomes eliminated them from consideration—he'd just have to change direction.

He was forced to start from square one, in a sense. But now he could add the two recovered emails to his search criteria. After a few more hours of sifting and cross-referencing, he finally came across one promising user profile, in a previously deleted Facebook account.

The entry contained the email that hadn't answered, and a name, and could be indirectly traced back to WIFRUN2345. Most importantly, it also indirectly referenced a physical street address. The real name of WIFRUN2345, the name of the girl behind the account on the MyNewFamily.com site, was *Jeanette Mallory*.

The name meant nothing to him, but there was enough correlation of the search criteria to suggest that the girl at the address he'd identified was Evangeline's sister, or at least, the owner of the *MyNewFamily* account Evangeline had contacted.

There was only one problem—the address wasn't in Victoria—it was on the mainland, in Vancouver.

XV

MCKLUSKEY

Rule #9: Allow a witness to tell their story in their own words. The flow often reveals details that will later be important evidence.
- **Shadow Mac's Comprehensive Guide to Private Investigation**

It had now been two days since the sailing trip, and in all that time, Jake hadn't seen or heard from Evangeline. Apparently their night of lovemaking had been less magical for her than it had for him. He told himself that was a good thing. Their relationship would either end, or return to what it should have remained—that of a client and contractor.

Even though he knew otherwise, he again found himself questioning whether the events of that night had really happened. He was becoming increasingly annoyed at Evangeline's erratic behaviour.

Other than buying the flea-market computer and security software, he'd spent almost none of her money. He'd come up with a solid lead on her sister—already earning a good chunk of his retainer. But if necessary he could easily return however much of the balance she thought she was owed, and forget the whole thing.

But he'd agreed to this hare-brained 'investigation', so until he managed to contact Evangeline to officially resign, or she fired him, or she told him she'd given up on her quest, he felt obligated to continue. He resolved to make the trip to the big city tomorrow, whether he heard from his client or not.

Technically, Vancouver was only thirty or forty kilometers away, but Victoria was on an island. A lot of the distance between the two cities was taken up by the Strait of Georgia. Flying was much too expensive. His only option would be to take the ferry, which meant an almost two-hour boat ride, then an hour's drive to the city—three hours each way. He might even have to stay overnight, depending on how much luck he had connecting with Jeanette Mallory.

In the afternoon, McCluskey came over, and they lounged in a pair of deck chairs on the *Rose's* aft deck. Jake took a swig of the R&B ale in his hand and sat the can on the arm of the chair.

"Kid, you gotta lay off the drink," McCluskey said.

"You're one to talk," Jake said, nodding at the can in McCluskey's hand. "Anyway, I *gotta* quit for the time being, that was my last beer."

McCluskey pointed a finger at him. "Hey, I'm doing you a favour taking it. You're gonna kill yourself if you keep this up."

"You *do* remember what I do for a living—they like what I'm playing at the Salty Dog, they buy me a beer. It goes with the job."

"Well, maybe you need another job," McCluskey said. "Anyway, you figure on playing piano in sleazy bars into your old age? Doesn't sound like much of a career plan."

"Hey, I'm sitting down—there's no heavy lifting involved."

"You should be grateful I set you on a new employment path."

"Being a PI? Yeah, now there's promising career."

"Hey, it forces you to use your brain," McCluskey pointed at his own head, "keeps your mind working, staves off dementia."

"Till some angry boyfriend or cheating husband caves in my skull."

"You go to unusual and exotic places..."

Jake nodded toward the water. "Like getting tossed in Victoria Harbour in the middle of the night with concrete blocks tied to my ankles? Am I supposed to be alive or dead when all this happens?"

"You meet interesting people..."

"Well, so far you're right on that one," Jake said, thinking not only about Evangeline, but about a few of his other prospective clients. "Bearing in mind the ancient Chinese curse about living in interesting times..."

"Anyway," McCluskey said. "There's less opportunity to drink."

Jake laughed, remembering his recent all-night binge with Evangeline. McCluskey took one last swig of his beer, got up, and headed for his own vessel. He returned a few minutes later with a new six pack.

"This is your strategy for helping me climb on the wagon?" Jake said.

"Like you pointed out," McCluskey answered. "I took your last one. I always pay my debts."

Jake glanced up at the walkway to the Wharf, just as a familiar figure entered it from the parking lot above. He swallowed hard as Evangeline made her way down the ramp to the commercial section, and headed along the dock toward them. Even from this distance, he could see heads turn, following her. A few minutes later, like a ghost out of the past, she was standing beside the *Rose*.

She was dressed in shorts and a tee-shirt, but looked no less stunning than before. He fought to suppress the luminous images drifting through his mind of their night of lovemaking, and of her body moving beneath him.

"Hi," she said, smiling, as if nothing had happened between them.

Jake had assumed he'd see her again eventually. He willed himself not to get angry, and for the thousandth time told himself she was just a client, though after the other night, that designation was no longer very convincing.

He hauled another deck chair over for her, and handed her a beer from McCluskey's case.

"I'm happy to finally meet Jake's manager in person," she said to McCluskey. "Jake tells me it was your idea for him to get into the PI business."

Jake laughed to himself.

"Somebody's gotta look after him," McCluskey said.

Jake turned to McCluskey. "So, as my 'manager', what do you *do* exactly?"

"What?" McCluskey asked, looking up.

"You, know," Jake continued, "what do you manage—what are your duties?"

"Well," McCluskey said, "I took your picture—"

"While I was passed out."

McCluskey shrugged. "I put the ad in—I got you this gig. Hell, you wouldn't be sitting here with this beautiful lady if it wasn't for me."

Jake let it go. He still wasn't sure he wanted to be sitting here, even with someone as gorgeous as Evangeline—especially with someone as gorgeous as Evangeline. And even after their lovemaking following the sailboat voyage, he felt a lingering resentment over her erratic behaviour, and hadn't forgotten waking up alone at the Screaming Dragon.

Evangeline eyed McCluskey's red weathered face, the wispy beard, the plaid shirt, baggy pants and gumboots.

"Do you manage any other clients—besides Jake?" she asked.

Jake snorted, almost spitting out his beer.

"No time," McCluskey said. "Too much happening."

Evangeline looked at him enquiringly.

"Helping out poor Jake here is just a sideline," McCluskey said. "My primary profession is philosopher." He leaned back in his chair. "Philosopher, and student of the human condition."

Evangeline smiled. "The human condition—that sounds like a pretty broad subject. Do you have a particular specialty?"

McCluskey set down his beer, and wiped his mouth on his sleeve. "Well, right now, I'm in the process of cataloguing the scourges of humanity."

"Scourges?" Evangeline asked.

"That's right," he answered, "as in—'major causes of suffering'." McCluskey eyed her intently. "For instance, you've got the POAFNABWICKs."

He leaned back, lifted his feet and set them on a nearby piling.

"Here we go," Jake said under his breath.

"What?" she asked McCluskey.

"Poaf-na-bwicks," McCluskey said. "P-O-A-F-N-B-W-C—'People On A First Name Basis With Cattle'."

"Oh."

He waved a hand back and forth in front of him. "You see them every day, driving around in their pickup trucks or muscle-cars. A lot of them have even got that bovine facial expression—you know, like they're not quite sure where they are, or what they're doing. My theory is that they're not even certain about their species."

Jake broke in. "She doesn't need to hear all this stuff—"

"Then there's the PYWPOITWOFs," McCluskey nodded sagely.

Jake stared at his beer and shook his head slowly.

"O...Okay." Evangeline raised an eyebrow, waiting for an explanation.

"'People You Wouldn't Piss On If They Were On Fire'," McCluskey said. "Just plain evil. Most of the people in authority, whether it's business or government, are in that category, too many to list right now—"

"Thank God," Jake said.

"By scourges," Evangeline said, "you mean they're dangerous."

McCluskey chuckled to himself. "When our civilization finally hits the skids big time, they'll be a good part of the reason."

"Of the two," Evangeline said, "which would you say is a bigger threat?"

"What? Between evil and stupidity?" McCluskey answered, eyeing her with a newfound respect. "That's a very astute and interesting question." He sat thinking for a few seconds. "Stupidity, I think. Evil usually has some kind of logic, some agenda. You can analyze an evil person's actions and make sense of them, maybe guess what they're going to do. With stupidity, all bets are off. You never know what they'll do, because they don't really know themselves. And what they do doesn't necessarily make any sense.

"They can be convinced of all kinds of ridiculous crap, conspiracy theories and such. And once they've made up their minds, such as they are, a stick of dynamite wouldn't convince them to think any different."

McCluskey paused for another swig of beer.

"The worst of it is," he continued, "you usually get the two groups working in tandem – or more correctly, a smart-evil person controlling one or more weak-stupid ones. That's a pretty lethal combination."

McCluskey put his feet down and leaned forward in his chair, a movement that always signaled he was about to expound on some weighty philosophical observation. "The fact is that history is an endless litany of the smart and powerful conning the weak and stupid into thinking and doing things that are against their own interests.

"Things like paying money for bottled water when they can have it out of the tap for free. Or eating crappy food that will make them sick when perfectly healthy food is sitting on store shelves in front of them.

"Then the same clowns pay big money for vitamins, hoping to replace the ones they would have gotten for free if they'd just eaten the healthy food in the first place. The sad thing is that the weak-stupid don't even realize it's happening. It's tragic, but it was ever so."

McCluskey closed his eyes, like he was contemplating the origin of the Universe.

Evangeline picked up her beer. "You say you're cataloguing—what are you planning to do with your findings?"

McCluskey re-opened his eyes, now deadly serious. "It'll all be in my book, which should be out shortly. Right now, I'm just watching. Watching and waiting to see what happens. At the moment, the social pendulum has swung toward the highest PPC rating I've witnessed in my lifetime.

"PPC?"

"'Pinheads Per Capita'," McCluskey answered, like it was obvious. "A shit-storm is coming. It'll be here momentarily. All we can do is pray for a change, or maybe just hang on for the ride. When the pendulum swings one way, it always eventually comes back and swings the other.

"By that time, my book will be firmly entrenched in the public psyche. And I'll be available—you know, for consultation."

"Consultation?" she asked.

"With the 'powers that be'," he held up two fingers of each hand like quotation marks. "It'll be such a shock they'll be splashing around like fish in a bucket, looking for direction. Most of them may be evil, and some of them may be stupid, but they're all we've got."

XVI

THE SHUTTERS

Rule #20: When tailing a subject, maintain a distance far enough away to avoid attracting attention, but close enough not to lose the subject if he does something unexpected.

- Shadow Mac's Comprehensive Guide to Private Investigation

Later that afternoon, after McCluskey had gone, Jake and Evangeline continued lounging on the aft deck. From the start she'd seemed reluctant to talk about her life, and about accidentally finding her sister on the DNA site. Now that Jake had come up with an address for the person they were looking for, his earlier doubts surfaced again.

Since they'd met, once or twice he'd tried to get more out of her to back her story, asking about France, her family, and Quebec City. She'd always given vague answers, or managed to evade the questions.

He'd even tried a couple of French phrases on her. She seemed to understand them, and as far as he could tell her replies were correct. Since he hardly remembered any of his high-school French, he couldn't say for sure. Anyway, that meant nothing, except that maybe she spoke French.

Through the whole process he'd felt an undercurrent of guilt—he was acting like his ex-girlfriend Julie, testing Evangeline to see if she measured up. For now at least, he resolved to accept her story as genuine. Still he wondered what would happen if and when he actually confronted Jeanette Mallory.

"I didn't want to mention it when McCluskey was here," he said, "but I might have come across a pretty important lead in finding your sister."

She pushed herself up, her expression brightening. "Really?"

"I traced the pseudonym from the *MyNewFamily* website to an actual name and address."

She smiled. "I knew you would come through."

"The girl's name is Jeanette, Jeanette Mallory—does the name ring any bells?"

He studied her reaction as she processed the information. Evangeline shook her head. She really didn't seem to recognize it.

"Only trouble is," he continued, "the address is in Vancouver—you're sure the account said she was living in Victoria?"

Evangeline shrugged. "Maybe she moved."

Jake took a sip of his beer. "I was planning to head over there tomorrow."

"You still have enough of my retainer for the trip?"

He nodded.

"I'm impressed," she said, smiling again. "See—the stars don't lie."

"You can come with me if you want. It might be a chance to meet your sister for the first time."

She gave him a strange look he didn't really understand.

She shook her head. "If she's the right one, there'll be time enough for me to meet her."

The lowering sun bathed her features in a golden glow, like some eternal sea-goddess. Jake picked up his phone. "Say cheese," he said, holding it up and pointing it at her.

"No!" she shouted, scowling, and holding her hand up to block her face.

"What?" he said, laughing. "You're shy?"

"No pictures," Evangeline snapped. "Ever."

"Okay, okay," he said, setting the phone down.

They sat silently for a while, watching the sun sink in the sky.

"I have to go," she finally said out of the blue.

Jake couldn't decide whether to be happy or sad. He wanted to spend more time with her, but he dreaded being swept up in another all-night binge. In any case, he was supposed to be playing at the Salty Dog tonight.

"I should get ready soon anyway," he said. "I gotta work." He swung his feet to the deck and sat up. "Why don't you let me take you home? You never have shown me where you live."

Her body tensed. "You don't need to come. I'm at the Shutters—it's just across the harbour."

She nodded toward the north, to the neighbourhood known as Esquimalt. The Shutters was a luxury resort style apartment block situated on the traditional territory of the Songhees indigenous people. The complex featured an onsite spa and surrounding water gardens, and had a fabulous view of the harbour. Jake had walked past it a few times, but had never been inside. You could actually see its sweeping white facade from the north end of the Wharf.

He raised an eyebrow. "Really? Wow—fancy place. I'd love to see the interior."

"I'd really rather not."

"I've got time. I don't have to be at the Salty Dog for a couple of hours."

She glanced at her hands on her lap. "My place is a mess."

"Come on, you've seen the inside of my place," he nodded toward the *Rose's* living area behind them.

"No!" she turned on him.

He flinched and leaned back.

"Sorry," she said, "It's just that I'm picky about it. Maybe next time..." She got to her feet.

"You're taking the water-taxi?" he asked, rising as well.

Evangeline nodded.

The water-taxis were mini-ferries that took foot-passengers to various locations around the harbour, including to the Songhees lands on the other side. Jake had taken them numerous times, mainly to frequent one of the bars on the far shore.

"Well, at least let me walk you to the landing," he said.

The taxi landing was a short walk from the *Rose*, on another jetty of the Fisherman's Wharf complex. They strolled along the dock, past the myriad shapes and colours of other houseboats, then through the commercial section.

Several giant tour buses were parked in the lot above, and a wave of tourists, probably from a recently arrived cruise ship, were gathered, getting ready to head down the walkway.

"Have you ever actually seen this book McCluskey's talking about?" Evangeline asked as they walked.

"You know the saying, 'Don't ask, don't tell'?" Jake answered. "That's where we stand at the moment. Let's just say I'm not holding my breath till it comes out."

"What's his story?"

"McCluskey? I've never been able to get him to talk about it. Deirdre, my great-aunt, who lived here before me, said she didn't like to gossip. Maggie, from across the way, claimed she knew something. She's told me a few things."

"Does he actually make his living from writing?"

Jake laughed. "In his dreams, maybe. Believe it or not, according to Maggie he used to be the VP of Finance for an Internet startup, back around the turn of the Millennium."

"I wouldn't have guessed that was his background."

"It might or might not be true. Anyway, from what I heard, the company he worked for were into something shady. It was years ago, just before the dot-com bubble burst. Every shyster drawing a breath was on the Internet in some way or other, selling puppies or artwork, or knitting needles—you name it.

"Eventually there was a government investigation of McCluskey's company. I think a few of the senior management actually went to prison."

"But not McCluskey."

Jake smiled. "McCluskey may be a lot of things, but he's not stupid. The story goes that he somehow extricated himself from the whole thing. And, of course, managed to keep a pretty big stack of money to boot."

"And that's how he bought his houseb... I mean 'floating home'?"

"I guess. Other than this book he talks about, which may or may not be for real, I'm not aware of him ever having done any other kind of work. He's got some source of income. Who knows? Maybe the book will actually sell."

They finally arrived at the launch point, just a demarcated section of the dock where the water-taxi would land.

At the moment, they were the only people waiting. In the distance he could see the ferry approaching. The quaint little boats, roly-poly and ungainly, bobbed in the water like something out of a Looney-tunes cartoon. They were always popular with the tourists, and were actually convenient for getting around the small harbour, which was basically in the center of town.

The taxi pulled into the landing, and a few passengers disembarked, stepping onto the dock.

Evangeline turned to Jake. "I'm sorry I can't invite you over."

He just shrugged. "Like you said, maybe next time."

He was shocked when she suddenly leaned forward and gave him a long, passionate kiss, before turning toward the taxi.

He tensed as the 'pilot' reached out for her hand, steadying her as she stepped onto the gently rocking vessel.

Jake glared at the pilot as he paid Evangeline's fare, and she took her seat on one of benches, along with a few others who'd finally showed up. She beamed at Jake and waved, as the little boat pulled out into the blue waters.

He watched as the little water-taxi bobbed slowly toward the other side, the sweeping multi-storey edifice of the Shutters apartment block looming over the rocks across the harbour.

On the way back to his vessel, he replayed the conversation they'd just had, her reaction to the photograph, her complete absence from the web, and her expression when he asked to see her place. At home, he suppressed another twinge of guilt as he rushed to grab a pair of binoculars from a drawer in the galley and made his way to the north end of the dock.

A few minutes later he could make out the water-taxi approaching the far side. He angled himself partially behind the corner of the nearest houseboat, and trained the binoculars on the vessel as it bumped against the landing. His grip tightened as the pilot again took Evangeline's hand, helping her onto the platform. She turned right and started walking, heading, as he'd expected, toward the Shutters complex.

As she entered the grounds, she encountered an older man with a pair of clippers in his hand—the gardener? She stopped and talked to him for a few seconds, then continued on.

A slight rise blocked the actual entrance to the building from Jake's vantage point. Evangeline continued along a stone path over it and down the other side, still heading toward the entrance. Just as she was about to disappear behind it, she stopped and turned.

For a second Jake felt as though she was staring straight at him. Instinctively, he lowered the binoculars and moved further behind the corner.

When he ventured back out and scanned the building, she was nowhere to be seen.

XVII

SLOW DANCE

Rule #33: Pay attention to the interviewee's body language, facial expressions, and overall demeanor. Non-verbal cues can often reveal more than what is being said verbally.
- **Shadow Mac's Comprehensive Guide to Private Investigation**

That night, the crowd at the Salty Dog was light. Max had booked Jake to work even though it was a Tuesday, expecting the arrival of a cruise ship. That arrival had been delayed, but it was already arranged, so he was up at the piano, as usual, lost in his music. He'd almost subconsciously drifted into Fats' *Handful of Keys*. It was a fast, intricate, technically demanding piece that usually impressed the audience, but at the moment he was oblivious to how many were listening, or even whether there was anybody out there.

When he finally finished, amid the smattering of applause, he heard the sound of enthusiastic clapping nearby. He looked up from the piano. Evangeline was sitting at a table not far away, wearing a light green sun dress adorned with images of flowered vines. She smiled and waved at him, and took a sip of what looked like a martini.

Jake slid his complimentary beer off the piano and joined her.

"This is a pleasant surprise," he said.

"That was wild!" she gushed. "Incredible! You see, the numbers are never wrong. You obviously have many talents. I hope you don't mind me coming here."

"Why would I mind?"

He scanned the room. Only a few tables were occupied. It was almost eleven. If the place was ever going to pick up, it would have by now. He walked over to the bar and talked to Max, who raised an eyebrow when Jake nodded toward Evangeline. Max smiled and nodded in return, and Jake rejoined her.

"I've got to finish this set," he said, "then I can join you. Max said I could take the rest of the night off."

About ten minutes later he picked up his half-full beer from the piano, brought it over, and set it on her table. James P. Johnson's *Bleeding-Hearted Blues* began to echo through the sound system.

Evangeline smiled up at him. "Something tells me this isn't their regular music feed."

"I also convinced Max to let me set up my own play list for the rest of the night," he said, sitting down across from her. "There's not much of a crowd—most of them aren't listening anyway."

Pushing down a new twinge of guilt, he decided to try digging for some more information. "You've never told me anything about yourself," he said, swirling the beer in his glass. "Have you got a job here in Victoria?"

Her hand froze in the middle of lifting her drink to her lips. She set down the glass. "I'm sort of between jobs at the moment."

"What did you do when you lived in Quebec City?"

She hesitated, and finally shrugged. "I worked for a while as a secretary for a law office. A few years ago I tried to get into modeling, but there's a lot of competition."

Jake tried to imagine Evangeline losing out in a modeling competition. Who was she competing against?

"I've always loved animals," she said. "I thought about being a vet, or maybe a vet's assistant..."

He thought back to her reaction to the seals, and Kong, and the orcas.

"Well, it's not too late," he said. "You could still do any of those things—don't you think?"

She shook her head. "I've got more important work right now."

She stared at her hands on the table, then looked away. It seemed like a strange statement. He decided it was time to change the subject.

"If I go to Vancouver and actually meet this girl," he said, "what exactly do you want me to say."

She looked up nervously. "Don't mention me—at least not yet."

"Well, I'll have to come up with some reason why I'm there, and confirm that she's the one who put up the account."

She cocked her head, thinking. "Fine, don't but give any details."

"If you want, I can call you from Vancouver tomorrow," he said, "let you know the status of the investigation—"

"Let's not talk about that tonight," she said, taking his hand.

There was a pause, where neither of them spoke.

"Have many of your girlfriends come to watch you play?" she finally asked.

He shrugged. "A few. Most of them didn't really share my taste in music. They're like everybody else—into rap and hip-hop and stuff like that."

"I love your music," she said.

As if on cue, a slow song came over the sound system. It was Fats' rendition of *Smoke Dreams*, one of Jake's favourites. He rose and took Evangeline's hand, and they made their way to the tiny dance floor in the center of the room.

The organ ebbed and flowed behind Fats' plaintive vocals, as they slow-danced. Her body pressed against his, and he could feel the warmth of her breath on his cheek. The bar was almost empty. They swayed together, barely aware of the music, lost in each other.

Half an hour later they were back at the *Honeysuckle Rose*, in Jake's loft. Again they made love, the light of the moon and stars streaming through the loft's skylight, lighting up Evangeline's amazing body and adding silver highlights to her hair as she moved beneath him. Then she was on top, and once more the swaying of the *Rose* intensified their movements.

After another hour of passionate lovemaking, she suddenly said. "I have to leave."

She got up and got dressed. Moments later, she was gone.

XVIII

THE BIG CITY

Rule #11: There are three modes of surveillance: from a parked car, on foot, or from inside a building.
- **Shadow Mac's Comprehensive Guide to Private Investigation**

The next morning, for once only mildly hungover, and still processing the events of last night, Jake made his way to the commercial section of the docks and had breakfast at one of the Wharf restaurants. Today, as he'd planned, he would make the trip to Vancouver and check out Jeanette Mallory's apartment.

It felt like a turning point. For the first time, he'd be going beyond sitting at a computer typing in Google searches. He'd be out there in the world, interviewing people, investigating leads, and generally assaulting his psyche with situations that were completely unfamiliar.

In many ways, it was a frightening prospect. And it brought home two important facts. First, that this wasn't a game—it could have consequences. The circumstances surrounding the removal of the *MyNewFamily* account might be totally innocuous—or they might not be. There was even a remote possibility that he might be placing himself in danger. Second, that he had no experience in any of the activities he was planning—he knew nothing about interviewing or gathering information on the ground.

As he approached the *Rose* on his way back from breakfast, a man stood waiting on the dock. Jake guessed that the visitor was another potential 'client'. McCluskey's ad had been gone for a week, but somehow people were still responding to it. He'd developed a nose for these things, and in any case, why else would a stranger be standing there at this time of the morning.

He was tempted to turn around, go back for another coffee, and wait for the guy to leave. But this was his home—he was damned if he was going to be driven away from it by some stranger. As he moved closer, he could see that the man was in his twenties, thin, with wispy blond hair and glasses.

"I'm not a detective," Jake repeated his standard line as he arrived.

"What do you mean?" the man said. "The ad said—"

"The ad on the web was a hoax." He tried to push past the man and step up to his vessel.

"But this job's a piece of cake," the guy said, quickly stepping in and blocking Jake's path. "Guaranteed. It's like free money. Just hear me out..."

Jake sat down on the deck, resigned. "What?"

"I want you to follow my girlfriend—I'm sure she's cheating on me."

"Sounds like a lot of work to me," Jake said.

"This is different." He counted off points on the fingers of one hand. "I can tell you where she works. I know when she gets off, and even where she goes.

"All you have to do is follow her. And take pictures—take lots of pictures. The last guy hardly took any."

Jake looked up at him. "Last guy?"

"Yeah," the man said. "The curtains were wide open—you could see everything. But he only took one or two."

"You already have proof that she's cheating?" Jake asked.

"Yeah. With different guys, too. In fact, I think it's with a different guy almost every time."

Jake scrunched up his nose. "Well, if you already know, what do you need me for? Anyway, why do you put up with it?"

The man hung his head. "Because I'm a bad person, I deserve it. Even Kelly, my girlfriend, agrees with me."

"She *knows* about all this?"

"Yeah, of course," the man said, as if it was obvious. "Why do you think she leaves the curtains open? See how easy it would be? Have you got a proper camera? A Nikon or Canon or something? With a good zoom lens. I don't want any cell-phone crap. I want good quality. But you'd have to get lots of pictures—that's important."

＊

Jake didn't own a car—in fact, though he knew how to drive, he had never owned one. Victoria was a relatively small town. Fisherman's Wharf was within easy walking distance of the downtown core and most of the places he wanted to go, and he could get almost anywhere else by taking the bus.

Even if he *had* owned a car, it would have cost a substantial portion of Evangeline's retainer to take it round trip on the ferry to the mainland. But Vancouver was a big city—and there he'd need transportation.

To get around this problem he'd signed up for the *EVO* car-sharing service. He could pick up an EVO in any of their specially designated 'Home Zones', unlock it with a special cell-phone code, and hit the road. To return it, he just parked in any approved zone. There was a zone within walking distance of the Vancouver Central Bus Terminal where he would arrive from the ferry.

He'd quickly brushed off the photograph guy, packed an overnight bag, and now sat in the back of a Pacific Coach Lines bus as it pulled out of the central bus station, headed for the ferry at Swartz Bay.

The bus, half full during the shoulder tourist season, made its way through the city, which hadn't changed substantially since Jake was a kid. Named for Queen Victoria, the iconic monarch of the British Empire, and known as the 'Garden City', Victoria was one of the oldest cities in the Pacific Northwest. British settlements were first established there in 1843, and its Chinatown was the second oldest in North America, after that of San Francisco.

Though the British hadn't had a major presence there for more than a hundred years, Victoria billed itself as a quaint remnant of the British

Empire. High Tea was still regularly served at the Empress Hotel. In town, souvenir shops sold trinkets bearing images of Union-Jacks and Beefeaters, English-style pubs proliferated, and red double-decker buses plied the streets.

The bus left the downtown proper in less than twenty minutes, and connected with the Pat Bay highway out to the ferry terminal, about twenty kilometers away.

The suburbs were soon replaced by farmland as they sped along the highway. Jake gazed out the window at passing fields dotted with grazing cows or carpeted with leafy produce, with the dark blue waters of the Haro Strait in the distance. The bus flew past the turn-off for Island View beach, where Jake had often hung out in his younger days, and where he had lost his virginity one night at a beach party in a secluded field, with a girl whose name he could no longer remember.

It was a weekday, still early in the season—the ferry terminal was only sparsely occupied. He'd booked the bus all the way into Vancouver, and they only had to wait twenty minutes to board. While a few passengers left the bus and ventured over to the terminal building for coffee or snacks, he stayed where he was, intending to sleep.

But his mind was still focused on his first true outing as a PI—that is, pseudo-PI, and his impending meeting with Jeanette Mallory. As an only child, he had no experience with siblings, and whatever emotional baggage having one might bring.

He thought back to the times he and Evangeline had talked about her sister, and tried to analyze her response. Of course, she'd never met this girl, and knew nothing about her. There was no reason why she should feel an emotional connection. But though Evangeline seemed fixated on finding her sister, she didn't seem that interested in actually meeting her.

It made him wonder: if the woman in Vancouver actually turned out to be the one he was searching for, what should he say to her? Like most decisions in his life until now, his current plan was to simply play it by ear.

＊

Half an hour later, he stood on the upper deck of the giant ferry, *Spirit of Vancouver Island,* and watched as the Swartz Bay terminal complex slowly shrunk into the distance. It was a sunny spring day, and dozens of gulls circled the ship's wake, gliding in the updrafts generated by its motion. The wind blew through his hair as he leaned forward on the railing, watching as they sailed past islands flanked by rocky bluffs and blanketed with thick green forests.

The Coast Salish First Nations peoples had inhabited Vancouver Island for thousands of years before the Spanish 'discovered' it in the late 18th century. Soon after that, the British had kicked out the Spaniards, and discovered it again. The massive island was one of several North American locations, including his destination, named after British naval captain George Vancouver, who explored the Pacific Northwest between 1791 and 1794.

The trip to the city of Vancouver would take just under two hours. After grabbing a self-serve plastic-wrapped sandwich and a cup of coffee in the cafeteria, he returned to the outer deck and sat on one of the many benches in the sun.

He breathed the sea air deep into his lungs and for a moment relaxed. He hadn't been to Vancouver for more than a year. The last time had been for what at the time had seemed like a promising gig with an old friend who'd sworn his band was headed for the big time.

The gig had been a fiasco, and his friend's bandmates had turned out to be assholes. But, Jake reflected, at least he'd done something. Whatever the consequences of this latest fiasco, at least it too was having the effect of catapulting him, willingly or unwillingly, out of what he now recognized was the serious rut his life had been traveling in for a long time.

You could actually buy drinks on the ferry, but Jake stuck with the coffee. As depraved, humiliating, and ultimately unpleasant as the Screaming Dragon episode had been, it had had the beneficial effect of putting him off excessive drinking, at least for the time being.

Anyway, he wanted a clear head. He was still processing his relationship with Evangeline—what her game really was, and why he was continuing with this investigation and traveling on this ferry in the first place. Last night had again been magical, but it seemed like every encounter with her was a crap-shoot—he could never be sure what would happen.

Of course, she *was* paying for his time, the ferry, and everything else. But in a way that made it worse—accepting her money committed him to continuing with the investigation. It meant he was effectively accepting his role as her employee.

An hour into the trip, the ship veered to port and rounded a bend into Active Pass, sailing to within a hundred meters of breathtaking rugged, evergreen-blanketed cliffs that plunged into the sea, interspersed with tiny gray scallops of gravel beach. Occasionally he spotted a home perched high on the surrounding bluffs.

He passed out for a while on his bench, and by the time he woke and rubbed the knot in his back, the long black promontory splitting the ocean and leading to the artificial island of the Robert's Bank coal terminal cut a line in the distance, and the Tsawwassen ferry terminal was in sight dead ahead. Seconds later, a booming voice on the public address system told everyone to prepare for arrival.

Down on the car deck, he re-boarded his bus, and slept fitfully for another hour, haunted not only by the prospect of what he would encounter in Vancouver, but by dreams of the client he was doing it all for. An abrupt stop shook him awake and he looked up. They had arrived at the main Vancouver Bus Terminal.

It was time for his initiation.

XIX

JEANETTE MALLORY

Rule #3: A good detective is like a chameleon. He can fit in anywhere, and get along with anybody.
- **Shadow Mac's Comprehensive Guide to Private Investigation**

Overnight bag in hand, Jake walked to a designated zone near the Central Bus Terminal and picked up one of the available EVOs, a black Toyota Prius. Until now, the investigation had cost him a considerable amount of his time, but not much money. But with the bus and ferry expenses, and now the car sharing, costs were beginning to pile up.

From the time he'd agreed to get involved, he'd deliberately avoided spending much of Evangeline's retainer. He hadn't yet abandoned the idea of tossing the whole ridiculous escapade and giving her money back. But he was here, so apparently, at least for the time being, he was still on the case.

The address he'd identified online was on Vancouver's East Side, a low-rent, working-class part of the city, actually not too far from the bus station.

Vancouver was a big city, with lots of big city problems. Its setting was breathtaking, bordering the blue expanses of English Bay and Burrard Inlet, with the spectacular backdrop of the snow-tipped North Shore mountains. A popular saying, at least in the winter, was that you could go sailing in the morning, and skiing in the afternoon.

But the city had more than its share of poverty and crime. Victoria had a few dangerous neighbourhoods, but they were dwarfed by those in Vancouver, such as the infamous Downtown East Side, where tent cities blocked large sections of sidewalk, the skeletal frames of addicts shuffled along the streets, and discarded condoms and syringes littered the alleyways. Jake had been in Vancouver enough times to know what and where to avoid.

Though he knew the general layout of the city, and you could always tell which way was north by looking for the mountains, in contrast to Victoria, you could easily get lost here. Since he didn't own a car, it took a while to figure out how to use the EVO's GPS system.

He eventually managed to punch in Jeanette Mallory's address. The device led him south on Main Street, past the Main Street/Science World Skytrain station and False Creek, the narrow finger of ocean that extended deep into the city. Eventually he reached East Van, with its maze of narrow side streets and decaying houses.

After a scouting run past what turned out to be an aging apartment complex with mildew-stained stucco walls, he parked the EVO a couple of blocks away, walked to the building, and climbed the creaky stairs to the third floor.

He'd come up with a cover story to explain what he was doing there. If a woman answered the door, and she was the right age to be Jeanette Mallory, he would start with a variation of his 'searching for an old school-friend' line, saying he was checking the addresses of several Jeanette Mallorys, looking for the right one.

If his contact actually turned out to be Jeanette, he would bring up the *MyNewFamily* account. Hopefully he could gain her trust and explain his real reason for being there.

If someone else answered, he'd simply say he was an old friend of Jeanette's looking to get in touch with her.

Standing in front of the paint-chipped apartment door, he heard the chatter of a TV somewhere in the interior. Since he had no idea who he would actually find on the other side, he had to be prepared to wing it. He took a deep breath and knocked. There was a shuffling sound inside. He knocked again. A moving shadow appeared in the bulb of the peep-hole.

"What do you want?" a muffled female voice said from the other side.

"Sorry to bother you," he said. "I'm looking for Jeanette Mallory?"

There was silence for a few seconds.

"There's nobody here by that name," the voice finally answered. "You've got the wrong apartment."

"Are you sure?" he said. "This is the address I was given."

The voice seemed anxious. Was that because she actually *was* Jeanette Mallory, or just the natural reaction to finding a male stranger at her door.

"I told you," the voice said, "There's nobody here of that name."

"Please," he said. "I've come all the way from Victoria. I just want to ask her—"

The latch turned, and the door opened a crack, with the security chain still attached. The face of a nervous woman appeared in the gap. She was wearing a loose-fitting sweat-shirt and jeans. She looked in her late twenties, too old to be Jeanette. She also looked ready to slam the door, but there was an expression of recognition on her face. The TV feed, some kind of sports game, now echoed more loudly behind her.

"Who's out there?" A male voice called from inside.

"Nobody," she turned and called behind her.

She turned back to Jake, speaking quietly. "That might be the name of the girl who lived here before. I think they said she'd disappeared— left town or something. They moved out all her stuff."

"Who's they?"

"Management," she said. "Just a minute."

She moved to close the door, and gave him a look when it struck his foot. He smiled, and removed the foot. She closed it, and he heard her walking away. He wasn't entirely sure whether she was planning to come back.

A few seconds later, the door-chain was unfastened and the door flung open. Jake had expected the woman, and he jumped back when instead he was confronted with a young guy in a wife-beater shirt and jeans, with tattoos and three days' growth of beard. The guy didn't look friendly.

"What do you want?" he said.

"I was just —" Jake started to say.

The girl reappeared beside him in the doorway, with a business card in her hand.

"These guys," she said, handing Jake the card.

He scanned it, and smiled at her, then at her friend.

"Get lost," the man said. He pushed the woman back and slammed the door.

"Thank you," Jake said through the closed door, and got out of there.

"What the hell was that?" he heard the man's voice inside the apartment as he walked away.

Sorry lady, Jake thought. *Hope I didn't cause you too much grief.*

"Of course," he said out loud, back on the street, flicking the card with his fingers as he walked back to the car, "what made me think it would be easy?"

XX

AN IMPERSONATOR

Rule #15: The ability to play a role is especially important for private investigators who work alone most of the time. Using his own identity could expose the investigator to recognition and danger.

- Shadow Mac's Comprehensive Guide to Private Investigation

The office of Fairways Property Management was in a far corner of a small, aging strip mall in Burnaby, the district next door to East Van. The office was nestled between a yoga studio and an accounting business. It didn't seem likely that the company would just give away Jeanette's belongings at the request of a stranger, but if they still had them, it was worth a try.

Jake willed himself to be calm as he walked through the front door. This type of cloak and dagger business was completely beyond his experience. He imagined a TV private eye adopting an outrageous persona to pry information out of a suspect. The woman from Jeanette's apartment had said that Fairways had removed Jeanette's stuff—she must have taken off in a hurry, and left some things behind.

He had no idea what the items would be—furniture? clothes? housewares? He hoped that there would be something to indicate who she was, and where she'd gone. The police might have come by and picked it up if there was any kind of missing persons investigation. If not...

"You're Jeanette Mallory's brother?" the woman at the front desk said, when Jake explained himself, coming up with a story on the fly. He couldn't decide whether or not her tone was one of suspicion.

"She moved to Calgary," Jake continued to ad-lib, surprised at how easy it was. "It's hard for her to get back here. She asked me to pick up her stuff."

"What took her so long?" the woman said.

"She's been busy—you know how it is."

"Can I see some ID?" the woman asked him.

Why didn't I think of that? Jake thought, as he froze momentarily, trying to maintain a calm exterior. It occurred to him that he couldn't have done anything even if he'd anticipated the question. He hadn't needed a fake ID since he was seventeen, trying to get into the liquor store, and he wouldn't even know where to get one.

He finally just handed her his driver's license.

She squinted at it. "Sommers?"

"Is there a problem?" he asked, cultivating a mild annoyance.

She nodded at the computer screen. "Jeanette Mallory—Jacob Sommers. I thought you said you were her brother."

"Oh," he answered. "Mallory's her married name."

"But it says here she was the lone occupant," the woman said.

Jake shrugged, almost enjoying his first attempt at serial lying. "She's separated."

"Hold please," the woman said indifferently.

She rolled her chair over to a filing cabinet, sifted through it and grabbed one of the folders, then rolled back to face him.

She read through the file. "Her rent was all paid up. She owed for the move-out fee. They found a bit of damage when they checked the place. But the security deposit covered everything. It looks like it all evens out."

She flipped a page in the file. "Sorry, according to this, they got rid of the furniture and clothes. You should have come earlier. All they kept was a box of papers that were easier to store. You're lucky you came now—we only keep this stuff for six months."

Twenty minutes later, Jake pulled up to a diner in another strip mall not far from the Fairways Management office. On the passenger seat beside him was the cardboard box full of knick-knacks and personal papers the company had given him. He'd lucked out, guessing that they were happy to unload Jeanette's stuff and not have to deal with it anymore, and wouldn't ask too many questions.

It had only occurred to him as he drove away that he should have checked the police Missing Persons website as soon as he'd come across Jeanette Mallory's name. It was possible that she'd done exactly what he'd suggested to Fairways—moved to another city, and just left her stuff behind. Then again, something more sinister might have happened to her—she could actually be missing.

He entered the diner, ordered coffee and a donut, set up his flea-market computer on a table in a booth at the back, and checked Missing Persons. His body tensed when he actually saw her name listed. In fact, a girl named Jeanette Mallory *was* missing. She seemed to match the profile he'd put together, and Evangeline's somewhat vague description.

Back in his car, he called the number from the site, and asked about Jeanette Mallory.

What is your relationship with the missing person? the woman on the line asked.

Jake didn't dare bring Evangeline's name into the discussion.

"I don't personally have any relationship. I'm looking into it for a friend—a family member."

I'm sorry sir, but we can't give out any information to you. Ask the family member to contact us directly, or they can provide a written affidavit stating who they are, and designating you as their representative.

"Can you at least tell me who made the Missing Persons call, and whether the investigation is ongoing?"

As I already told you, sir, we can't release any details about the case. If her information and her picture are up on the site, the investigation is active at some level. I can't tell you any more than that.

Once more he thought about TV shows where the private detective impersonated someone, or adopted some persona. But he'd already played his hand—it was too late to try that now. Anyway, it was one thing to play the part of Jeanette's brother at Fairways, but with the cops? He didn't think he was ready for that level of deception.

Jeanette's presence on the Missing Persons site also cast a new light on the stuff in the box in his car. They could still just be the belongings of someone who skipped town without leaving a forwarding address— or...

Anyway, if the cops were worried about it, why hadn't they looked into it already?

Hanging up, he decided there was nothing else to accomplish in Vancouver. There was an outdoor supply store at the other end of the strip mall. He bought a backpack with some more of Evangeline's money, and stuffed it with the contents of the Jeanette Mallory's cardboard box. He didn't want to go through it all now, and risk losing the items he'd gone to the trouble of acquiring.

After dropping the EVO back at its designated spot, he made his way to the bus station on foot, now loaded down with the overnight bag and backpack. He wasn't in a hurry—his bus wasn't scheduled to leave for another hour.

On the way, he stopped at a hot-dog cart and grabbed a Smokie with all the fixings. Looming over his head was the giant sphere of Science World, the silver-latticed Geodesic dome constructed for Expo '86, and now housing a collection of interactive science demonstrations open to the public.

He took a bite of his dog, and stopped outside the front entrance, where a small crowd stood watching a giant moving art exhibit go through its convoluted motions. It was basically a Rube Goldberg-like ball machine about ten meters high. A chain-driven carrier conveyed a stack of billiard balls up, dumping them into a trough at the top, where they rolled downwards, triggering levers, running across chime-like ramps that played a musical scale, bouncing off tubular bells, dumping into round dishes then circling like miniature planets before finally dropping through a hole at the bottom. The trajectory of each ball changed with the device it encountered, until it finally reached the bottom and was carried up for another run.

He munched on his Smokie as he watched the mechanism. It occurred to him that the machine was like a microcosm of his life. Events came at random, pushing him in directions he wasn't expecting, and usually didn't want to go. He would be bounced and rattled around like a pachinko ball, distracted into confusion by chimes and bells, and redirected by forces over which he had no control, only to hit bottom and begin the process anew.

The bells and clanging noises echoed behind him as he continued on his way.

XXI

A PICNIC

Rule #23: Good detectives are stubborn They don't quit easily. They continue to pursue an investigation long after the average person would have given up.
- **Shadow Mac's Comprehensive Guide to Private Investigation**

Late in the evening back in Victoria, Jake took out his phone and checked for messages as he ambled along the dock toward his vessel. During the junket to Vancouver, he'd texted Evangeline to let her know the status of his investigation. He'd heard nothing back.

It was confusing—at times she seemed desperate to find her sister— at others she really didn't seem to give a damn. Back aboard the *Rose*, he dropped his travel bag and the backpack, then climbed up to the loft and crashed, beyond exhausted.

Jake almost fell out of bed the next morning, as his phone beeped loudly with a new text message.

Still only half awake, he rolled over, grabbed at the offending phone on the nightstand, missed it, and knocked it to the floor. Groping blindly, still hoping to avoid getting out of bed, he managed to wrap his fingers around the device just as he lost his balance and fell to the floor. He dragged himself to his feet. Somehow he'd inadvertently set the ring tone volume to maximum. He lowered it, then checked the time, thinking it was early. It was actually ten o'clock.

Finally, he brought up his messages. The offending one was from Evangeline. It said: *Have a look up at the parking lot.*

Resigned, he made his way down the ladder, across the room, and up to the deck of the *Rose*. Rubbing his sleep-gummed eyes and shading them from the bright morning light, he gazed up at the lot above the Wharf.

A figure sat on a motor-scooter parked near the edge, beside the walkway. Even at a distance he could see it was Evangeline, though she looked different, with her hair up.

She saw him and waved, gesturing for him to come up and join her. He texted her to wait, got changed, locked up the *Rose*, and headed off. When he arrived she was still straddling the scooter, a Vespa. A wicker basket was strapped to a frame at the back. She was wearing a yellow retro-style miniskirt and had her hair done up in a beehive. She looked like a character from a sixties Italian movie.

"I rented it," she said, in answer to his glance at the Vespa. "I thought we could have a picnic."

She motioned to the space on the seat behind her. Jake climbed on and wrapped his arms around her waist as they headed north and out of the city. Reaching the outskirts, they turned onto the Malahat highway, the first of a series of routes that eventually ran the length of the Island. Faster vehicles blew past as the overladen scooter chugged up the numerous hills on the way out of town.

About twenty minutes later, after climbing a long hill, Evangeline pulled into a gravel turn-off. They unstrapped the picnic basket and scrambled up an embankment and over a low rise, to a flat grassy area, out of sight of the highway, and overlooking the blue of Saanich Inlet. Jake couldn't help wondering how Evangeline knew about this place, and who else she'd brought here.

She opened the basket, unfolded a large, red and white checkered blanket, and Jake helped her spread it out onto a wide section of grass. Broken clouds opened up and a brilliant sun moved out to light up the entire inlet.

They unpacked the lunch: sandwiches, a fresh baguette, a block of cheese, and a bottle of red wine. Far below, sailboats and ships sailed through the inlet, headed for Brentwood Bay and parts north.

Evangeline opened the wine and set out two glasses. Jake was gratified that there was only one bottle—there shouldn't be an opportunity to descend into another blackout-inducing binge.

She unwrapped the sandwiches and they each took one. For a time they sat in silence, gazing at the beautiful vista below.

Finally Evangeline looked at him and spoke. "I know I haven't always behaved myself—I guess sometimes I get carried away."

"It takes two to tango," Jake answered, happy that she'd at least acknowledged some of what had happened. "I could have walked away any time I wanted."

"I've always had a hard time connecting with men," she said. "I've pretty much driven away all I've ever met—" She locked eyes with him. "Except you."

She reached out and put a hand on his. He wasn't sure how to respond, trying to decide whether the remark was actually a compliment. She folded her legs under her, leaned back, and closed her eyes, the morning sun casting a golden glow on her upturned face.

Her eyes opened again as a large yellow butterfly flitted nearby, finally hovering just above her shoulder. She raised her right hand, and smiled as the butterfly drifted downward and alighted on her finger. There it sat, slowly opening and closing its wings. A ray of sun pierced through a break in the clouds, enveloping her and the worshiping creature. It was like nothing Jake had ever seen before.

Forgetting her objection to photographs, he scrambled for his phone to capture the moment, but seconds later the insect beat its wings, lifted into the sky, and flew away. Evangeline refilled both their glasses, then lay down, propped up on one elbow.

"If it wasn't for all that's happened..." her voice trailed off.

"All what's happened?" Jake asked. "You mean with your sister? I've actually been trying to get ahold of you. I've got news about my trip yesterday. I found the apartment, but your sister didn't live there anymore."

Her face fell. "Really?"

"But I did make some progress..."

"We can talk later," she interrupted him, looking away. She turned back, her eyes brightening. "For now, let's just enjoy the moment."

She emptied her glass, put it down, and moved close to him. The sunlight seemed to move with her, until they were both bathed in its golden glow.

He dropped his own glass, reached up and brushed her cheek, then began to unpin her hair. The highlights shimmered in the sun as it tumbled to her shoulders.

They lay down on the blanket, undressed, and made love out on the bluff, surrounded by the gliding gulls, flitting birds, and chirping crickets.

From a state that was like a dream, Jake felt her hot breath close to his cheek, and her voice whispered in his ear: "I know I'm bad, but the truth is I really do love you."

Afterwards, they lay in each other's arms, the sun pouring down from a now cloudless sky. A boat far in the distance below noticed them. The people on board whistled and waved. They both waved back, smiling.

That afternoon, Jake emptied the contents of the backpack from Vancouver onto the table in his dining nook. Evangeline had dropped him off around lunchtime and left, saying she had stuff to do. Finally resigned to her quixotic personality, he didn't bother to ask what. Now he studied what was left of Jeanette Mallory's possessions, scattered randomly over the lacquered wooden surface. They seemed to be mostly letters and bills, with a few knick-knacks and photographs thrown in.

One envelope that caught his eye had a letterhead from MyNewFamily.com.

Excitedly, he opened it up, and smiled. As he'd hoped, it was the bill in Jeanette's name for the DNA analysis—the first conclusive proof that Jeanette Mallory was, in fact, the mystery girl that Evangeline had contacted.

The bill was yellowed and crinkled, with transaction dates of almost two years ago. He glanced at the address, and straightened on the bench. Unlike almost all the other documents in the pile, it *didn't* refer to Jeanette's apartment.

It was an address in Victoria, in the district of Fairfield, just to the southeast. Jake thought back to Evangeline's claim that the site had said her sister was living in Victoria. His pulse quickened. Was it possible that it would be this easy—that he could already have solved the 'case' he'd been hired for?

He left the rest of the stuff where it lay, and headed for Fairfield.

XXII

JEANETTE'S STUFF

Rule #44: *Before beginning surveillance, always conduct a preliminary investigation.*
- **Shadow Mac's Comprehensive Guide to Private Investigation**

Jake stood solemnly watching the shovel of a yellow front-end loader tear a chunk of earth from the pit that now filled the lot at the address from the *MyNewFamily* bill, wondering if some omniscient power was somehow aligned against him.

The machine swiveled around and dumped its load in a large pile on one side. A wooden sign in one corner listed the developer's name, and showed a picture of some kind of low-rise to be built on the site.

A worker in a reflective vest was repositioning the sandbags reinforcing the fence surrounding the property. It was a long shot, but it didn't hurt to try. The man stood up as Jake approached and waved.

"Hi," Jake said.

The worker eyed him expectedly.

Jake nodded at the pit. "I just wondered if you had any idea who was living on this property—you know, before."

The man shook his head. "The company tells us to do a job, we do it. No idea about anything else." Jake turned to walk away. "I can tell you what used to be here though," the worker said behind him.

Jake turned back. "Yeah?"

The man nodded at the driveway. "I used to drive by it every day on the way to work. It wasn't a regular house—it was a group home for wayward kids."

"Is that right. I don't suppose you remember the name?"

The worker looked at the ground, thinking. "Something with an 'R'—Rainbow, I think it was—Rainbow something..."

Jake thought back on McCluskey's comment about detective work improving your mind, as he spent another marathon session back at the *Rose* sifting through recent historical records and city directories, searching for the group home at the demolition address. He eventually found it: Rainbow House, which had sheltered various unattached youth in the city for more than two decades. It had finally shut its doors just under a year ago.

An archived picture of Rainbow House showed a stately old building with forest green wooden siding, gables, and a huge porch that wrapped around the entire structure. He searched through the records, but the information on its residents was confidential. It did reveal that most were 'Crown Wards', meaning they were children of the state, with nobody to look after them.

He would keep the place in mind for later, but with no way to determine when, or even if, Jeanette Mallory lived there, for now it was a dead end.

Meanwhile, he continued to sift through the rest of Jeanette's belongings. There were more bills—hydro, phone, and a couple of food deliveries, all referring to the apartment he'd visited in East Van. There was nothing to say that Jeanette was anything other than an ordinary girl living alone. There was also no record of where she might have worked, where she'd gone, or how to find her.

And his difficulty in finding her in the first place was suspicious. She'd clearly once had a presence on social media, but all of it had been scrubbed clean. She'd been almost completely erased from the Internet. If Jake hadn't used specialized search tools and accessed the Deep Web, there would have been no trace. Clearly someone had done their best to make her Internet presence disappear.

The thought was a little disturbing. That, along with the fact that Jeanette was missing, were the first hints that maybe this was more than just a simple case of locating the owner of a deleted account.

There were a few photographs in the pile, all apparently of Jeanette. She was pretty but not spectacular—though she did bear a slight resemblance to Evangeline—blond hair, with a smattering of freckles. The only photograph that included another person showed Jeanette with an older man, tall and withered, probably in his mid-fifties, though his face looked much older.

Her companion had the hollow, used-up look of someone who'd spent time on the street—possibly even in prison, with sunken eyes and a horseshoe moustache. A section of a crude-looking tattoo poked out of his right shirtsleeve. Both he and Jeanette were smiling, outdoors, surrounded by trees, in what looked like a park somewhere. But there was nothing to indicate who the guy was, or their relationship. None of the photographs had anything written on the back.

Jake stuck the photograph of Jeanette and the older man on his fridge beside a few of his own photographs, to maybe think about later, emptied the rest into a cardboard box, and stowed the box in the storage area under one of the nook benches.

He put his findings aside, to let them percolate for the time being, satisfied that he'd at least identified the girl Evangeline was looking for.

Not bad, he congratulated himself, for a guy who'd never done any real detective work in his life.

XXIII

ANOTHER PARTY

Rule #38: When tailing a subject, wear clothing that makes you feel at ease. The more at ease you feel, the less likely you are to attract attention.
- **Shadow Mac's Comprehensive Guide to Private Investigation**

Later in the afternoon, as Jake lounged on his aft deck, he tried to push aside the distraction of this morning's picnic as he replayed the events from his trip to Vancouver: confronting potentially violent tenants, lying to the management company, fraudulently claiming the belongings of a girl who'd turned out to be a missing person. This was supposed to be a straightforward search for a DNA pen-pal. Things were getting a bit complicated.

On the other hand, he was making headway. He contacted Evangeline, reminding her that he had news she might want to hear, and to his surprise, she responded quickly. They arranged to meet at a café near the Wharf in two hours.

He got to the meeting place first. It was cosy and casual, serving home-style fare, and with a reasonable view of the harbour. At the moment there were only a handful of customers. He found a table near the window and ordered a coffee.

He watched with a tangle of emotions as Evangeline appeared and strolled past the window heading for the entrance. She was dressed casually, in a pair of mauve slacks and an unassuming light blue top. Even so, the eyes of the few men around him followed her form intently.

Lately, Jake had come up with a game of guessing which of what seemed like a myriad of Evangelines would show up at a given time. This time, his guess was correct—she was all business. He thought back to her moaning, crying out, clawing at his shoulders, and bending her body beneath him this morning, and to her whispered declaration of love. There was no trace of that passion now.

She ordered coffee, and he brought her up to speed on what he'd found so far, describing the trip to Vancouver—how he'd actually visited Jeanette's apartment in East Van and found she was gone.

"I checked with Missing Persons," he said. "She's listed, but they said I couldn't get any more information without permission from one of her close relatives. If you were willing to go there, or give me—"

Evangeline straightened up and her eyes went wide. "You contacted the police?" she said loudly. "Did you mention me?"

A couple of people at other tables turned to look.

Jake pushed his hand down for silence. He shook his head. "I remembered your instructions. I just asked about the status of the case."

Her hands clenched into fists. "Please don't contact the police again."

"Why not?"

She sat staring at him.

"Okay," he finally said. "But that's going to make things a lot harder."

After her reaction, he decided not to mention that he'd managed to snag Jeanette's box of papers. Now that he knew Jeanette was the subject of a Missing Persons case, he assumed that he should be turning it over to the police. Maybe he'd tell Evangeline later, once he'd thought all this through.

"I'm pretty sure she's the one we're looking for," he said instead. "And I think I found an address for her here in Victoria," he added, careful not to mention the *MyNewFamily* bill. "That would fit with what was posted on the website."

She eyed him suspiciously for a few seconds, the wheels turning.

He took a sip of coffee, and set down his cup. "Anyway, that's a lot farther along than I expected to be by this time."

Suddenly her demeanor changed and she was smiling, with her signature little-girl smile.

"That's great news," she said, clapping her hands together. "Let's celebrate."

Once again Jake had occasion to question why he steadfastly refused to listen to his little voice, as they made the rounds through a set of bars and night clubs, some he'd never seen before.

"You're not much fun tonight," Evangeline said, pouting her lips as she steered him toward yet another establishment halfway down the block.

Jake had always thought he could party with the best of them. He'd lost track of the times he'd shut down the Salty Dog with rambunctious clientèle, and many of those times he'd continued on with the debauchery long afterward at other locations.

But Evangeline took partying to another level, one he'd never experienced. It was as if plain, ordinary reality wasn't enough for her — as if the everyday world was too drab and boring, or devoid of excitement and meaning. Her excesses seemed like an attempt to transport herself to some plane that she couldn't find here on Earth.

It occurred to him that in a sense he was the same way, with his fleeting relationships and haphazard manner of drifting through life. Maybe he too was looking for something more beautiful, more exciting than reality had to offer.

Evangeline seemed driven to hammer her foot on the gas as hard as possible, as if something horrible was chasing her, something she could only escape by extreme behaviour.

"Is there a point to all this?" he asked her as they stumbled down the street toward a new bar. He was beginning to recognize that there was an upper limit even to partying.

Evangeline frowned and looked away. "Putting in time," she said. "Putting in time, until things are made right."

He stared at her, not really understanding what she was saying.

After an interval that was all a blur, they somehow found themselves at low-rent bar with a table full of bikers. Jake scowled as Evangeline alternated between sitting on one or the other of their laps. A wizened old guy named Walter, with grey stubble, a missing tooth, and worn-out leathers, claimed he could divine people's futures. He went around the table, picking out candidates and generating 'oohs' and 'aahs' as he reeled them off.

"How about this one," asked the biker on whose lap Evangeline was currently sitting. She giggled as he bounced her on his knee.

Walter studied her. He hesitated, as if he was reluctant to give a prediction.

"She's burnin' up the fast lane for somewhere," he finally said, his expression turning serious. "I don't know where she's goin', but wherever it is, it ain't gonna be fun."

The table went silent for a few seconds.

Walter shrugged and laughed. "Anyway, I don't think you need any psychic powers for that one. She's trouble—trouble with a capital T."

"What do you think of him?" Evangeline nodded over at Jake.

Already annoyed and angry, Jake felt his face flush red as the biker seer swiveled around and eyed him intently.

"Him?" Walter said, thinking again, then chuckling. "I think he's in way over his head."

XXIV

THINGS FALL APART

Rule #27: A good detective recognizes that clerks and secretaries run the world, and cultivates close contacts with them.
- **Shadow Mac's Comprehensive Guide to Private Investigation**

"Never again," Jake managed to croak as he opened his eyes the next morning, and immediately fought to return to unconsciousness.

Somehow, he was in his own bed on the *Rose*. This time he honestly couldn't remember where he'd been at the end of the night, or how he'd gotten home. But he was here, so it must have happened. An explosion reverberated through his skull as he lifted his head and blearily scanned the room, checking to see if anything was missing. His vision too blurry to tell one way or the other, he finally gave up and lay back down, once again praying for death.

He awoke sometime later to a burbling sound, and the smell of brewing coffee. Slowly, wary of the possible consequences of the blood rushing to his head too quickly, he raised himself up on both elbows and looked down to the living area. The coffee maker in the galley below was bubbling away, but the room was empty. A thundering tsunami of pain crashed against the inside of his skull.

"Ugghh," he groaned, as once he collapsed and passed out.

When he woke, the coffee machine had finished, and a single empty cup sat on the counter beside it. There was no sign of anybody. He dragged himself out of bed and carefully, to avoid any sudden movement, descended from the loft, crossed the room, opened the door, and climbed to the outer deck. He was just in time to make out Evangeline's unmistakable form moving from the exit ramp into the parking lot above.

He staggered back to bed in pursuit of further unconsciousness. He'd no sooner laid his head on the pillow when the *Rose* swayed a little and there was a shuffling sound at his door. He didn't dare move quickly, dreading another avalanche of pain. The vessel swayed again as somebody stepped back to the dock, and he heard footsteps moving away.

He carefully climbed down again and opened the front door. Whoever had been there was gone, but a piece of paper was now taped to the wall beside him. It was a request to meet with Harold Filbert, the president of the Fisherman's Wharf Resident's Council. The meeting was scheduled for ten o'clock tomorrow morning.

"Shit," Jake said. "That's all I need."

Crumpling the page in his fist, he went back inside, climbed up to the loft and got back into bed, sleeping fitfully. One thing he'd always liked about his floating home was that its gentle rolling on the waves usually rocked him into a restful slumber at night. Even in the darkness with the curtains drawn tightly shut, it was clear that wasn't going to happen today.

His inner voice had warned him, but he wasn't sure whether the crushing apprehension he was feeling was because he knew he was a fraud, because he sensed the 'investigation' would somehow end badly, or because the experience had tossed a cluster bomb into the comfortable rut his life had become.

By the time he hauled himself out of bed it was two PM. It occurred to him that today was Friday—he was supposed to be working at the

Salty Dog in a few hours. He called Max, told him he was sick, and held the phone away from his ear so that the yelling at the other end wouldn't kick-start his new headache to another level of intensity.

Resigned to being awake, and grateful for the pot of coffee Evangeline had left on the galley counter, he filled the cup, turned on the radio, and sat back in the nook, his eyes closed and his head resting against the wall.

"...have released the name of the woman whose body was found washed up on the beach at Spanish Banks two weeks ago," a newscaster was in the middle of saying. "Nineteen-year-old Jeanette Mallory had apparently been dead for several months." Jake opened his eyes and lifted his head. "Police are currently investigating," the voice continued. "At the moment, no foul play is suspected."

He climbed to his loft office and checked the news feed on the computer. A few minutes later he'd come up with the story. He grabbed the photograph of Jeanette and the older man still pinned on the fridge, and compared it to the attached picture of the deceased girl. There was no doubt.

Jake shut his eyes. So, this was it. He'd reached the end of his journey. His short, pathetic stint as a pseudo-private detective was over. It occurred to him that, ironically, in a tragic twist, he'd cracked the case. He'd successfully located Evangeline's sister.

The focus of his investigation, a young girl he never knew, and now never would know, was gone from the world forever. It was a tragedy, but there was no longer any reason to look for her. The affair had ceased to be his concern. He felt a strange combination of sorrow, disappointment and relief.

All along he'd believed Evangeline's story about innocently searching for her sister. The news had said there was no indication of foul play, but his gut now told him that something more sinister was going on.

Since the bizarre sequence of events last night, he had yet to hear from her. The betrayal and confusion he'd felt after the Screaming Dragon showed themselves again, more intense now, as his frustration and confusion increased.

He was actually relieved that his private investigation career was finished, almost before it started. He texted Evangeline saying he wanted to see her—that he had important new information he could only deliver in person.

He wasn't sure why, but he was curious to see her expression when he told her about her sister's death.

XXV

THE WHARF COUNCIL

Rule #40: A professional private investigator can communicate effectively, has great listening skills, and can quickly establish a rapport with others.
- **Shadow Mac's Comprehensive Guide to Private Investigation**

Like all members of the Wharf Council, the president, Harold Filbert, lived in one of the floating homes at the Wharf. Filbert's home, thankfully pretty much as far away from Jake's as it could get, was also the polar opposite of the *Rose*. It had a modern, squarish, almost industrial design, with walls of metal and plastic. The place had almost no decoration or embellishment and, Jake thought, very little character, much like its owner.

Just before ten the next morning, Jake's footsteps echoed along the wooden dock as he wove through the sparse tourist traffic, steeling himself for the meeting. He'd only officially met Filbert twice. The first time was when Deirdre had introduced him as the prospective heir to her home. Jake suspected Filbert, and probably the rest of the council, would have preferred to reject him right then and there as an owner, but Deirdre had been very ill at the time, and they probably hadn't wanted to cause her any more stress.

He stopped for a second and closed his eyes, as the memory of her last day surfaced, unbidden and unwanted. Dierdre, emaciated and grey in a hospital bed, her eyes closed, an oxygen cannula hanging from her nose, the smell of disinfectant and the beeping of machines filling the room.

He'd held her hand as her breathing became more laboured. She stirred and opened her eyes.

"Auntie," he said, holding back his tears, "thank you for all you've done for me. I can never repay you."

She smiled and squeezed his hand weakly. "I can't think of anyone I'd rather spend my final days with. I know someday you'll discover your purpose and become the person you were meant to be. I'm so sorry that I can't be there..."

The tears had begun to flow, and he'd sobbed openly as her eyes drifted shut and she went to sleep, never again to awaken.

He pushed away the memory and continued walking. He'd met with Filbert a second time on the day he'd actually moved in, after Deirdre's death. The president's nose had risen as if he'd smelled something bad when Jake arrived with the black garbage bag containing all his worldly possessions slung over his shoulder, and his portable keyboard under his arm. Since then they'd nodded politely to each other in passing, but had never progressed beyond that.

At ten AM sharp he arrived at Filbert's front door, where he was confronted by a black display panel with a bright green LED light at the top. A small round bulb of shiny glass, apparently a camera, was mounted just above that. When Jake moved within range of the panel the green light blinked several times.

He knocked, and a few seconds later Filbert's unsmiling face appeared in the display.

"Good morning, Mr. Sommers," the video image said. "Thank you for being punctual."

The door opened and Filbert, a tall, dour, fifty-something man, extended a hand to invite him in. They sat across from each other at a small table in Filbert's austere dining area. Jake didn't know if there was a Ms. Filbert. If there was, she wasn't around. His host looked nervous. His hands worked over each other on the table in front of him. He offered Jake a coffee, which Jake declined.

Jake did his best to portray the image of an earnest, responsible owner, but the remnants of his hangover and the events of two nights ago were still occupying his mind.

"I'll get right to the point, Mr. Sommers," Filbert said. "We've had a number of complaints concerning your activities, both from tourists, and from your fellow residents."

"Is that so."

Filbert ran a finger down what looked like a long list on the screen of a computer tablet positioned in front of him.

"There have been reports of lewd behaviour on your vessel —" Filbert said, reading from the entries.

"Lewd behaviour?" At first Jake was confused, then he remembered Maggie's face when he'd dropped his hat, the day he'd met Evangeline.

Filbert continued to scroll down the list, which apparently spanned multiple pages. "Recently you were seen half-undressed and passed out on the outer deck of your vessel in the middle of the day. You understand that our little community is open to tourist traffic, including young children. We have a certain responsibility to maintain decorum."

Jake nodded, dreading what would come next.

"Strangers have also been seen loitering around your vessel," Filbert continued, "and there have been rumours that you may be conducting unsanctioned and possibly unsavoury business activities..."

"What?"

Filbert looked up from his list. "We've had complaints in the past, but for the most part they've been minor. Lately, they seem to be escalating.

"You were given a copy of our bylaws when ownership was transferred to your name..." His expression registered disappointment at the memory of that event.

"There are numerous bylaws governing behaviour in our community. Consider this a warning. Continued violations could result in fines, and possibly even eviction."

Jake sat up straight in his chair. He could actually lose the *Honeysuckle Rose*?

"Look, there's been no illegal activity on my vessel," he said, as firmly as he could manage. "The incidents you're talking about were isolated, and won't happen again."

Filbert attempted a smile, obviously unconvinced. "I'm glad to hear that. To be honest, there was a certain apprehension among the residents when Deirdre announced her intention to bequeath her craft to you, but she assured us that you would be a valuable member of our community—I hope you will live up to her faith in you."

"Absolutely," Jake said, trying to sound conciliatory. The thought of losing the *Rose* had rattled him. "Most of the complaints were just misunderstandings. As for the others—I'll clean up my act—I promise."

Jake's body tensed as he stepped back on board his vessel and looked around him. This could all be taken away?

XXVI

BREAKING THE NEWS

Rule #21: When possible, avoid looking directly at a subject. Use reflective surfaces, peripheral vision, and estimation of the subject's position whenever possible.
- Shadow Mac's Comprehensive Guide to Private Investigation

That evening, Evangeline finally contacted him. Again, she said nothing about the events of two nights ago, or how she'd gotten him home, and again he didn't ask. They arranged to meet at the *Rose*.

She smiled as she climbed aboard, and took a seat across from him in the dining nook. She placed a small purse on the table in front of her, and stared at him as her hands moved over it.

He studied her, trying to reconcile the woman sitting facing him now with the one from their latest bar-hopping spree less than forty-eight hours ago.

"You've found out something," she said, resuming her client persona.

"I assume you haven't heard. I'm sorry to tell you this, but it looks like our little investigation is over. The girl, Jeanette Mallory—the one I thought was your sister—it turns out she's dead."

It had been a blunt statement. He watched Evangeline's face as she processed the news. It registered shock, but she seemed surprisingly unaffected, considering her original excitement at the prospect of finding her long-lost sister.

"How did she die?" she asked, a trace of sadness finally making its way into her features.

"It was on the news. They didn't say, apparently it's still under investigation. They don't suspect foul play at the moment. But they had her name, and her picture. There's no doubt."

Not wanting to upset her, he didn't mention how they'd found the body.

"I'm sorry," he added. "If she really is your sister the authorities might want to talk to you eventually."

She straightened up and her eyes widened. "You didn't call them..."

He shook his head. "No, but they could probably find traces of your communications with her on the *MyNewFamily* site if they looked hard enough."

Her hands gripped her purse tightly. He could make out the impression of a gun inside. "They can do that?"

"I don't think most of that stuff is ever really erased. It's a shame — it's not the way I would have liked the investigation to end. Anyway, I'm going to have to contact the police, and I may have to bring you into it to explain everything I've been doing."

An expression of horror crossed her face. "No, you can't!" she almost shouted.

"Look, this isn't what I signed up for," he said, getting angry himself. "There's a record of me calling Missing Persons looking for her, and I've got some of her stuff..."

"Stuff?" She wildly scanned the room as if she was looking for it. "You didn't tell me that. What kind of stuff?"

"I got a box of her papers when I went to Vancouver. I thought maybe she'd just skipped town or something. Now, it's possible I might be withholding evidence of a crime. I looked through it all when I first got back here. There were just a few bills, almost all of them referring to the address I already checked."

She glared at him, her tightened fists trembling. For a second, he thought she would hit him. "I need to see it."

"It's all under your bench."

He nodded at the bench she was sitting on and she stood.

"You haven't been around or I would have told you earlier," he said as he hauled out the cardboard box with Jeanette's things and dumped it on the table. "There was only one useful piece of information anyway—a bill with a Victoria address from MyNewFamily.com, for the DNA test Jeanette had requested."

Evangeline moved her hands frantically over the bills and papers, spreading them out on the table. Jake slid the yellowed *MyNewFamily* receipt in front of her. "This proves she's the one who created the account—the one you tried to contact," he said. "She must be your sister."

She ignored the bill, picking out the photographs and studying each of them closely.

"That's all?" she said, frustrated.

"There's one more, stuck on the fridge—of her with some older guy."

"What?" she asked excitedly. "Give it to me."

She moved to the fridge, scanning the crowd of papers and photographs stuck there.

"Where?" she said. "Show me!"

He picked out the picture of Jeanette and the older man and handed it to her. Evangeline studied the girl's image for a few seconds. Her gaze quickly moved to the older man. She brought the photograph closer and stared at him, as if through a microscope.

"What? Do you know him or something?" Jake asked.

She finally turned to him. "That's it?"

He nodded.

"Are you sure?" she asked, shaking.

"What—you think I'm lying to you?"

She stared at him. "No," she finally answered. "Of course not." She held up the photograph. "I need to keep this."

"The cops are going to want it," he said. "All of it. Maybe after that..."

She ignored him, grabbed her purse on the table, opened it, and stuffed the photograph inside.

Their business, at least as far as his 'investigation' was concerned, was over. He'd have no need for the photograph. And he was reluctant to cross her at this point. If the cops wanted the picture, it would be on her.

"I'm sorry about what happened," he said, "and I'm sorry it had to end this way. I've fulfilled my end of the bargain—I've found your sister. I've spent some of your money, and I might need some to pay for a lawyer if there's a problem with the cops."

She looked up at him intently. "You must continue your investigation. You have to find the man in the picture."

"What?"

Images flooded into his mind of the night two weeks ago at the Screaming Dragon, two nights ago at the bar, and Filbert's threat to kick him out of Fisherman's Wharf.

He shook his head. "Look, when I agreed to this job, I wasn't expecting this kind of trouble. You know I could lose the *Rose*? I've had it with this relationship."

"No, please!" her angry voice transformed into a pleading one. "You are the only one who can help me!"

"Then you better start leveling with me," he said, watching her hands, which still held her purse.

"What are you talking about?"

"There's more to this than you just looking for your long-lost sister." He counted off on the fingers of one hand. "You claim you innocently found this girl on an ancestry website. The girl's account disappears shortly after you contact her. Then *she* disappears. Then she ends up dead. I may not be a real detective, but..."

She looked away, her jaw set.

"If you're looking for justice for your sister, you should leave it to the police."

"No," she snapped, turning back. "No police."

"Why not?"

She bowed her head. "The truth is, I haven't been a good person. Please don't make me go into detail..."

She put out a hand and placed it on his. "Please—you have to help me—you're my only hope. I'm sorry for the trouble I've caused you."

She turned to leave. He followed as she climbed to the deck outside and they stood at his front door. His eyes were on her hands as she opened her purse. He tensed, ready to react if she went for the gun. She fished through the purse, and he let out a breath when she pulled out a wallet and removed two one-hundred-dollar bills.

"I'm satisfied that you've fulfilled the terms of your original retainer," she said. "Here's some more. I beg you—please continue the investigation. Find the man in the picture. It means everything to me."

Her hand reached in again, emerging with the photograph from his fridge, and she took a picture of it with her phone.

"You'll need this," she said, quietly, holding it out.

For a few seconds he was frozen in place, staring at her. Finally, he reached out and took the cash and the photograph.

She then turned and walked away.

XXVII

INSPIRATION LODGE

Rule #6: When interviewing, good detective takes note of the facts, and avoids including derogatory or inflammatory statements.
- Shadow Mac's Comprehensive Guide to Private Investigation

In the morning, Jake sat in his nook with a cup of coffee, staring at the pair of hundred-dollar bills Evangeline had given him the night before.

Was that enough? Would any amount be enough, considering the direction events seemed to be leading? He shook his head, took one last sip of coffee, picked up the bills and transferred them to his wallet.

He decided to hold off contacting the police, at least for a day or so. He would probably have to give up all of Jeanette's stuff, including the only picture of the man who was supposedly the object of his new mission. He used his phone to take his own pictures of items he thought were important, just in case.

Strangely, even beyond Evangeline's pleas and her additional retainer, he felt a compelling urge to know what had happened. His sense of justice and the desire for closure now galvanized his need to uncover the truth.

And he was haunted by the possibility that whatever he was involved in might be related to Jeanette Mallory's death.

He thought back to Evangeline's Numerological analysis when they'd first met. *Determination and persistence underly everything you do. That's the kind of person I need—one who's stubborn, and won't quit.*

And anyway, there was one important connection he had yet to explore.

Later in the morning Jake lay in the lounger on his aft deck, his phone in hand. He'd determined that the former Rainbow House director, Caroline Matthews, had been hired as the director another group home, *New Day Lodge*, after Rainbow had closed its doors.

He called Ms. Matthews. He'd considered coming up with another lie like he'd used with Fairview Management, but she would want to check his credentials, and he wasn't keen on giving out his ID again.

Jeanette Mallory? A year ago? Ms. Matthews answered. *The name isn't familiar. I was actually brought in as an interim director, to oversee the shutting down of Rainbow House. Maybe she'd already gone by then.*

I wouldn't be at liberty to tell you anything even if I knew, she continued, *at least not without some kind of valid credentials. Are you a relative?*

"Just looking on behalf of a friend who used to know her," Jake said.

The Ministry would probably know where she's living now, Ms. Matthews said, *but they couldn't legally tell you either—not without more information.*

She didn't seem to be aware of Jeanette's death. Not wanting to complicate things, Jake neglected to tell her. Anyway, he suspected he'd already visited Jeanette's last known place of residence.

"You say you were an interim director," Jake said. "What happened to the one you replaced?"

I'm afraid I'm not at liberty to talk about that either, Ms. Matthews answered, an edge of nervousness entering her voice. *Again—you might want to contact the Ministry...*

That afternoon, Jake paused in front of a paint-chipped door set into the mold-stained, graffiti-plastered wall of a crumbling building in the Victoria neighbourhood of North Park. The district had the dubious distinction of having by far the highest crime rate in the city. A homeless guy wrapped in a sleeping bag sat on the pavement just outside the entrance, his head nodding.

After some additional digging on the history of Rainbow House, Jake had quickly come across the reason for Carolyn Matthews' nervousness around the topic of her predecessor. Just over a year ago, irregularities were found in the institution's finances. An auditor was brought in to investigate, and the finger soon pointed at the director at the time—a Maxine Sharpe.

There was talk of her going to prison, but in the end Ms. Sharpe agreed to pay back money she'd misdirected, and got away with mere termination. Since Rainbow House was scheduled to be closed anyway, Ms. Matthews had been brought in to replace her until the operation wound down.

It looked like Sharpe had been director for five years before her sacking, so she would have been in place when Jeanette was there. Jake eventually tracked her down, still in a director's role, at this place—a drug rehabilitation facility called *The Inspiration Space*. From this perspective, it didn't look very inspiring.

He climbed the creaking, urine-stained stairs to the second floor. Ms. Sharpe had obviously taken a big step downward since her time at Rainbow House.

A heavily-pierced young girl at a desk in the middle of the room took his name. He didn't have an appointment, but the place didn't look all that busy. The girl leaned into an open office doorway and spoke to someone, then came back and gestured for him to go in.

Maxine Sharpe was in her late forties, with sallow cheeks, nicotine-stained teeth, and brittle, frizzy black hair laced with grey.

They shook hands, and he sat and asked about Jeanette Mallory.

"I understand that the information is supposed to be confidential..." he said.

"I gave up caring what those bastards at the Ministry want a long time ago," she said. "They've done enough to me already."

She pulled a cigarette out of a pack on her desk, lit it up, and took a long drag.

"Jeanette?" she said, blowing out a cloud of smoke and smiling. "Yeah, I remember her well. She stayed with us for a couple of years. She was a smart, level-headed, well-adjusted girl—quite a surprise, considering."

"Considering?"

"Her mother had an off and on drug problem, and finally died of an overdose when Jeanette was fifteen. We had no record of who her father was. She had no one really. That's why she ended up at Rainbow House."

As with Carolyn Mathews, it appeared that Ms. Sharpe hadn't yet heard of Jeanette's death.

"Do you know what happened to her?" Jake asked.

The director shrugged. "She 'aged out' of the system last year, so she was free to go where she pleased. We were always on good terms, but we haven't kept in touch. I don't know where she went."

"You say she had no one?" Jake said. "No one ever came to see her?"

Ms. Sharpe stared at the wall as she blew out another puff of smoke. "There was one man—I don't remember his name… middle-aged, tall, beaten-up looking. I remember because we investigated his background and found he had a lengthy criminal record. We were reluctant to allow him access, but he convinced us that he'd been clean and gainfully employed for many years. And Jeanette really wanted to see him. In the end we agreed to supervised visits."

Jake pulled the photograph of Jeanette and the older man from his wallet and handed it to her. "Is this the guy?"

She held the photograph close and studied it, then nodded.

"But you don't remember a name?"

She shook her head. "Sorry. I do remember he worked as some kind of landscaper, on the mainland. Part of our due-diligence confirmed his employment status. His company had a name like 'New Eden' or something." She looked away for a second. "'Gardens'—'New Eden Gardens'—or something like that."

XXVIII

STONE COLD

Rule #41: *An eye for detail is a must-have for a PI. The smallest piece*
of evidence can make or break a case. Every clue is
important, so it pays to be thorough.
- Shadow Mac's Comprehensive Guide to Private Investigation

On the way back to the *Rose*, Jake stopped for a six-pack of beer, and picked up an Italian sausage pizza from a shop nearby. By the time he arrived home, the light was beginning to fade. He sat in the nook, hunched over the flea-market computer.

The thought surfaced yet again that Evangeline had preferred to run off rather than tell him the truth. For the moment, he pushed aside the question of why he was continuing to pursue this investigation. At least, he told himself, there were no laws against doing regular research on the Internet.

He tore off a pizza slice, cracked one of the beers, and continued the now familiar deep dive into the web. It didn't take long to come up with a name: *New Eden Garden Works*—a company based in Vancouver.

It looked like New Eden was now toast, so there were only indirect references to it anywhere. As Ms. Sharpe had said, and as the name implied, the business had done landscaping and gardening work. It had ceased operations a few months ago. He managed to locate a phone number and tried calling but, as he'd expected, it was no longer in service.

He eventually found one or two clients the company had worked for. The name of the largest one made him raise an eyebrow—*Stone Cold Production*. He'd actually heard of them before in his dealings with various musicians and bands, though he'd never dealt with them personally. Stone Cold was one of the most important music production companies in Vancouver. Unlike New Eden, the company was still in business, and had a huge presence on the web.

He drilled down into the maze of web references to Stone Cold. Their company website featured an animated collage of their facilities: studios, sound boards, instruments, vocal booths, with a few cameo endorsements from some well-known recording artists.

The founder and CEO was a guy named Tommy Skylar. The 'About' page featured a tasteful portrait photograph of Skylar—a slim, good-looking, forty-something man with longish curly hair. Further digging revealed that it was Skylar's home address in the British Properties neighbourhood of Vancouver that was listed on the New Eden work history.

Given the dearth of information on New Eden, Jake decided to dig deeper into Stone Cold. An archived article dated nineteen eighty-eight featured a photograph of three young men with big hair, heavy eye makeup, and silver suits with wide shoulders. There were two tall ones, and a shorter one in the middle. Skylar was the tall one on the left, back then sporting a lion's-mane of hair.

Jake didn't recognize the shorter middle guy, but he dropped the pizza slice he was holding when he came to the taller one on the right. The man in the picture was clearly the same person as the one in the photograph with Jeanette, only much younger, minus the moustache, and much less worn out. The caption underneath read: *Tommy Skylar, Larry Karlsen and Owen Bailey—members of the band 'Stone Cold'.*

The article went on to tout Stone Cold as one of the breakout bands of Victoria for that year. On a hunch, Jake returned to his deep dive into New Eden Garden Works—it took time, but eventually he was able to confirm that its single proprietor was listed as Owen Bailey.

And according to Evangeline, finding Bailey was Jake's revised mission.

Jake studied Bailey's image in the old photograph—a tall young kid with deer-in-the-headlights eyes, who looked like he didn't understand what he was doing there. Older pictures from Stone Cold Production also showed the third member of the band, Larry Karlsen, as a principal in the company. So, Tommy Skylar had run a wildly successful music production company with one of his bandmates, and hired the other as his gardener?

Further digging resolved the mystery. Apparently, after the breakup of the Stone Cold band, Skylar, Karlsen and Bailey had started the music production company of the same name in Victoria. As the business expanded, they'd moved it to the more lucrative market of Vancouver, where it had become massively successful. Stone Cold was famous in its day, producing records for some of the biggest bands of the eighties and nineties, though it didn't seem like they'd done much lately.

By the early two-thousands, Bailey wasn't working out. For years the others had tolerated him, but he wasn't contributing to the running of the company, and his descent into drinking and drugs was making him a liability. Larry Karlsen had been instrumental in ejecting Bailey from Stone Cold Production, citing his substance abuse problems.

Bailey was enraged. A few weeks later he assaulted Karlsen as the latter was entering a gala at the Orpheum in downtown Vancouver. Bailey had roughed up his former bandmate, and probably would have done him serious injury if the security people hadn't pulled him off.

Bailey was charged with assault, and spent six months in prison. Less than two weeks after Bailey's release, Karlsen was found beaten to death in the lobby of the Stone Cold offices. Bailey was charged with his murder, found guilty, and this time sentenced to twelve years in prison.

Larry Karlsen was long dead. There was almost nothing on the web about New Eden, and Owen Bailey seemed to have disappeared. Jake considered trying to call or email Skylar, or even visiting Stone Cold's offices in Vancouver, but guessed that he'd never get past the gatekeepers.

That meant there was only one avenue open to him — Tommy Skylar himself.

XXIX

THE MANSION

Rule #25: When tailing in a vehicle the detective needs to be close enough to maintain eye contact, but not close enough to attract attention.
- Shadow Mac's Comprehensive Guide to Private Investigation

It was a breathtaking sunny day the next afternoon as Jake made his way up the steep incline of the Upper Levels highway in West Vancouver. Far below, in the distance, beyond the carpet of forest, lay the crowded beaches that bordered the shimmering blue expanse of Burrard Inlet.

Early that morning he'd left the Wharf and once again caught the bus and the ferry over to the mainland. He picked up an EVO near the bus station, and traffic was light as he now powered up into the hills above. Nestled just below the towering North Shore mountains lay his destination: the British Properties, a neighbourhood packed to the gills with Vancouver's elite and their fabulous multi-million-dollar mansions.

He found Skylar's address and drove past once, checking it out. Its pure white walls, set with massive plate-glass windows, were surrounded by a substantial hedge, and a wall of huge trees on the periphery provided an additional layer of privacy. Jake parked on the street a block away and walked, the huge edifice looming above his head as he climbed the steep driveway and through an open wrought-iron entrance gate.

The grounds featured several terraces, each with its own immaculately maintained garden of flowers, shrubs and small trees. As Jake headed up a set of stone steps and through an unlocked gate, he noticed a man on a terrace just above him, shoveling mulch from a wheelbarrow and spreading it around the nearby trees.

Jake reached the man's level and headed over. As he approached, the man straightened up and turned to him, leaning on his shovel. He looked Filipino, and wore a name tag that said 'Armando'. The gardener's hands tightened on the handle as Jake asked him about his predecessor. He said he'd heard of Bailey, but had never met him, and knew nothing about him.

Armando turned away and headed for to his wheelbarrow.

"Are you sure," Jake asked to his back. "Wouldn't the have had to show you the ropes or something?" The gardener was studiously ignoring him as a man came out of the front door of the mansion and approached them. He was tall and thin, with a ring of frizzy grey hair circling his largely bald head.

Though he was considerably older and less attractive than in his website promo photograph, Jake recognized him—it was Tommy Skylar. Skylar wore a tee-shirt with the AC-DC logo, battered jeans, and running shoes. He didn't look happy.

"What are you doing on my property?" he asked. "Can I help you with something?"

The gardener glanced at his boss sheepishly, and bent down to continue his work.

"Are you Mr. Skylar?" Jake asked, trying to look and sound as non-threatening as possible. "I'm looking for a man I've been told used to work as your gardener—Owen Bailey?"

Jake thought he saw Skylar flinch, but if so, he recovered quickly. A middle-aged woman in what looked like some kind of uniform appeared in the mansion's doorway.

"Yeah, I'm Tommy Skylar," the man said. "What's your interest in Owen?"

"Jake Sommers," Jake said, reaching out his hand, which Skylar shook. "I have a friend who's lost touch with him. They're concerned about him. They just want to know if he's okay."

"A friend?"

"I think they'd rather I didn't reveal their name."

Skylar turned toward the mansion's front door.

"It's alright, Mona," he called to the woman. She shot Jake a suspicious glance, then disappeared inside.

"Owen?" Skylar said. "Yeah, he was my gardener for years, but he took off somewhere a few months ago. I haven't seen him since."

"Have you got any idea where he might have gone?"

Skylar shrugged. "To be honest, I never even knew where he actually lived. I think his mail went to a box number. He was a part-time musician. Maybe he finally found a paying gig somewhere. Or maybe— you know, he had a problem..." Skylar made a motion like injecting something into his arm. "What's the connection? Are you a musician?"

"Yeah, I am," Jake said. "Sort of, though that's not the connection..."

Skylar cocked his head, straightened up, and pointed a finger at Jake. "Wait a minute—Sommers." He narrowed his eyes. "I've seen your act. In Victoria, in that little place down by the Inner Harbour..."

"The Salty Dog," Jake said.

"Yeah—yeah, I was there six months ago. You're good. I was impressed."

"Thanks."

"You play that old-time stuff—Fats Waller and all that. Too bad nobody listens to it anymore."

"I do," Jake said.

Skylar nodded toward his mansion. "Why don't you come up for a drink? I'm in the business, you know."

Jake hesitated. Skylar took a step back and swept a hand toward his front door.

"Okay," Jake finally said. "Maybe just one."

He followed his host up a set of steps to an imposing carved wooden doorway. Skylar walked inside. Jake turned back for a second and looked behind him. Armando had stopped working and was talking to someone on his cell phone.

Jake caught up with Skylar as they moved along a hallway, climbed a half-dozen carpeted stairs then down a short passage, and emerged in a massive, opulent living area. Almost the entire south wall was glass, and a glass door on the right led out to an expansive patio and lush garden, with a stone stairway leading down to a spectacular infinity pool.

Jake froze for a second, staring in awe at the stunning panoramic view of Burrard Inlet and the Lion's Gate Bridge. Far below, the rays of the afternoon sun glinted off the water, sparkling with a million dancing points of light. In the distance, tiny sailboats heeled in the wind across the waves, and a giant cruise ship approached from the open ocean.

"Scotch?" Skylar's voice woke him from his trance.

He turned to face his host, who was now holding a bottle of Bruichladdich. "Uh—yeah, sure."

Mona appeared, and Skylar handed her the bottle.

Jake inspected the interior of the giant living area. The walls were festooned with gold records and awards, and there were shelves and tables crowded with trophies and pictures of musicians and bands, a few of which Jake recognized. The labels on the albums and trophies listed some of the biggest Vancouver acts of the eighties and nineties. The final remains of a joint sat in an ashtray on one of the coffee tables. On another, the butt of a handgun was barely visible under a magazine.

In a far corner of the room stood a gigantic Fazioli grand piano. Jake unconsciously took a step toward it—he'd seen pictures, but had never actually played one.

"Try it," Skylar said behind him.

Jake turned back. His host, now with a drink in each hand, nodded his head toward the piano. Jake walked over and sat down on the bench. He turned back toward Skylar, nervous.

"It's okay," his host said. "I trust you—go ahead."

Jake put out his hands, hesitated for a second, and finally, at first hesitantly, played a few notes, checking out the action, finally settling into Debussy's *Arabesque No. One*. The instrument was amazing. The action was clean and positive, like nothing he'd experienced before, the keys answering the movement of his hands as if they were part of him. The bass notes seemed to echo from somewhere deep under the earth, and the full-bodied mid-range responded to the slightest change in nuance.

The tumbling waterfalls of notes in Debussy's sublime masterpiece seemed to drop from heaven, echoing through the room and out the open patio door to envelop the world. Jake immersed himself in the interlocking curly-cues that wound in and out of existence like the shoots of a flourishing vine in the morning sun.

"It's great, isn't it," Skylar's voice came from behind him.

Jake surfaced and stopped playing. He'd forgotten where he was.

He turned back to his host.

"Looks like there's more to you than old-time jazz," Skylar said, smiling. "I don't really play anymore, but I like to have it around."

"It's fantastic," Jake said, truthfully.

Skylar handed him a drink, and they moved toward the luxurious leather couches in the center of the room.

On the way, they passed a table with what looked like an old photograph—blown up, the original taken with a cheap camera. Jake stopped and studied it. It was the same one he'd seen in the article on the web, with the three bandmates.

"I was nineteen," Skylar said.

Jake looked more closely. His host moved up beside him.

"We had a band in the eighties, called 'Stone Cold'. That's where I got the name of my production company—'Stone Cold Production'." He pointed at the kid on the right. "That's Owen, the guy you're looking for. He was our bass player."

Again Jake studied Bailey's youthful features.

"We thought we were really going places," Skylar laughed. "We weren't. I played a 'Keytar'—you know, one of those synth keyboards that you hold like a guitar." He held his arms up in a guitar-playing stance.

Jake looked at him. "I guess you wouldn't remember," Skylar said.

Jake's eyes moved to the shorter kid in the middle. "Larry Karlsen," Skylar said, nodding at the picture. "The three of us formed Stone Cold Production, way back when."

"Yeah," Jake said. "I heard about the whole thing between him and Owen..."

"Well, like I said," Skylar shrugged, "Owen had a lot of personal problems—drinking and drugs. They pretty much destroyed any chance he had at a career. At the time I didn't realize how far gone he was. It's tragic.

"Owen did twelve years for Larry's murder. He was never the same after he got out. I gave him the gardening gig more or less out of sympathy. He actually turned out to be pretty good at his job. I never had any complaints."

Jake continued to study the picture.

The newspaper version had been cropped. In this one, more of the background was visible. Off to one side, almost out of the picture, was a blond woman, smiling. She'd been cut out of the one on the web. Something about her looked familiar.

Jake bent down for a closer look. "Who's the woman?"

"Oh, I don't remember," Skylar said, gesturing with one hand. He took Jake's arm and guided him away. "I think she was one of Owen's. Owen did pretty well with the babes back in the Stone Age."

Skylar swept a hand toward one of the couches.

"How's the Bruichladdich," he said, nodding at the drink in Jake's hand.

"Nectar of the Gods," Jake said, taking a seat. Skylar sat in an armchair beside him. Jake set his drink down on an end table. "You say you didn't know Owen that well anymore. Do you think it's possible he had a daughter?"

Skylar seemed to freeze momentarily.

Jake removed the photograph of Jeanette and Owen from his wallet and handed it to Skylar. "I think the girl's name is Jeanette Mallory — you know her?"

Skylar stared at the photograph. "Daughter?" he finally said. He handed it back to Jake. "First I've heard. We were pretty tight years ago, but not for a long time. He just worked for me, that's all."

"And you have no idea what happened to him?"

Skylar shrugged. "I think he used to live in a dumpy place in Burnaby, but I wouldn't know where. Everything went to the PO box."

He rose, called in Mona, and whispered in her ear. She left, and a few minutes later returned with a slip of paper. Jake glanced at it—as Skylar had said, it was a box number, in what looked like downtown Vancouver.

"He was actually on the street for a while," Skylar continued. "Maybe he's back there..." He moved a hand toward Jake's glass. "Have another one."

Jake looked down and noticed his drink was empty. "I'd better not— driving. I should be going."

He rose and turned toward the hallway. Skylar walked over to a small box on one of the tables. He opened it, removed a business card, and handed it to Jake.

"If you're looking for work, let me know. I might be able to get you something in the studio."

Jake glanced at the card, decorated with vibrant splashes of colour surrounding a guitar-shaped space in which was written: 'Tommy Skylar—CEO : Stone Cold Production'.

"Thanks," Jake said. "I'm not really used to playing with other people, but I'll think about it."

He turned and took one last glance at the magnificent view.

"So who is this 'friend' that wants to know about Owen?" Skylar asked, annoyance edging his voice.

"Like I told you," Jake answered, smiling, "they'd rather not give their name."

Skylar walked him down the stairs and out the front door.

"If you have any luck finding Owen," he called as Jake walked away, "say hi for me."

Jake waved his acknowledgment. He had a pleasant buzz from the scotch as he hiked back up the road, passing stupendous mansion after stupendous mansion. He thought back to the photograph in Skylar's living room, and it occurred to him why the woman in it had looked so familiar.

The features and hair colour were slightly different, but the expression was a dead-ringer for Evangeline.

XXX

A SECRET MEETING

Rule #22: When preparing to tail a vehicle, study it closely. Make note of make, model, year, colour, license plate, tail-light configuration, bumper stickers, dents, items hanging from the mirror, etc.

- Shadow Mac's Comprehensive Guide to Private Investigation

The address Skylar had given Jake was a non-starter. Bailey had used it online as his business address, and Jake had already checked it out. There was no way he could access it legally. It had probably been shut down with the business anyway. On the other hand, Skylar's current gardener, Armando, had behaved in a way that implied he knew more that he was telling.

It was late afternoon by the time Jake left Skylar's mansion, and as he passed by Armando, it looked like the gardener was packing his stuff into his truck. Jake walked back to his car and drove to a location on a hill, where he could watch the curving road leading back to Vancouver. A gut feeling told him it might be worthwhile tailing Armando's truck, which luckily was pretty distinctive, with a giant 'Green Tree Landscaping' logo on the side, and towing a small trailer with all his tools.

Twenty minutes later, the truck drove around a corner below him. Jake had parked in the shadows, behind a cluster of trees. He pulled out and moved in behind it. The truck quickly made its way back to the Upper Levels highway and headed east toward the city.

Jake had never had occasion to tail anybody. It was tricky staying close enough to keep the target in sight, but at the same time not being 'made'. Traffic was light, but there were enough cars for him to remain out of view.

Luckily, there were lots of EVOs in the city, so his didn't really stand out. They all looked more or less the same, like taxis. It wouldn't be that unusual to find one behind you on one block, then a different one behind you on the next. Since he'd parked some distance away and walked to Skylar's place, Armando wouldn't have seen him driving it before.

Another twenty minutes later, the gardener took the exit ramp for the Second Narrows bridge, and continued on the highway toward East Van. He took the exit for Boundary Rd., eventually turning right onto a side street, and into the maze of the suburbs.

It had been easy to tail the truck on the highway, but now, among the short and narrow side-streets, it became more difficult. Also, seeing the same vehicle, even an EVO, behind you for an extended period of time might raise alarm bells. Jake was forced to hang back, and even take detours that allowed him to keep Armando in view, in order to avoid detection.

One positive development was that it was beginning to get dark, and therefore easier to avoid been seen, and the EVO's largely black colouring blended in well with the shadows.

After a series of convoluted twists and turns through the suburban streets, where Jake had almost lost it, the truck finally pulled up to the curb. It seemed unlikely that Armando was going home. He'd been slowing down and speeding up periodically, like he hadn't been totally sure where he was going.

Jake came to a stop a half a block away, switched off his lights, and watched. Armando got out and headed up the street, toward a small commercial strip mall on the main road. Jake slouched down in his seat as the gardener glanced nervously up and down the block, before entering the parking lot. He made for a Circle K convenience store on one end of the strip.

Shit, Jake thought. He'd been hoping that if Armando was actually meeting Bailey, it would be at Bailey's home. As Armando approached, a figure emerged from the shadows. The two men stood in an alcove, backlit by the glare from the store window. Armando's contact was considerably taller than him. He looked middle-aged, and could be Bailey, but from this distance, there was no way Jake could tell for sure.

Now Jake was torn. He was close enough that if he were to leave his car, his targets would probably notice. If he didn't, it was unlikely he'd be able to see the contact well enough to say for sure if it was Bailey. In the end, he decided to stay. At least he'd be able to watch what went down between the two men.

They spoke for a few minutes, then Armando's contact put a hand in his pocket, removed something, probably an envelope, and handed it to Armando.

A payoff, Jake thought.

Armando took the package and stuffed it in his own pocket, then quickly headed for his truck. The movement distracted Jake for a few seconds before he realized that Armando's contact had disappeared from the back of the parking lot.

Jake started up the car, made a U-turn, and sped around the block, hoping to catch up with his target. He let out a breath when he spotted the man, still in the shadows, quickly crossing the street and heading east. Jake followed for two blocks, but he dared not get too close.

His quarry reached an intersection and turned right. Jake accelerated and turned the corner, but the man was suddenly gone. Jake drove as slowly as he dared without drawing attention, scanning the shadows, but Bailey, if it was him, had disappeared. Again he gunned the engine and circled the block, hoping to catch the man on the other side, but there was no sign of him.

Jake pounded the steering wheel with his fist. It was over.

The houses were set ten or fifteen meters back from the street. If the man had entered one of them, Jake should have seen it. It was as if his quarry had suddenly vanished. It was possible that he'd spotted Jake's car and gone on the run, but Jake didn't think so.

He stopped, brought up a map on his cell phone, and made a note of his current location, the Circle K, and the block where Bailey had disappeared. There was nothing more to see here. If he delivered the EVO right away and caught the next bus, he'd still have time to make the eight o'clock ferry.

During the long bus and ferry ride, Jake thought back on his meeting with Skylar, and the rendezvous between Armando and the man in the shadows. Their transaction, along with Armando's previous phone call, implied that Bailey, if it was Bailey, had paid Armando to inform him of anyone asking about him.

That, in turn, implied that Bailey was somehow in hiding. But in hiding from whom? And who was the woman in the picture at Skylar's place? From the similarity of their features, Jake was convinced that she had some connection with Evangeline—her mother? The picture was almost forty years old. That implied that the woman had been living in Victoria, not Europe or Quebec City, long before Evangeline was born.

Back at the *Rose*, he fired up the flea-market computer and dove back into the search engine, reconstructing a picture of the drama surrounding Stone Cold Production and the murder of Larry Karlsen.

In the same way that individual musical notes could come together to form a chord, the clues in a case could combine to form a theory. It took a couple of hours, but Jake was finally able to tease the identity of the woman from the photograph at Skylar's out of the sea of data.

Her name was Esther Franklin. She was one of a number of women who regularly hung out with the band. He dug up additional pictures of her with Bailey, Skylar, and Karlsen, though he found nothing to indicate her relationship with any of those men.

There was passing mention of her in various articles for several years, but at one point it seemed that all mention of her ceased. Jake's eyes opened wide as he worked out the timeline of her disappearance. There was no way to pinpoint it exactly, but it seemed to roughly match the day of Karlsen's death.

That didn't prove anything, but it was an interesting coincidence. Exactly who was this Esther Franklin, anyway? His gut told him she was somehow involved in the whole business.

He'd finally put a name and a persona to the older man in the picture from his fridge. But what was Owen Bailey to Jeanette Mallory? According to Maxine Sharpe, there had been no father of record on Jeanette's birth certificate. And yet Jeanette and Owen Bailey clearly had a close relationship. Was it possible that Bailey was her father? And if he was *Jeanette's* father, then...

One thing was becoming abundantly clear: Evangeline's original story was shot full of holes.

XXXI

FACE OFF

Rule #30: *The ability to recall accurately the facts and events or the physical characteristics of a suspect is one of a detective's most valuable skills.*
- Shadow Mac's Comprehensive Guide to Private Investigation

"You've been shitting me," Jake said to Evangeline the next evening, his hands bunched into fists on either side of his bowl of Pho Bo. They sat at a table in the 'Pho Better' Vietnamese restaurant on Belleville Street in James Bay. As usual, he willed himself not to be distracted by her stunning looks, or her equally stunning knitted outfit, this one pure white.

Jake had booked an early time, hoping the place would be sparsely occupied. It turned out to be two-thirds full, though at least he managed to find a table in an empty corner.

He'd spent the afternoon replaying in his mind what he'd learned about Jeanette Mallory, Owen Bailey, and Esther Franklin, and the evidence pointed at one conclusion.

He picked up his spoon and dipped it into the bowl. "The person you originally said you wanted me to find turned up dead. That should have been the end of it, but now you say you want me to look for the man in the picture. From what I've been able to work out, there's a good chance that man is Jeanette Mallory's father—and if he's her father, according to the DNA site, he's yours as well."

She feigned indifference as she stirred her own bowl with her spoon.

"I have a theory," Jake said. "Want to hear it?"

Evangeline looked up at him.

He took a sip and put down the spoon. "I don't think you were looking for your sister in the first place."

She stuck out her chin defiantly. "Of course I was. It's just that—"

"Let me continue," he interrupted.

She scowled, set down her own spoon, and crossed her arms on her chest.

He looked her in the eye. "You did the DNA test, like you said. But it wasn't out of an innocent desire to connect with your family—you had a specific purpose—you were looking for your father. The story about him being dead is bullshit, like so many other things you've told me."

She turned and looked away, as if trying to ignore what he was saying.

"The DNA test finds people related to you," Jake continued, "*all* people. It didn't find anything on your father, but it did find your sister—the sister you didn't even know you had—at least that part might be true."

She stole a glance at him, and again looked away.

"How am I doing so far?" he asked. "When you found Jeanette Mallory on the DNA site, you realized that she might lead you to your father—the person you'd been looking for all along."

She finally turned to look at him. "Well, what if I *am* looking for my father? What's wrong with that?"

"That's what I've been asking myself," Jake answered. "Why would you go through this pretext of looking for your sister all this time, unless..."

She picked up her spoon, but it slipped and dropped into her bowl with a splash.

Jake smiled. "Unless there was something about your father you didn't want me to know."

Evangeline fished out the spoon and wiped it with her napkin, then looked down at the steaming bowl. "I admit I haven't been completely truthful."

"Well, maybe it's time to start," Jake said. "Your parents didn't die in a car accident, like you said."

She looked up earnestly. "When we moved from France, my father stayed behind. We left when I was very young, and I never saw him again. I don't even remember what he looked like. My mother would never talk about him. I always assumed he had died, but I didn't know—"

"And your sister?"

She turned away again. "I was an only child, and my mother didn't have any siblings, so when I found the match for my sister, I knew she must be my father's child. But I didn't know whether she was born before he died, or whether it meant that he was still alive."

"So most of what you've been feeding me has been lies."

She sat silently.

"Why didn't you just tell me you were looking for your father in the first place? What is it about your father that you didn't want me to know?"

He was reluctant to mention the woman from the photograph—the woman he suspected might be her mother, until he had more information.

Evangeline set her jaw. "That's none of your concern," she snapped. "Your job before was to find my sister, now it's to find my father. I've paid you a generous retainer. What I do with the information you uncover is my business."

He stared at her and a chill settled over him. He had to admit she was right. He'd allowed himself to get too close to her, to think that their relationship was something beyond client and contractor. Her words now brought home the truth.

"I've had enough," he said. "You can find another guy for this investigation. Like I told you right from the beginning, I'm not even a detective. And this relationship isn't working for either of us."

She straightened in her chair and her eyes opened wide. "No! You must continue—the numbers—our spiritual planes—the universe has spoken—there can be no mistake. Only you can help me."

"Well you better find somebody else on the same 'spiritual plane'," he said. "I should never have gotten into this mess in the first place—"

"I can give you more money," she interrupted. She hauled her purse onto the table and withdrew her wallet.

"I don't need more money!" he shouted, pushing the wallet away.

The other patrons in the restaurant turned and looked over at them.

"I'm getting out of here," he said.

He called the waiter over.

"You'll continue your search?" she asked. Suddenly her features softened again. "Please—we're almost there. I promise I'll tell you everything—just not yet." She reached out and placed a hand on his.

He ignored her as he paid, rose, and turned for the door.

Evangeline followed, and put her arm through his as they stepped through the front door and turned right.

"I'll call you a cab," he said.

"Please," she said. "Don't abandon me."

He booked the ride on his phone, and they moved into a parking area beside the restaurant to wait. The lot seemed unusually silent. It was a quiet night and there was no movement anywhere. Inexplicably, Jake heard a familiar sound to their right—one he hadn't experienced since Basic Training: the metallic click of a gun being primed.

He glanced toward the source, and saw a moving shadow. Instinctively, he jumped on Evangeline, throwing her to the ground. A silenced gunshot blasted a divot out of the wall over their heads. He dragged her toward a nearby dumpster and another shot ricocheted off the pavement beside them.

"Stay here," he whispered, pushing her behind the dumpster.

He peeked around the far corner, just in time to see the shadow disappear down an alley.

"Don't move," he said to Evangeline. "I'll be back."

He took off after the fleeing shooter, turned a corner and saw him turn left down another alley. He followed, running flat out, constantly scanning the shadows, his lungs bursting. The fleeing shadow of his quarry was always one step ahead. The next alley was empty, lined with alcoves accessing doorways. Jake stole forward slowly, sticking near the walls, studying every darkened corner, testing each door as he moved.

All were locked. When he reached the far end, he poked his head around. Ahead was a bustling square lined with shops and people. He scanned the crowd, hoping to spot the shooter, but there were too many people—the attacker could be any one of them, or could have ducked into one of several adjoining alleys.

There was no point in continuing his pursuit. He made his way back to the lot where he'd left Evangeline, and checked behind the dumpster.

She was nowhere to be seen.

XXXII

CONNECTING THE DOTS

Rule #35: In detective work, all is often not as it seems. The good detective can sift through the superficial details, and dig down to find the truth.
- Shadow Mac's Comprehensive Guide to Private Investigation

In the morning Gordon, the giant sea lion, was sprawled across the aft deck of the *Honeysuckle Rose*, his expansive body a dark grey glistening blob in the rising sun, his whiskers twitching as he fended off the flies that routinely hovered around him. A greasy patch on the deck in front of Gordon's nose marked the final resting place of what had once been his breakfast: a dead fish.

Jake lay in a lounge chair beside him—eyes closed, head tilted back, feet extended out on the deck. Careful to expend as little effort as possible, Gordon slid his whiskered snout close enough to sniff the soles of Jake's shoes. Not finding any scent of interest, he lay his head back down and closed his eyes.

Jake hadn't heard from Evangeline since the night before, when she'd disappeared after he'd chased her attacker. A part of him was grateful—their relationship was finally well and truly over. But last night someone had tried to kill her. He couldn't just let it go. He'd tried to both call and text her, but there had been no response.

He knew he should inform the police, and was still wrestling with the decision, replaying her violent reaction whenever they were mentioned. And while he knew he should let the whole thing go and walk away, the intricacies of the case continued to surface unbidden in his mind.

Like a discordant note in an arpeggio, something stood out from everything else—something didn't belong.

Which of these is not like the others, he thought back to the old picture puzzles he'd seen as a kid.

He straightened up in his chair and turned to Gordon. "So was Jeanette Mallory really Evangeline's sister? Is Owen Bailey her father? Was Esther Franklin her mother?"

Gordon made an indifferent honking sound, and blew out a spray of something disgusting from his nose and mouth.

"But more importantly," Jake continued, "why do I even care? I don't owe her anything. I've already more than earned her retainer, and I didn't care that much about the money anyway. And why did I get mixed up in all this in the first place? I'm twenty-six years old—you'd think I would have learned something by now."

Gordon half-heartedly flapped one of his flippers on the deck, and shifted to a slightly more comfortable position.

Jake didn't really believe Evangeline's revised story any more than he now believed the first one, but the image surfaced of her expression last night when she'd talked about her father. There had been a momentary transformation—an intense emotion; he wasn't clear exactly what that emotion had been. His thoughts returned to Esther Franklin's face in the grainy photograph at Skylar's.

Somehow all the pieces must fit together.

He hadn't changed his decision to end their relationship, as both lovers and business associates, but only after he'd confirmed Evangeline was alive and safe. If she'd been the target of one attack, it seemed likely

171

another would be coming. The image spun through his head of her gunned down in some dark alley or bar, or of her body rolling against the surf, like Jeanette Mallory's.

The drone of an engine made him look up. One of the little water-taxis was chugging across the harbour, headed for the Songhees. Looming on the far shore was the white expanse of the Shutters complex.

It was a long shot, but it might be worth a try.

He made his way to the taxi landing, took the next one across to the Songhees lands, and headed for the Shutters building. The imposing front entrance was almost entirely composed of plate glass. Inside was a concierge's desk with a woman in uniform sitting behind it.

He strode to the front door and pulled, and wasn't surprised when it didn't open. There were no familiar names on the tenant panel beside it. The concierge had her head down, reading something on her desk. Jake waved at her, but got no response. Finally, he pounded on the glass wall.

The concierge looked up, annoyed. Jake motioned that he needed to get in. The concierge shook her head and pointed toward the entrance panel. Jake motioned to the woman, who finally got up and came to the other side of the glass.

"I need to get in touch with somebody who lives here," Jake said loudly, to breach the barrier.

The concierge again pointed at the panel beside him.

Jake shook his head. "I already looked. I'm not sure about her apartment number. I just want to know if she lives here—she's a very attractive young girl—blond, with blue eyes."

The woman shook her head. "Sorry, I can't give out information about tenants." She turned toward her desk.

"Wait," Jake said. "She's in her early twenties — well dressed, beautiful..."

She turned back. "I'm sorry."

Well, it was worth a try, Jake thought as he headed back toward the water taxi. It occurred to him that he knew so little about Evangeline, if she didn't call, he might never actually find out whether she was dead or alive.

As he hiked back over the same rise he'd watched her cross what seemed like an endless time ago, he spotted a man painting an ornamental chain-link barrier around one of the trees on the property.

He was old, with grey hair and a grey beard. Jake couldn't be certain, but it could be the guy he'd seen Evangeline talking to as he spied on her through his binoculars. The man paused his painting and stood as Jake approached.

"Can I help you with something?" he asked. He leaned down and laid the paintbrush he was holding on a paint can on the ground.

"I'm looking for someone that lives here—an attractive young girl—blond, with blue eyes. I think you might know her—Evangeline?"

"Evvie?" the handyman said, laughing. "Living here?"

"You *do* know her?"

"Yeah, sure, I know her. She's a looker alright. But she doesn't live here."

"What do you mean?"

The man shrugged. "She's my neighbour."

"What?"

The man nodded to his right. "Sunset Apartments—514 Barrington Place. It's about half a klick that way."

Jake asked him a few more questions, then began to walk away. He hesitated and turned to face the handyman.

"Have you seen her lately?"

The man cocked his head, thinking. "Saw her yesterday, I think. She comes and goes a lot."

Relieved, Jake headed for the new address. A few blocks away from the Shutters was an aging apartment block, with stucco walls and sagging windows. It reminded him of the one he'd tracked down for Jeanette Mallory. He walked down the chipped concrete sidewalk that divided a neglected lawn, and past a line of scraggly bushes, to the entrance.

As with the concierge at the Shutters, the handyman had been unwilling to give him Evangeline's apartment number, citing security. A dilapidated metal box with rows of mechanical buzzers was mounted beside the paint-chipped door. Almost all the names beside them said 'Occupant'. The one or two others didn't resemble any name that might be Evangeline.

"Why am I not surprised?" he said to himself, standing back and gazing up at the block of windows.

Back at the *Rose*, Jake was relieved when his phone beeped to indicate he'd gotten a text message. It turned out to be from Max, the manager at the Salty Dog—an invitation to come and talk. He'd missed several gigs at the bar since he'd taken up with Evangeline. His performances had been suffering, and he hadn't been on the best of terms with management even before his recent plunge into private investigation — he figured the news wouldn't be good.

So he wasn't surprised when he heard the strains of *Piano Man* echoing through the bar as he walked in the back door, and guessed what the meeting would be about. On the way to Max's office, he strolled through the darkened space, past tables with chairs inverted on top, and stopped for a few seconds to watch the kid at the piano. He was pretty good—Jake had to admit he was probably a better fit for this place than himself.

There was a light on in Max's office at the end of the hall. The door was open, and he walked in. Max looked up and smiled, then swept a hand toward a chair on the other side of his desk, and Jake sat down. The news was pretty much what he'd been expecting.

"What? Just because I missed a couple of nights?" Jake said.

"That didn't help," Max answered, "but it's more than that." He avoided direct eye contact as he shuffled some papers on his desk. "Nothing personal. You're just not really gelling with our current set of clientèle."

"Gelling?" Jake said. "Is that some modern slang word I haven't heard about, like 'noob', or 'finsta'?"

Max smiled sadly. "To tell the truth, I'm surprised you care. I didn't get the impression your heart was all that in it anyway."

He leaned forward and put a hand on Jake's shoulder. "Look Jake— you're good—probably too good for this place. And like I said before, personally I like the stuff you play. Maybe you'll find a place around town that's more in tune with your style."

"In tune," Jake said, shaking his head. "Good one. You're turning into a regular Oscar Wilde."

"Good luck, Jake," Max said, his expression indicating that the meeting was over. "I'll send you a cheque with your final pay. Come by anytime. Check out the new guy—he's good. I'll even give you a discount on the beer."

Jake walked out into the late afternoon. He wasn't sure whether he was happy or sad. But he had to admit, it was probably for the best.

Back home, he sat down in the dining nook, and glanced up at one of Deirdre's paintings on the wall. In it, a naked female figure (who Deirdre once admitted was herself), strolled down a narrow dirt path into a magical wood. A host of trees and animals lining the path shimmered in the early morning sunlight, and were positioned in such a way that they seemed to beckon her on.

He thought back on the day she'd first showed it to him, and they'd talked about her art.

"But you've done okay financially—with your painting," he said.

"I paint because I love doing it," she answered, "not for money. I've always believed that if you follow where your heart leads, Karma will find a way to sustain you. I've never painted for money—the money just came, because people recognized that my art was coming from within, and they wanted to be part of that."

"But it's different with music," he'd said. "You can't even get gigs anymore. Everything's recorded, and they all listen to the same boring crap."

"Art is art," Deirdre said, "whether it's painting, writing, or music. If what you create comes from your heart, people will be drawn to it like moths to a flame. Not everyone, of course. You don't need everyone to love what you do, just enough to get along."

She looked at him and smiled. "In the end, you have to decide—do you want a hundred-meter yacht, or do you want to be happy?"

That night he would normally have been playing at the Salty Dog. At six, he actually showered and started to get ready before he remembered—he didn't work there anymore. Another part of his life was gone, chipped away like a flake of stone from a sculpture that was gradually being whittled to nothing. And what would happen when the final chip was removed?

He dug a bottle of cheap scotch from the cupboard under the sink, and poured himself a glass. Moving to his own keyboard, he pulled out the bench from its usual location underneath, sat down, and put on his headphones, resting the glass on the top.

His fingers, seemingly with minds of their own, explored snippets of tunes he'd learned over the years, searching for one that would capture his current mood. He paused for a sip of scotch, and cringed at the difference between what he was drinking and the heavenly Bruichladdich he'd savoured at Tommy Skylar's place.

When darkness entered his life, and even sometimes threatened his sanity, music had always come to his rescue. It was his friend, teacher, physician, shrink, and psycho-stimulant drug all rolled into one.

His fingers found their places on the keys, and settled into a mournful rendition of one of Satie's *Gnossiennes*. Its off-kilter tune and strange rhythm were somehow soothing, as if the music had been discovered in some primordial cave once occupied by an ancient race, long before the first human took a breath.

He wasn't sure why he found it comforting. He didn't ask—he simply let it wash through his psyche, let it transport him to a place where there was no trouble, no sorrow, no pain.

He played and drank until his eyelids became heavy and he began to nod off. He finally slid from the bench and curled up to sleep on the floor.

XXXIII

AN UNEXPECTED ENCOUNTER

Rule #43: *In the event that a private investigator is approached or stopped by a police officer, they must heed the officer's instructions.*
- Shadow Mac's Comprehensive Guide to Private Investigation

That night Jake dreamed he was walking along a dusty dirt road in blinding sunlight and searing heat. He was on a journey. There was no indication where he was, or where he was going, and no maps or directions, but somehow he knew he was headed for some centre for personal development or healing, like a Buddhist monastery or an Indian ashram. Just as he was about to arrive, he somehow made a wrong turn, and no longer knew the way.

Every time he changed direction, the path seemed to be more confusing. And when he approached someone to ask directions, they would turn away, or simply disappear.

He woke in a panic, his forehead and palms sweaty, still dressed and lying on the floor in front of his keyboard. It was light outside, and his body tensed when he heard footsteps on the dock, heading his way.

Inexplicably, in a replay of the day he'd first met Evangeline, his vessel was swaying, the water sloshing against the hull below, and the swaying was soon accompanied by pounding on the door.

Jake lay back, pretending not to be home. It was probably McCluskey, and it was possible that his annoying neighbour would eventually give up and go away.

But the pounding continued, eventually followed by a male voice shouting: "Open up—police!"

The pounding and swaying continued. Jake finally got up and answered the door.

Two cops, in uniform, really were standing on the dock outside. He glanced left, toward the parking lot, and noticed a third blocking the ramp he'd have to use if he tried to run away. He was too shocked to speak.

The two on the dock began to move forward, and the vessel swayed again as they climbed aboard. He didn't see any point in running—he was in no condition, and there was nowhere to run anyway. The cops now stood on the deck, an arms-length from him. His eyes moved to the guns on their hips.

"Are you Jake Sommers?" One of them asked.

He nodded.

"We have a warrant to search your vessel," the cop said, holding up a document for Jake to read.

Jake's vision was still blurry as he took the piece of paper. He rubbed his eyes, blinked a few times, then read. It really was a search warrant. He cringed when he saw the target: 'Records relating to Ms. Jeanette Mallory'.

The cop from the ramp joined them.

"I was going to give them to you," he started to say, "I just hadn't..."

They ignored him and pushed into the space.

Jake followed them, and made a move toward the head. One officer put out a hand to stop him.

"You'll be sorry if you don't let me in there," Jake said.

The cop pushed him aside, stepped into the head and checked for a few seconds, then came back out and nodded. After emptying his bowels, washing his face, gulping down a massive drink of water, and capping it off with the standard pair of Ibuprofen, Jake emerged, and the cop led him toward the door.

"Jeanette's stuff is in a box under there," he said on the way, pointing at the bench in the nook, hoping to minimize the dismantling of his home.

He swayed on the dock bleary-eyed with one cop, while the other two began systematically tearing the interior apart.

Maggie's curtains parted and her face appeared, horrified but maybe not terribly surprised to see the police at his door. Jake cringed as he imagined Filbert with his tablet, tacking another set of infractions onto the end of his already long list. One of the cops soon emerged with the box of Jeanette's belongings.

"There's nothing else," he said to the cop holding the box.

The cop didn't answer, and his partner continued the search. Finally, a half hour later, the second cop emerged, and nodded at the others.

"We'd like you to come with us, please," the cop said to Jake. "We have a few questions we'd like to ask you."

They allowed Jake to lock up the vessel. He glanced at the interior as he closed the door. The state was surprisingly similar to the way it had looked before he'd met Evangeline. All his hours of cleaning...

Back on the dock, one of the cops turned and extended a hand toward the ramp, then started walking. Jake followed him, now sandwiched between him and the other two, one of them carrying the box with Jeanette's belongings. As they neared the top of the ramp, a police car was waiting.

Shit, now what? He thought, as one of them held his head and he was guided into the back seat.

The police interrogation room looked pretty much the way he imagined one should look—just like the ones he'd seen in cop shows on TV. But he'd never expected to actually find himself seated in one.

The car carrying him had arrived at the main Victoria police station, and the cops had led him inside and deposited him there. Right now he was sitting at a small table, alone. The walls were bare, and a single empty chair was positioned across from him. Some kind of device—probably a video camera—was mounted on the wall high above his head.

He'd been sitting there for more than ten minutes. He wasn't sure whether the wait was a psychological strategy meant to soften him up, or whether the interrogator had actually been held up for some reason. After another five minutes, he decided the tactic was deliberate.

If Mom could only see me now, he thought to himself.

He imagined the expressions that would have crossed his parents' features, knowing their only son was at a police station and under investigation—at least for his fraud at Fairways Management, but probably for something worse. It would be funny if it wasn't such a tragedy. Luckily, if you could call that luck, neither were around to see how far he'd fallen.

The Ibuprofen was finally beginning to kick in, but his head was still pounding, floaters were swimming across his corneas, and he felt nauseous. It wasn't the condition he would have chosen to be in while being interrogated.

Finally the door opened. A middle-aged guy with a grey brush-cut walked in, wearing a rumpled suit and carrying a file folder.

"Hello, Mr. Sommers," he said in a non-committal tone. "My name is Detective Harrow. I just want to ask you a few questions."

"What's going on here?" Jake asked, though in truth he had at least some idea.

"Can I get you anything?" the detective asked. "Coffee? Water?"

Jake shook his head.

"Wait," he said, changing his mind. "maybe a coffee—black."

Harrow opened the door, leaned out and talked to somebody, then came back in and shut it behind him. He opened the folder, removed a single piece of paper, and slid it onto the table in front of Jake. On the paper was written a single telephone number—it was Jake's.

"Is this your number?" Harrow asked.

Jake scanned the number more than once, hoping he might have misread it the first time. He hadn't.

"Yeah," he nodded.

"You called Missing Persons in Vancouver a little over a week ago, using this number—is that correct?"

Jake swallowed.

"You were asking about Jeanette Mallory," Harrow continued.

There was a quiet knock on the door. Harrow opened it and a hand appeared with a paper cup. He took the cup, closed the door, and placed it in front of Jake. It smelled bad, but Jake had a feeling he'd need it. With a shaking hand, he picked it up, and managed to get it to his lips without spilling any. It tasted as bad as it smelled, but hopefully the caffeine would help clear his head.

Harrow walked away a few paces, turned and came back. "Fairways Property Management in Vancouver have your name on record as receiving Ms. Mallory's belongings. Apparently you told them you were..." He pointedly leaned down, opened the file folder and double-checked, "her brother." He straightened up and looked at Jake. "Are you Jeanette Mallory's brother?"

Jake's body stiffened. Things were going from bad to worse.

The detective closed the folder again. "Are those the items we retrieved from your vessel at Fisherman's Wharf?"

Jake nodded.

"Somebody closely matching your description came looking for Jeanette Mallory at her former apartment in Vancouver," Harrow said. "Was that you?"

Jake took another sip of coffee. He finally felt awake enough to say something. "There was a thing about Jeanette's death on the radio a week ago. That's the first I heard about it." He shakily set down the cup and returned Harrow's gaze. "I had nothing to do with it, if that's what you're thinking."

"So you knew about her death," the detective said, "but you still neglected to contact us about her possessions."

Jake remained silent.

"The body had been in the water for quite some time," Harrow continued. "Performing a proper medical examination took longer than usual. Initial evidence implied death by accident or suicide, but the detailed medical exam has confirmed that Ms. Mallory was murdered."

Jake's knuckles whitened on the arms of his chair. "How did she die?"

"We can't release that information," Harrow said. "Anything you can tell us would be useful. What's your interest in Jeanette Mallory?"

Jake leaned back in his chair. "I think this is the point where I tell you I'm not saying anything more without a lawyer present."

Harrow bent down and put both hands on the table. "You know, it so happens I served in the Navy under your father for a couple of years. He was a good man. So I'm inclined to cut you some slack. Right now, we're just asking a few questions. If you cooperate, you can be out of here in no time."

The detective smiled. "Anyway, we're reasonably satisfied that you had no involvement in Jeanette Mallory's death." He locked eyes with Jake. "Despite the fact that your behaviour over the past week and a half almost seemed deliberately contrived to make you look guilty."

Jake reflected on that unfortunate sequence of events.

Harrow left the room for a few minutes and returned with a laptop. He opened it, fired it up, and clicked and typed for a few seconds.

He swiveled the computer to face Jake. "We were about to pick you up for questioning regarding the Missing Persons call and the fraudulent claiming of Jeanette Mallory's possessions, so imagine our surprise when you turned up again."

What looked like a blurry stopped-motion frame from a video feed was frozen on the screen.

"A few days ago, we investigated a report of shots fired in a parking lot near a Vietnamese restaurant on Belleville Street," Harrow continued. "We managed to acquire some video footage from one of the businesses nearby. Guess who happened to be in the picture?"

He pressed the 'play' button. The action began, and clearly showed Jake and Evangeline standing in the parking area, then diving for cover after the gunshot.

Harrow stopped the recording. Jake continued to stare at the screen, now showing only the empty lot.

"It's apparent from the video that either you or the woman beside you were the target. You didn't consider reporting this to the police?"

Jake shrugged. "There didn't seem much point. What can I say, there's a lot of lunatics running around the city these days."

"I think it's time you started talking to us," the detective said, making eye contact. "We're not sure what you're mixed up in, but whatever it is, I can tell you that you're in way over your head, and if you keep it up, you're going to find yourself in a world of trouble."

"I don't suppose this video of yours shows who the shooter was?"

Harrow shook his head. "We were hoping you could shed some light on that. All we could see is shadows. The video does show you running after him. I assume you didn't catch him—otherwise you'd probably be dead now. But I don't suppose *you* got a good look?"

Jake didn't see much point in continuing to deny his involvement. "Like you say, all I saw was shadows. The guy was too far ahead for me to see, then he blended into a crowd and he was gone."

Jake looked at his hands on the table for a few seconds. "I have no idea who shot at us or why," he finally said, raising his head. "That's the truth. The shot came totally out of the blue. I know I should have reported it..."

Harrow backed up the video and nodded toward the frozen image of Jake and Evangeline on the screen. "You know, it happens that we're already acquainted with your little friend."

Jake tensed. Evangeline's words came drifting back: *The truth is, I haven't been a good person.*

XXXIV

THE TRUTH

Rule #8: Everybody lies. Never assume that a suspect is telling the truth. Always check their alibi.
- **Shadow Mac's Comprehensive Guide to Private Investigation**

"Betty?" Jake said, almost in a whisper, after Harrow shut down the video and brought up the police file of the woman appearing in it.

Jake realized that he didn't have to feel guilty about spilling the beans to the cops: they already knew about Evangeline—seemingly a lot more than him. Except that Evangeline wasn't her real name. He felt as if he'd stepped through a door into another dimension.

"Not that there's anything wrong with that," he added hastily. "It's just... Betty who?"

"Rumford," Detective Harrow answered. "Betty Rumford is her real name. At least, as far as we can determine. What exactly is your relationship with this woman?"

Jake shrugged. "We're friends."

"Friends..." Harrow said skeptically.

For a moment Jake was silent. Finally he decided it was time to open up. He detailed Evangeline's entire story: her family history, how she'd wanted him to find her sister, and how he'd established that her sister was Jeanette Mallory. He didn't mention that Evangeline had paid him—that would lead to pesky questions about things like whether he had a PI's license.

"Grew up in Lyon, France?" Harrow threw his head back and laughed. "That's a new one, I must say. And you bought all that?"

"Well...not completely, but—so, she's not..." Jake said.

Harrow smirked and shook his head.

"Well, who the hell is she?"

The detective scrolled down, clicked on one of the entries and read for a few seconds.

"We don't have a lot of details about her," he said, finally looking up, "but as far as we know, she was born here in Victoria, and there's no indication that she's ever left this country. I'm surprised Betty even knows where Lyon is."

Jake felt like he was drifting through some kind of dream, or had entered some alternate reality. "You say you're familiar with her—familiar how?"

Harrow smiled. "She's one of the better-known call girls in the city."

Jake put a hand down on the table to steady himself. "Is that so..."

"We've known about her ever since she got here a few months ago, but she's been pretty smart—we've never been able to connect her to anything that would allow us to make a bust."

The warmth Jake had felt on his cheeks after Harrow's original revelations was still there, as he realized how completely he'd been duped. "I guess that explains all the money, and the way she dressed. But I've done searches on the web, even on the so-called Deep Web, and found nothing."

"People in her profession go through names like we go through pocket change," Harrow said. "If you wanted to find her, it wouldn't make much sense to use her name."

Jake shook his head slowly, still in shock.

The detective slid his finger along the mousepad and continued reading. "We believe that she and her mother originally lived here in Victoria, then for a short time in Vancouver. There's no record of who her father was. Twenty years ago, when Betty was a young child, the mother skipped town and moved across the country, to Halifax, under the name of Eleanor Rumford. We're not sure why, or whether that was her real name."

"How old was ...Betty when all this happened?"

"When they first arrived in Halifax? She was four." Harrow scrolled further through the file, reading. "Eleanor got a job cleaning rooms in a motel, and they spent years just scraping by. Over that time, Eleanor made repeated calls to nine-one-one, claiming someone was stalking her. The police were never able to substantiate her claims.

"They chalked it up to general paranoia. Apparently, that paranoia eventually deteriorated into full blown mental illness. Somehow Betty fell through the cracks, and was never apprehended by children's services. She continued to live with her mother."

Jake thought about the frozen image of Evangeline he'd just seen on the display. Beyond the immediate fear from the attack, there had been a deeper, crushing terror in her eyes.

"She was a wild child," Harrow continued, "always acting out and running away. Her relationship with her mother became more and more strained."

He scrolled further down the display, then continued. "When she was eighteen, Betty moved out, though apparently she and her mother maintained contact. We think that's when she first started her life as a call girl.

"Then, a year ago, Eleanor was found dead in her apartment, of a gunshot wound to the head. The death was deemed a suicide. About eight months later, Betty moved back here to Victoria, and a month or so after that we started to get wind of her activities."

Jake closed his eyes momentarily. "You wouldn't happen to have a picture of the mother?"

Harrow clicked the mouse button, sifting through the files, then turned the machine around again to face Jake. On the screen was the image of a woman, lying sprawled on a carpeted floor, obviously dead. Jake flinched at the sight of the body. There were shadows, she was much older, and the shot was at a weird angle. Still, Jake had no doubt—the woman in the picture was Esther Franklin.

He told Harrow and the detective made a note on the file.

"But why the accent," Jake asked, "and the big convoluted story about her family?"

Harrow shrugged. "Beautiful girls like that—a lot of times people don't take them seriously. Maybe she thought you'd be more likely to believe her if she came across as someone more sophisticated. Or maybe she was acting out the persona she wished she'd had, the life she wished she'd lived."

Jake suddenly sat up straight. "Do you think Evang... I mean Betty, could have had anything to do with Jeanette Mallory's death?"

Harrow shook his head. "We're pretty certain she wasn't even living here at the time Jeanette was killed."

"Like I told you," Jake said, "at first she claimed she was looking for her sister. But after I confronted her with Jeanette's death she admitted she was actually looking for her father. Any idea why?"

"It's not that unusual," Harrow answered, "a child wanting to understand where they came from—wanting to connect with their birth parents. Especially when her mother had been absent for most of her life, and had died violently. If her father is still alive, he might be her only living blood relative. That could be all it is."

"But then why lie and say she's looking for her sister?"

Harrow shrugged again. "I'm afraid only she can answer that. Some people lie the way they breathe. It's part of who they are, a power thing—they know something you don't. You haven't heard anything from her in how long?"

Jake nodded at the laptop. "Since the shooting—a couple of days. But none of this explains who was trying to kill her—or why."

"Are you sure you're telling me everything?"

"About the shooting, and about Jeanette Mallory's death? Absolutely. Am I going to be charged with anything?"

Harrow waved a hand dismissively. "There's no law against being the target of an attempted murder. Technically, we could charge you with interference with our investigation, tampering with evidence, fraud, and so on, regarding Jeanette's things, but we'll leave that alone—at least for now.

"We brought you in mainly to see if you could throw any light on what happened. But as long as you're here, I'll warn you again: give up on this mission—whatever it is."

Jake was escorted out of the police station. "We'll look into the Esther Franklin angle," Harrow said as Jake opened the door. "I'll let you know if we come across anything important. And be careful—I'm assuming that the shooter was after Betty, but I guess it's possible he was after you."

In the loft of the *Rose*, Jake shook his head slowly as he fired up the flea-market computer, still stunned by Harrow's revelations. He'd never had a reason to look for sex online, so he wasn't sure where to start. He also wasn't completely sure he wanted to know, wanted to see what presence Evangeline had set up in pursuit of her 'profession'.

He'd done searches for her name before, and found nothing, but as Harrow had pointed out, call girls and those with other illegal occupations weren't likely to use their real names, or advertise in regular social media.

He remembered Evangeline's look of surprise when he'd explained to her about the Deep Web—it occurred to him that she probably knew more about it than he did.

He started typing a search for a sexual partner, to see if she would come up, but decided that he really didn't want to know. Anyway, the fear persisted that the assassin, whoever they were, might have struck again and succeeded. At any time he expected to hear from Harrow that she'd suffered the same fate as Jeanette Mallory.

He'd just given up and flopped down on his bed when his phone beeped with a text. It was from Evangeline.

The text said: *It's vital that you continue with your investigation. Please—I'm begging you. I'll be in touch.*

XXXV

A NEW TARGET

Rule #17: Danger is an inherent part of a detective's work. A good detective must always be vigilant, and alert to any unexpected threat.

- Shadow Mac's Comprehensive Guide to Private Investigation

Jake crashed for a while, hoping to clear his head, but when he awoke in the afternoon, he was still stressed out, processing the latest information from the police and Evangeline's latest terse text.

He thought about Harrow's revelations. A part of him wasn't surprised. Again he was impressed with the power of denial—that he could have continued to believe every lie Evangeline told him day after day, even though his gut told him otherwise.

As for the task she'd set for him—it was dead in the water, and as far as he was concerned, their relationship was dead with it. He'd replied to her earlier text, saying that he had nowhere to go with the case and wouldn't continue even if he could. He'd suggested that she abandon her search, and leave it all to the police. He'd also asked if she was okay. So far, he hadn't heard back.

Even if he had been willing to continue, he couldn't see a path forward. He could go back to East Van and scour the set of blocks where he'd lost Bailey. But that would probably be a waste of time. The only real clue left was Skylar's current gardener, Armando. It looked like he knew how to contact Bailey, but Jake had no idea how to make him talk. Again, Jake reflected on how little he actually knew about being a private detective.

That night, he didn't feel like hanging around, letting his destructive thoughts hijack his brain. He took Max up on his offer, and visited the Salty Dog—as a customer. Despite his vow that it was all over between them, he couldn't shake the image of Evangeline maybe showing up, like she had all those days ago.

He watched and listened to his replacement on the piano. He had to admit the kid was good, and unlike Jake, he seemed happy to crank out the bland, forgettable tunes that had been produced in the current century.

Jake had a couple of discount beers and headed home, with no more than a pleasant buzz. Somehow, the excesses with Evangeline were accomplishing what years of empty vows and guilty self-recriminations hadn't—he seemed to be losing his desire to drink to excess.

He'd just stepped aboard the *Rose* when he got a phone call.

Mr. Sommers, the voice on the line said. *It's Detective Harrow.*

Jake moved to the lounger on the aft deck and sat down to speak to the detective. *I thought you should know,* Harrow said, *we contacted the police in Halifax regarding Eleanor Rumford. You were right—she and Esther Franklin were one and the same person.*

There are also new developments in the investigation into Eleanor's death. Apparently a witness recently came forward and claimed they'd heard the gunshot from her apartment, and had seen a man rushing away just afterwards.

"They're re-assessing the whole suicide angle?" Jake said.

They are taking another look at the case, Harrow answered. *Back then, the witness had been afraid to get involved, but I guess since then they've had an attack of the guilts.*

Jake's body tensed, and his fingers tightened on the phone in his hand.

You still there? Harrow said.

"Yeah, I'm here," Jake answered.

Anyway, just to let you know, Harrow said. *It's not clear what exactly is going on, but I think it's even more important than before that you be careful.*

For a second, Jake debated with himself whether he should tell Harrow that Evangeline had finally contacted him. In the end, he kept silent. He ended the call, stood up, and turned to go inside. Out of the corner of his eye, in the distance, he spotted a moving shadow on the dock. It was late. All the businesses and restaurants had closed.

At first he felt silly—he was being paranoid. Harrow's call had spooked him, and he was seeing shadows and danger everywhere. Just the same, he moved behind the corner of the cabin and poked his head out.

There was definitely something. For a moment he thought it was one of the otters that sometimes scurried around the docks at night, or even Gordon looking for late-night handout. But when he looked closer, he could make out a human figure dressed all in black slinking along the dock between the now silent businesses, then the houseboats, heading in the direction of the *Rose*.

When the figure's hand happened to fall under a patch of light, Jake froze. It was holding a gun. When Jake had first arrived, a few of the workers had still been packing up and leaving the Wharf. His attacker must have been watching him and waiting. Jake scanned the dock. It was now completely dark and empty. There was nowhere for him to run. If he stepped onto the dock or tried to re-enter his home the assassin, as he was now certain the figure was, would see him.

There was only one way out. He made his way to the far gunwale of the aft deck, still behind the corner of the cabin and out of sight of the killer. He climbed over the side, and silently slipped into the water, fighting to keep from crying out as his muscles were paralyzed by the cold.

He hung from the far side of the *Honeysuckle Rose* with his phone in his teeth, and felt her sway as the killer stepped silently aboard. Holding onto the gunwale, Jake worked his way hand over hand toward the dock. He heard the man try his door, which was still locked. The assassin might not have seen him move to the aft deck. Would he think Jake had gone inside? Or would he grasp that he'd had spotted him and was hiding?

Footsteps moved along the deck to the back. There was no longer any doubt. Jake's body was quickly turning numb in the freezing water, as he silently made his way closer to the dock, his frozen fingers barely able to grip the wooden beams and pylons.

He passed underneath, his head barely above water, and the wooden dock only a hand's width above him. Faint bars of light from the gaps in the planking cut across his face as he slowly glided toward the other side, careful not to make any noise, or produce ripples that would give away his location. He remembered that the life expectancy in water this temperature was about twenty minutes.

He heard a faint pop, as apparently the killer had broken open the door to his living area. The *Rose* tilted back and forth slightly as he prowled around the interior. There was another, much louder, pop-pop, followed by the muted rain of debris on the roof of cabin. The assassin must have shot up into Jake's loft from underneath. Soon, the footsteps moved quickly back across the deck and stepped onto the dock.

Jake's body began to shiver as the footsteps passed directly over his head, shaking loose dirt and debris, which fell onto Jake's face. If the killer was to look down...

Jake remembered that McCluskey had a balcony at the back of his place. McCluskey's lights had been on. Now on the other side of the dock, he worked his way, shivering, toward the back of McCluskey's vessel and around it, still shielded from the attacker's sight. He reached the balcony, grabbed the wooden railing, and tried to pull himself up, but his fingers were numb, and he was cold and exhausted.

He heard the muffled footsteps of the killer slinking along the dock back toward shore. Had he checked Jake's bed and found he wasn't there? Would he wait somewhere to see if Jake came back? That seemed likely.

A door opened on one of the nearby houseboats, then another.

Somebody shouted: "What's going on out here?"

Seconds later, Jake could barely make out the faint tap of footsteps moving up the exit ramp and into the parking lot.

His body was now shaking violently, and he was losing the feeling in his extremities. His fingers were no longer able to maintain their grip on the balcony. They opened and slipped off the slime-coated wooden posts, and he slid deeper into the freezing water. He began to feel light-headed, on the verge of losing consciousness.

McCluskey came to the back window and peered out. He must have felt the motion from Jake's weight on the balcony. He spotted Jake and was about to yell something when Jake frantically raised a shaking finger to his face and shook his head. McCluskey silently opened the door, came out, and helped drag a soaked and shivering Jake over the railing and inside.

"What the hell are you doing?" McCluskey said.

Jake spit the phone into one hand, and pushed the other down for silence. McCluskey sat him on a chair, shut the door and rushed to get a towel and a robe for him to wear. Jake was shivering uncontrollably.

"There's never a dull moment with you, is there," McCluskey whispered, as Jake rose shakily to his feet, got out of his soaking clothes and toweled himself off.

McCluskey helped him to a cot in his spare room, and draped him with warm blankets. Jake collapsed on it and knew no more.

In the surreal eternal twilight of the high arctic, Jake stepped out of the mess trailer and down a small set of steps to the wooden walkway connecting the buildings of the training base. It was late November, and the sun was already sinking below the horizon, even though it was only three in the afternoon.

He was halfway to his destination—the recreation building, when the sun finally winked out altogether and it was dark. A flash of light shot across the blackness. He zipped up his parka, crossed his arms, and patted his mittened hands on his shoulders as he stopped and studied the evening sky. The show—the Aurora Borealis, or Northern Lights, was about to begin.

A dome of white blasts like spotlights began to march across the horizon, firing into the heavens beneath a deep green halo. Soon the reds and purples joined in, dancing and swirling around and through each other before pouring across the sky like a giant celestial river. A few other soldiers exited the rec building and joined him. The cold was forgotten as they stood for more than ten minutes, transfixed by the spectacle.

Jake blinked his eyes, now awake. At first he was confused. Still shivering slightly, he stared up at the unfamiliar ceiling. His body felt trapped—

he was unable to move, and there was a strange sound emanating from the area of his stomach. He soon realized that heavy blankets had been wrapped around him. He felt additional weight on his midsection. Lifting his head with difficulty, he stared down toward his feet.

It was dark, but he could make out a hot-water bottle lying on his chest. Just behind it, curled up and purring, his black-and-white face half-buried in the blanket, was Kong the cat. Kong complained and jumped to the floor as Jake pushed against the covers, rolled over and hauled himself out of bed. Still wrapped in the blankets, he opened the door and walked into the next room.

XXXVI

LEAVING THE ROSE

Rule #19: *A common mistake PIs make is to pre-judge a situation. Your client may believe someone is guilty, but that doesn't make it true.*

- **Shadow Mac's Comprehensive Guide to Private Investigation**

McCluskey was sitting on his couch with a laptop on his knees, a pair of glasses pushed down on his nose.

"How long was I out?" Jake asked, as he staggered forward, still half asleep, and still shuddering with the occasional tremor of cold. Kong wove a path between his feet.

"About half an hour," his neighbour answered, looking up and studying him. "Imagine my surprise, looking out my window and seeing a guy floating in the harbour with a cellphone in his teeth..."

Jake gave McCluskey a quick explanation of what was happening while he changed into the jeans and plaid shirt that McCluskey had set out for him to wear. He wondered in passing whether his neighbour ever wore anything else.

McCluskey shook his head slowly, and ran his fingers through his thinning hair. "Here I set you up with a cushy career in pseudo-law enforcement, and this is what you do with it. I don't want to have to peel your bullet-riddled body off the dock—or my balcony."

"Sorry," Jake said sarcastically, "I'll do my best not to bleed on any of your property. I better call Harrow and let them know what happened."

"You hungry?" McCluskey asked. "I've got some leftovers from my dinner."

"I'm starving," Jake answered. "Thanks, that would be great."

Jake made the call while McCluskey disappeared into the galley. They put him through to Detective Harrow, who said they'd be on their way.

While he waited, he strolled through McCluskey's living room, which was considerably larger than his own. Jake had spent time on his neighbour's back patio, but had never actually been inside his place. A number of certificates hung on the walls. He checked out a few: a Master's degree in Physics from UBC, a degree in Philosophy from McGill, a membership in the Chartered Professional Accountants Association of BC, and a membership in the BC Historical Society.

There were also several pictures of someone who might or might not have been McCluskey posing with what might or might not have been some of the most important business and political figures in BC. Jake recognized a former Lieutenant Governor, a former BC Premier, and a well-known TV host.

A seventies-era fabric couch with floral patterns sat in the center of the room, decorative wooden studs extending from the top of each corner like wings. An ancient, but well-preserved fifties-era dining room table took up one corner, and a small TV, currently off, rested on a wooden stand in the opposite one.

Jake glanced through the open door of another smaller room, which he assumed must be McCluskey's 'office'. A large white board, resembling a police investigation board, dominated one wall. Numerous newspaper clippings and photographs were stuck to it, connected by marker lines.

Beside it was a desk on which sat a computer with three large monitors. One appeared to be displaying world news and events, the second showed some kind of social media feed, the third displayed a word-processed document.

McCluskey appeared with a plate of pasta and a tall glass of water.

"You're gonna be dehydrated," he said, as he set them down on the dining table.

Jake had no sooner wolfed down his dinner when the police showed up. Standing beside the *Honeysuckle Rose*, Detective Harrow scanned around the Wharf area, analyzing the crime scene.

"The attacker came this way?" Harrow asked Jake, nodding his head toward the down ramp from the parking lot.

"I don't know," Jake answered. "He was already on the dock heading my way before I noticed him."

Two uniformed policemen stood guard on the dock as Jake, Harrow, and a forensics guy climbed onto the *Rose* and down into the living area.

"Don't touch anything," Harrow warned him.

Jake smiled. "I thought they only said that on TV."

Harrow gave him a look. They continued to the back of the room, and stood beside the piano keyboard, in the space underneath Jake's loft and bed. Jake swallowed. A pair of holes pierced the underside of the loft, directly under where the bed was positioned.

They climbed to the loft. The holes continued on through the bed and into the ceiling, through which a tiny glimpse of night sky was now visible.

"It's a good thing my bed's in the loft," Jake said. "If he'd shot downwards, the *Rose* would be taking on water now."

Harrow stared at him. "I think that's the least of your worries at the moment. You're incredibly lucky to be alive."

They headed back outside.

"And you have no idea who did this?" Harrow asked.

Jake shook his head. He was pretty sure the detective didn't believe him.

"Better avoid any of your regular haunts, including here, until we sort this out," Harrow said.

Avoiding the Salty Dog didn't really matter, since he no longer had a reason to go back there. But being separated from the *Honeysuckle Rose* struck deep at Jake's heart. The vessel was more than a home. It was his being, his persona. It symbolized his freedom of movement, his individuality, and his connection to his Great-aunt Deirdre—his family—his past—and the sea.

He stayed the night at McCluskey's, but after tonight's incident, it was too dangerous to remain at Fisherman's Wharf. Apparently, whoever had tried to kill Evangeline was now after him, and obviously knew where he lived. Or was it possible they'd been after him in the first place?

And if he was now the target, did that mean that Evangeline was already...

XXXVII

THE INVESTIGATION ENDS

Rule #14: There is only one firm rule when tailing a suspect—don't get caught.
- **Shadow Mac's Comprehensive Guide to Private Investigation**

The next morning, fighting a sense of doom and depression, Jake arranged to crash for a few days at the apartment of Ricky Halpern, an old friend of his from back in Basic Training. Halpern was a kid from the Prairies who'd somehow or other picked up playing the clarinet.

There had been a piano in the mess hall at the base, and when he and Jake had spare time, they used to get together and jam. Ricky had since moved to Victoria, and they still got together occasionally.

"You? A Private Eye?" Ricky said at dinner. "Have I suddenly entered some kind of alternate universe?"

That night Jake couldn't sleep, missing the gentle sway of the *Rose*, the lapping waves, and the cries of the gulls. Instead he lay thinking. It was as if fate was somehow dragging him back to the case against his will. He was still angry at Evangeline for lying to him and using him. Even so, having had his own run-in with the assassin, he hoped she was still alive. Reluctantly, he texted her one more time but got no response.

He also hadn't heard from his little voice recently. Apparently it had given up on him and gone silent in disgust. Still, every shred of his common sense told him to cut his losses and run. But he couldn't abandon Evangeline now that her life was obviously in danger.

In the morning, he let out a breath when he finally heard from her, suggesting they meet. She said nothing about where she'd been, or why she hadn't contacted him earlier. They couldn't go back to the *Honeysuckle Rose*. He arranged for them to get together at a diner called *John's Place* downtown in an hour.

He got there first. The walls around him were plastered with images from the worlds of sports, movies and pop music. A giant painted mural of Detroit's Tiger Stadium filled the wall on the far side, which was lined with old-style dining booths. The breakfast rush was over, and there were only a few other patrons.

Jake picked out a booth in the back corner, far from the other customers, and ordered a beer—he'd need a drink, considering what he had to say. He ordered another one for her.

As usual, heads turned as Evangeline walked in, dressed in a short, light blue baby-doll dress with spaghetti straps. At least Jake's latest conversation with Harrow explained her choice in outfits. Her eyes were red, as if she'd been crying.

"I can't stay long," she said, as she took a seat across from him.

He stared at her. It was as if he was looking at a different person, which, when he thought about it, he actually was.

"I guess I should call you Betty from now on," he said, curious how she'd react.

A wave of shock washed over her face, but it was fleeting.

"You went to the police," she said, an edge of anger in her voice. "You said you wouldn't."

Jake laughed. "I don't have to go to the police—they come to me."

"Anyway," she said, matter-of-factly, "that's right—Betty Rumford is my real name."

He was surprised. He'd expected her to deny everything. The fine pronunciation and trace of an accent were suddenly gone. She sounded like any other young girl from the neighbourhood, maybe with a slight maritime lilt. He paused for a few seconds, still processing the truth.

"So—everything you've told me was a lie," he finally said, leaning forward. She turned away. "Everything. This whole thing about France and Quebec City and mansions and your parents' murder-suicide... It must have given you a good laugh."

He studied her as if he'd never seen her before. "Tell me if this is somewhere close to the truth: you picked me to conduct your little 'investigation' because you wanted somebody off the grid—not a certified PI who'd be constrained to follow the rules and maybe report anything illegal."

Her upper lip quivered and her eyes moistened as he continued.

"You wanted somebody inexperienced, somebody you could con into doing the initial investigation. You figured you'd get me to find the sister, hoping that it would somehow lead to your father. Then you could ditch me and do the rest yourself."

She sat silently, still avoiding eye contact.

He grabbed her by the wrist and twisted her around. "Come on!" he snapped. "Admit it for once. You lied about everything. Right from the day I met you."

She pouted her lips and again turned her head away.

He shook her arm. "Isn't that true?"

She finally turned back. "Not everything—not the way I feel about you."

He choked off a laugh, as he let go of her, reflecting on the power of telling someone what they wanted to hear. But he had to assume that this too was a lie.

"What happened to you back in the parking lot?" he finally asked.

"I was scared. I just wanted to get out of there."

"What the hell's going on? Why would somebody want to kill you?"

Evangeline looked away again, as if that would shut down all talk about the incident.

"I found some stuff about your mother," he said. "She wasn't from the 'old country', like you told me. You both lived right here—here in Victoria. Isn't that right?"

She turned back, anger in her eyes. "Leave my mother out of this."

He pounded the table. "I want the truth for once!"

Her body shook and she began to sob. She pulled a tissue from her purse and dabbed her eyes. "That's right—we lived here—then we had to leave."

"What else?"

She put down the tissue, composed herself and glared at him. "Nothing else. Have you found my father?"

Jake was still trying to get used to the missing accent. "What? You're still on about that? Somebody's trying to kill you—that's what you should be worrying about."

"Well, have you?"

He shook his head resignedly. It wasn't his problem anymore. "I found a guy who might be your father. I tracked him to a place in Vancouver—in East Van."

She straightened up excitedly. "Where? Tell me right now!"

"Not until I get some answers. Who's after you?"

She waved her hand dismissively. "Some crazy person—how do I know? What about my father?"

Jake was getting tired of the whole exercise. "It was at night," he answered. "The guy was on foot—at least I think it was him. I was in my car. I followed him to a set of streets behind a strip mall, then I lost him."

Her fists were clenched. "You lost him? How could you lose him? Where? Show me!"

He pulled out his phone and brought up the map, and the area where he'd been tracking Bailey.

"Here," he said, pointing at the strip mall, and the cluster of city blocks behind it. She grabbed the phone and stared at it. She shrunk and expanded the zoom a few times with her fingers. Suddenly her body stiffened and her eyes went wide, as she studied the screen intently.

"What?" he said.

"Nothing." She reset the zoom and handed the phone back to him.

But now she seemed restless and anxious to leave. She put a hand on her purse and turned from the table.

"You know, somebody came after me," he said.

She turned back and stared at him. "What?"

"Yesterday—they know where I live. A guy came to the *Rose*. He had a gun—I barely got away. I can't go back there. This isn't a game. We're both lucky to be alive. I can't protect you if you won't tell me what's going on."

She turned again and stood up, stuffing the tissue in her purse. "You can't protect me anyway. Don't worry, in a few days it'll all be over."

"What will all be over?"

Her body trembled, and again her eyes moistened. "I'm sorry," she said, looking down at him. "I'm sorry about what happened—about all of it. I wish we could have..."

Despite everything, Jake's first impulse was to comfort her. Then he remembered that it was his impulses that got him into all this.

"You can keep whatever's left of your retainer," Evangeline said, her voice breaking. "Your services won't be required anymore."

She hurried toward the exit.

"For God's sake," he stood and called after her, but she was already out the door.

XXXVIII

DETECTING

Rule #39: One of the most important parts of an investigation is connecting the dots between individuals and uncovering patterns that may relate to a case.
- **Shadow Mac's Comprehensive Guide to Private Investigation**

The streets and buildings seemed to swim around him as Jake made his way from the diner. Even after Harrow's revelations, it was shocking to hear the truth from Evangeline's, or Betty's, own lips. How could he have let himself be duped so completely? Even McCluskey had warned him.

He headed for the Wharf. It was mid-afternoon, and it would be crowded with tourists. He'd decided to take a chance and check on the *Rose*. He immersed himself in a mob exiting a tour bus as he approached the down ramp, keeping an eye out for anyone who looked out of place. Everything seemed to be clear.

The day before, he'd hired a guy to go and replace the lock the killer had broken. Now, still scanning the crowds around him, he made his way to his vessel, double-checked the lock, retrieved the key from its prearranged hiding place, and had a quick look inside. Nothing had been disturbed. He placed a bucket on his bed under the bullet holes, in case it rained.

He assumed it wasn't safe to hang around, but he stopped by McCluskey's place to thank his neighbour again for saving his life, and to congratulate him that he'd been right all along. McCluskey invited him in, and got them each a beer.

They sat on McCluskey's back patio. Jake filled his friend in on his investigation up to that point: Jeanette Mallory, Owen Bailey, Esther Franklin, and the real Evangeline.

McCluskey shook his head, marveling at the convoluted stream of events. "Hey, you're not the first guy that's put his brain on hold for a beautiful woman. But it's finished now—right?"

Jake stared at the deck beneath his feet.

"It's *not* finished?" McCluskey asked, incredulous.

Jake looked up. "Whatever 'Betty', or Evangeline, or whoever she is, said or did to me, it doesn't change the fact that somebody tried to kill her, and they'll probably try again."

"You're forgetting that they tried to kill you, too."

Jake gave him a look. "She doesn't even seem to care about the danger. She's totally preoccupied with something. I'm still not clear what her game is, but I know she's not going to stop. She's obsessed with this father thing. Even after all the lies and deception, I don't want to see her get hurt."

"Let's just keep calling her Evangeline," McCluskey said, setting down the beer in his hand. "It'll make things a lot easier. Let's see if we can analyze all the elements of the case. She never told you *why* she wanted to find her father?"

Jake shrugged. "Like Detective Harrow said. It's natural for a child to want to know where they came from—to know who their biological parents are and connect with their family."

"But why not just *tell* you who she was looking for? Why all the secrecy? And like you say, she seemed kind of fixated on it—almost obsessive."

"That's true. But everybody's different. I guess for whatever reason it's important to her—having lost her mother..."

McCluskey gazed out at the harbour for a few moments, thinking.

"If what you're saying is right," he finally said, "this Esther Franklin person was Evangeline's mother."

"It looks that way. A few weeks before she died, Esther complained that a guy was hanging around her building and following her. The cops interviewed her, but they concluded she was just being paranoid. Apparently, she'd made complaints like that numerous times before. According to Harrow, she was suffering from some kind of serious paranoia."

McCluskey shook his head. "So, Esther complains about somebody stalking her, and soon after that she ends up dead. Harrow mentioned there were some new issues with the scene of Esther's death. Did he say what they were?"

Jake explained Harrow's recent call about the Halifax police reopening the case.

"Meaning it's possible Esther didn't commit suicide," Jake continued. "Maybe she was murdered." He put down his beer, as a thought occurred to him. "From what Harrow said, Esther really was mentally ill, but maybe there was more to it than that—maybe she had good reason to be scared. I guess with her diagnosis, they didn't take her seriously—looks like they should have."

"When did all this happen?"

"According to Harrow, about a year ago."

"It sounds like Esther wasn't just being paranoid—she'd been hiding from someone—maybe for a long time. Evangeline might have been a young child when it started, but kids can be pretty perceptive. She might still have understood a lot about her mother's situation."

Jake stared at his friend.

McCluskey leaned back in his chair. "How about this for a theory: twenty years ago, Esther Franklin and her daughter are living here on the West Coast. Esther either witnesses or learns something—something bad. Somehow, she knows the identity of the person responsible, and somehow the perpetrator *knows* that she knows. What does she do?"

Jake straightened up in his chair. "She runs and hides—runs as far away as possible..."

"And changes her name," McCluskey added. "From what you've said, she was involved in the music scene, where drug use is part of the lifestyle. Back then, you could go to jail for having a leftover joint in the ashtray of your car. Maybe Esther didn't trust the cops and was afraid to report what she'd seen. Or maybe she didn't think they could protect her from whoever was after her.

"The question is, who was she afraid of? Whenever you see these newscasts on TV about women getting beaten or murdered, it almost always turns out to be a particular person..."

"The husband—the 'intimate partner'," Jake said. "Esther was afraid of her husband, or boyfriend or whoever, ran to the farthest place in the country from here, and changed her name, to hide from him."

McCluskey nodded. "And maybe the husband, Evangeline's father, finally found Esther, and did her in. Her father killed her mother."

Jake shook his head. "It makes sense."

"So," McCluskey continued, "say Evangeline somehow figures out the truth—that her father ruined her life by effectively taking her mother away when she was a child, then having her mother killed.

"But she doesn't know who the father is. She was four years old when it all went down. She might remember the event her mother saw—it might have been pretty traumatic—it's probably etched into her memory. But she doesn't remember him, or even what he looks like. There's no record of the father. Maybe her mother was the only one who knew who the father was."

"And she's conveniently dead."

Jake got to his feet and started pacing, gesturing with his hands. "Right—so Evangeline goes on this DNA site, and finds out she's got a sibling. She's not really interested in her sister, but she realizes the entry could be a connection to her father. But when she tries to make contact, it all gets taken down."

McCluskey took up the thread. "She comes out here, makes up the whole long-lost sister thing, and hires you. She doesn't want you to know she's actually looking for her father, because she doesn't want you to know *why* she wants to find him..."

Jake stopped and looked down at his feet, thinking. "She showed some kind of powerful emotion the other night when she talked about her father. It didn't register at the time because it didn't fit with what she was telling me, but now I recognize it—it was intense, all-consuming rage."

He lifted his head and locked eyes with McCluskey. "She doesn't just want to reconnect with her father... she wants to *kill* him—Jesus Christ."

"You're getting to be a real detective, kid."

"Maybe I should tell Harrow. Somehow, we need to warn the guy in Vancouver. I can't say for sure that he's Owen Bailey. Even if he is, there's no proof he's Evangeline's father, or even Jeanette's father. He might not be guilty of anything."

McCluskey shook his head. "The cops won't do anything. It's just our theory. Even *we* don't know that it's right."

Jake sat down. They were both silent for almost a minute.

"If that theory is correct, who tried to kill Evangeline? And me?" Jake finally said.

McCluskey made an opening gesture with both hands. "Jeanette Mallory puts up the entry on the DNA site. As soon as Evangeline answers, somebody takes it down. It doesn't seem likely that Jeanette herself would do that. If she put it up, she must have expected that she might get a response.

"My guess is that somebody else found out about it, and didn't want it to stay up—especially after someone contacted her. It was probably somebody close to her—somebody in authority."

"Like her father."

"And if Jeanette is Evangeline's sister..."

"Maybe the father saw the message and guessed that Evangeline would be in town snooping around. He killed Jeanette after he found out about the website, to keep her quiet. Then he also tried to kill Evangeline, then me because I'm helping her."

McCluskey put down his beer. "If Evangeline connects with this Bailey guy, the shit's gonna hit the fan, one way or the other. The question is, how good a detective job did you do? How close were you to actually finding him?"

"I trailed him to an area in East Van," Jake said, "but I never actually found where he lived. We *should* be safe on that score, at least for now. I showed Evangeline a map of the general area, but that's all she knows."

"Are you sure? Is the exact location something she's likely to figure out? She may look like a bimbo, but my impression is that she's got more brains than the both of us put together."

Jake waved his hand dismissively. "I don't see how."

He suddenly froze, and closed his eyes momentarily.

"What?" McCluskey said.

"When I saw her at the diner this morning, I showed her the map of where I'd lost Bailey. She'd been desperate for more detail about the address, but after she looked at the phone, her expression seemed to change. She basically 'fired' me on the spot and walked out."

Jake hauled out his phone and brought up the map he'd shown her. He glanced at it for a few seconds, but saw nothing of interest. He handed it to McCluskey.

"You can see the blotch of grey marking off the strip mall where Bailey met Armando," Jake said, indicating on the map.

McCluskey put on his glasses, studied the map and nodded.

"Just to the south," Jake continued. "Behind it, there's a jumble of streets—that's where I lost him. But that's all I know, and that's all Evangeline knows."

"Is this the zoom level you had set up when you showed her?"

Jake shrugged. "Yeah, I think so. Let me look."

McCluskey handed the phone back.

Jake stared at it. "That's where I had it when I handed it to her, but then I think she compressed it, zoomed it out."

He repeated what he guessed she'd done and examined the streets. Again, he saw nothing.

"It's even harder to see anything at this size—most of the street names don't even show up."

He handed the phone back to McCluskey. "I couldn't see it that well, but I think it was like this."

Again McCluskey studied the map, and his fingers played with the zoom level. "What was that pseudonym you said Jeanette was using on the DNA site? 'Wifrun', or something?"

Jake's body tensed. "Yeah, why?"

McCluskey handed him the phone. "Take a close look."

Jake studied the now zoomed out map. "What? I don't see anything."

"Not in East Van," McCluskey said. "In Burnaby—next door."

"Burnaby?" Jake stared at the map intently. Written along one of the streets in the adjacent district of Burnaby, far from where he'd lost Bailey, was the name *Wifrun Street*.

"Shit," he said. "Is that right?"

He left McCluskey's, ran across the dock to the *Rose*, rifled through the documents he had stuffed in a drawer, and came up with the paper Evangeline had given him what seemed a lifetime ago.

He unfolded it and read it— *WIFRUN2345*.

Back at McCluskey's, his hands shaking, he typed the address into the map—*2345 Wifrun Street*. A marker tag popped up around the center of the block in Burnaby. He closed his eyes. He remembered the outline of the gun he'd seen in Evangeline's purse.

"If that's what Evangeline saw," said McCluskey, "we're in trouble."

"I gotta find her," Jake said, jumping up from his chair. "Find her and stop her before she does something we'll both regret."

"Are you crazy?" McCluskey called after him, as he rushed out the door. "You've done enough for that girl. Chances are she's going to shoot somebody, and it might end up being you!"

XXXIX

WIFRUN2345

Rule #7: You will need patience, courtesy, tact, and understanding to secure the vital facts and information required to conclude an investigation.

- Shadow Mac's Comprehensive Guide to Private Investigation

Jake had no idea where Evangeline had gone after their meeting at the diner, but if the theory he and McCluskey had come up with was correct, and she'd worked out Bailey's address like they had, he knew where she'd ultimately be headed. In fact, chances were pretty good that she was already on her way.

If it *was* Owen Bailey who had met before with Armando in Vancouver, Jake's guess was that the former gardener was in hiding, and had offered to pay Armando to keep an eye out for anyone skulking around looking for him. Why? That was a question only Bailey himself could answer. Did Bailey live on Wifrun Street? Was he still there now? Jake could only hope not.

He put together a small carry bag, rushed to the depot, and caught the first bus back to Vancouver, determined to find Bailey and warn him. On arrival, he picked up yet another EVO, and headed immediately for Burnaby, for 2345 Wifrun Street. By the time he got there it was mid-afternoon.

He drove past to confirm the address. It was an older, dated, but well-maintained house in a pleasant, if working-class, district. He parked a block away, got out, and walked.

His impression driving by was reinforced when he arrived at the address. The place was probably built in the fifties or sixties, and had wooden siding with a newer paint job, a decent lawn, and a pair of well-kept shrubs on either side of a set of the steps leading to the front door.

He walked up to the entrance and pressed the little button for the bell.

"Did you have trouble finding the..." said a shaky female voice as the door opened.

"Oh," said a white-haired older woman standing in the doorway. "Sorry, I thought you were someone else." She turned her head toward the interior. "We seem to be unusually popular today, don't we, dear."

An older man appeared beside her. "Can we help you?" he asked Jake.

Jake's body tensed. "Someone was here already?"

"Oh, yes," said the woman. "A very nice young lady."

"When was she here?" Jake asked.

"About an hour ago," the woman answered. "At first she thought we were someone else, but I explained that we'd bought this place a few months ago. She said she was looking for the previous owners."

"You knew them?"

"No, but when we bought, the real-estate agent told us a sad story. He said the owner had lived here happily with his daughter for more than five years." She shook her head slowly. "They had some kind of falling out and the daughter ran away. Then she disappeared. The father didn't want to live here anymore, so he sold to us."

"The woman that was here earlier," Jake said, "can you tell me where she went?"

"Are you a friend of hers?"

Jake had to think fast. "Yes—actually, we were supposed to come here together, but I got delayed. Do you know what happened to the previous owner?"

"Not exactly," the woman answered.

"Not exactly?" Jake said, relaxing a little at the news.

"I know he lives somewhere in East Van," she said, "not far from the Kensington shopping centre—do you know the area?"

"And that's what you told the woman who was here?"

The old woman looked over at her husband.

"The car," he said, to her.

"Oh, yes," she said. "We drove by this house for a look before we bought it. There was a car parked in the driveway. It was quite distinctive—"

"A seventies-era BMW 2002," the husband put in.

The woman smiled and turned to her husband. "Albert's a bit of a car enthusiast. The car was in very bad shape. It was originally green, but you could hardly tell. It was dented all over and covered with rust. The realtor mentioned that it belonged to the owner. If he still has it, and it's parked outside, you might be able to spot it."

"And you told the woman all this?" Jake asked.

"She seemed very excited. Said the man was her long-lost father... Such a touching story."

"Thanks," Jake said. He turned and rushed away.

"I hope the young lady finds her father," the woman called after him.

God, I hope not, Jake thought, as he waved behind him.

The area the old couple had described matched the one where he'd lost Bailey earlier. He parked nearby, got out, and walked to the intersection where Bailey had disappeared. The district was a lot more run-down than the one around Wifrun Street. The houses were ancient and decrepit, with chipping paint and moss-covered roofs, and the yards were run-down and unkempt.

He was relieved to find there was no swarm of cop cars with blue and red flashing lights, and no indication of trouble. He wasn't sure how long it would have taken Evangeline to get here. He was already familiar with this area—she would have to search for it. He guessed that she wouldn't be at all familiar with Vancouver, but it also seemed likely that she would have a big head start on him.

He thought back to that night, after Bailey's meeting with Armando, when Bailey seemed to have disappeared. *Disappeared,* he thought. *People don't just disappear.* He started at the intersection and strolled along the street, trying to look as inconspicuous as possible while scanning the houses on either side.

The yard of a house halfway down the block had a tall hedge bordering the sidewalk. In the darkness, and in his panic to catch up to Bailey, Jake had failed to notice an important feature. At first glance the hedge appeared to be a solid wall of vegetation. On closer inspection he saw a narrow opening in the center.

The opening had once been a much larger doorway leading to a sidewalk, but was now so overgrown it had almost closed up. He pictured Bailey pushing through it, then waiting out of sight on the other side until Jake's car was gone.

Had Bailey made him, or was he just being cautious? It didn't really matter. And was the house on the other side of the hedge actually Bailey's, or had he just been using the hedge to hide?

✳

Jake took a chance, squeezed through the opening, and strode down the cracked and weed-infested sidewalk. The place was a broken-down sixties-era stucco bungalow that would probably be scheduled for demolition sometime in the near future.

A set of concrete steps accessed a gabled entrance enclosing the front door, with a single light bulb hanging on a bare wire above it. None of the lights inside were on. He walked to the door, knocked, and waited. Nothing. He glanced to his left. There was a driveway, with recent tire tracks, but nothing was parked there. He knocked again, stepped forward, and peered through a peephole. It was too dark inside to see anything, but it didn't look like there was anyone home.

Another path, even more neglected and crumbling than the sidewalk, led around the left side of the house. He followed it to three cracked concrete steps that led down to a paint-chipped door. A number scrawled on a piece of wood attached to the wall beside it confirmed it was a basement suite. A light, that looked like it was bleeding in from one of the inner rooms, dimly illuminated the interior.

He knocked on the door, and got no answer. He moved to the closest window and tried to peer through a ragged set of curtains, half expecting to see Evangeline with a smoking gun standing over Bailey's dead body. There was no sign of anyone.

The path continued to the back of the house. He followed it to a large back yard with the remnants of what had once been a lawn, with a rusted-out child's swing-set at the center. A gabled back exit hallway projected from the rear wall.

Then he saw it, on a patch of gravel between the back wall of the house and the gabled exit—an ancient, rusted-out BMW, up on blocks. This had to be where Bailey lived. Evangeline wouldn't have known the exact location where Jake had lost him that night. And she wouldn't be able to see the car from the street. Could she still have somehow worked out the location of this place?

XL

OWEN BAILEY

Rule #31: Interviewing is a fundamental skill for any aspiring private investigator. Through interviews, crucial information can be extracted from people, enabling you to uncover the truth.
- Shadow Mac's Comprehensive Guide to Private Investigation

Returning to the side door, he knocked at it again and waited. Nothing. He pounded harder, then stepped forward and peered through the peephole. A faint shadow moved across the hallway inside, heading for the rear of the house. Jake retraced his steps along the path to the back.

Using the rusted car for cover, he worked his way around to the exit. On its left side, a half-dozen steps led to the upstairs of the place. On the right, beside them, another set led down to the rear door of the basement suite. He was trying to decide whether to descend the stairs on the right when he heard the basement door unlatching.

He quickly crept down, thinking back on his combat moves from Basic Training, something he'd spent the past few years trying to forget, as he stood just outside the door. It opened a little, then stopped, and a middle-aged man's head poked out, scanning the yard and to either side. Just below it, Jake could make out a hand holding a gun.

The man spotted Jake, pulled his head back in, and tried to push the door shut. Jake jammed his foot in the opening, and threw his full weight against the door until it burst open, throwing the man back. He landed on his ass on the hallway floor. The gun dropped from his hand and now lay in a corner out of his reach.

Before his adversary could react, Jake picked up the gun, rushed forward and put his foot on his chest, pinning him. Jake studied the man's face. There was no doubt—it was Owen Bailey, the guy from the photograph with Jeanette.

"Not again," Bailey groaned.

"Don't move," Jake said, aiming the gun at Bailey's head. "Keep your hands where I can see them."

The man's eyes were like pin-pricks, and were wandering around the room.

"You're on my property illegally," he said nervously, his speech slurred. "What do you want?"

"Are you Owen Bailey?"

The man hesitated, then said. "What if I am?"

Jake hauled Bailey to his feet, quickly frisked him, and found nothing.

"Turn around," Jake said. Bailey complied, and almost fell over as Jake pushed the gun into his back. "Walk."

They moved forward, and Jake kicked the door shut behind them. They continued through the short hallway and into the apartment's living area. It was a cramped, dingy room, with a threadbare couch, a couple of tubular metal chairs, and a beaten-up cardboard box for a coffee table, on which lay a syringe and elastic strap.

On the fridge in the kitchen Jake could make out a photograph, similar to the one he'd taken from Jeanette's things, of Bailey smiling with his arm around Jeanette.

Jake kept prodding Bailey until they were facing the nearest wall.

"Put your hands against the wall," Jake said.

Again Bailey complied.

"I think your life may be in danger," Jake said to the man's back.

Bailey grunted. "Well—yeah, I guess. Some lunatic's got a gun shoved in my ribs."

"No..I don't mean from me," Jake said. "Well, maybe from me," he corrected himself, "if you try anything."

"You're not making much sense," Bailey said.

"What did you mean, 'Not again'?" Jake asked.

"What?"

"Just now—you said 'Not again'. Somebody else has been here?"

Bailey nodded, unsteady on his feet. "Some crazy bitch—with a gun—babbling on about how I was a murderer. That's why I had my own gun—I thought maybe she came back."

Jake tensed. "A woman?"

"Yeah," Bailey answered. "A real looker. I thought I was a dead man. She was totally out there..."

"Well, you're still alive. What happened?"

"Look," Bailey said. "I feel weird having a conversation like this. "Can I at least sit down?"

Jake stepped back. "Turn around."

Bailey turned to face him. He still had the horseshoe moustache, but it was now almost lost in two or three days growth of beard. His body was emaciated, his hair scruffy and thinning, his skin sagging, and his nose red and laced with veins—the nose of a drinker. Jake swallowed, as the memory surfaced of the young Owen Bailey in the photograph of the Stone Cold band. He thought about his own drinking, and what he might look like in a few years.

Bailey looked harmless enough—beaten-up, like the apartment he lived in. He was swaying, in danger of falling over if he had to remain standing. He was a tired old addict who looked like he no longer cared about much of anything.

"Yeah, okay," Jake finally said.

He motioned with the gun toward the couch, and held it on Bailey as the old man lowered his hands, turned and flopped down. Jake sat on one of the chairs opposite, his gun trained again on Bailey's chest.

"Now talk."

Bailey looked up at him. "She asked me about a woman. She showed me a picture."

"A picture of Esther Franklin."

Bailey's eyes widened with surprise. He nodded. "Yeah, she said Esther was her mother, and that I'd had her killed. I asked her if I looked like a guy that had the money to hire a hit man."

Bailey's head sagged downwards—as if he was going to nod off.

"Hey," Jake said loudly.

"Wha? Oh, yeah," Bailey said, looking up.

"A woman attacked you," Jake reminded him.

Bailey nodded. "She said Esther was murdered, and the murderer was her father."

"And she figured that was you," Jake said. "But she left you alone. What did you say to change her mind? You *did* know her mother—"

A light seemed to come into Bailey's eyes. "Esther?" he said, gazing wistfully across the room. "Yeah—that was a lot of years ago. She was a beauty, that one. She was one of the women that hung out with the band. One of the few that was worth anything."

He told Jake about his time as the bass player in Stone Cold. Jake tried to hurry him along, imagining where Evangeline might be at this moment. Bailey wouldn't be rushed.

"After the band didn't work out," he continued, "we had the idea for the production company. I was part of it for years, but then one day that all got thrown out the window."

"By Larry Karlsen," Jake said.

Bailey nodded and gritted his teeth. "That asshole. He ruined my life."

"So you killed him."

Bailey's body swayed on the couch, his eyes half-shut. "I guess..."

"What do you mean, *you guess*?"

Bailey shook his head. "I hardly remember anything. I don't even remember where I got the statue."

"Statue?"

"The one they said I used to beat him to death. I was totally out of it, you know?

225

"I remember the three of us were supposed to meet at the production studio after hours. We were going to have it out about me being dumped from the company, and maybe get me some kind of compensation.

"When I got there, I'd already shot up. I was bombed. The last thing I remember I was lying on the floor in the bathroom. When I woke up, a cop was shaking me. Somehow I was in the lobby, in a chair beside Larry's body. The cop was holding a plastic bag with the blood-covered statue.

"I was a known addict and I'd already done time for attacking him. My fingerprints were on the statue. It was a pretty airtight case. After prison, I got back into drugs, and I ended up on the street."

Again he bowed his head, but continued speaking. "I was homeless on the Downtown East Side. Tommy was passing through, going to some party nearby."

"Tommy Skylar," Jake said.

Bailey nodded. "He gave me his business card—said maybe he could help me out. For once I got my act together. I contacted him, and he gave me the gardener gig." He shook his head. "Poor Esther—it's a cryin' shame."

"Where does Jeanette fit in?"

Bailey looked up and his lower lip began to quiver. "Jeanette?" He clenched his fists and closed his eyes. He finally opened them again. "Jeanette's mother Angie came to Tommy's one day when I was there working. I knew her from when we had the band in Victoria, and we got together."

His features sagged. "I was a drug addict and a convicted murderer. I'd never had a family, anyone to care about... She and Jeanette changed my life. For them, I cleaned up my act. Jeanette spent a lot of time at my place on Wifrun Street. We had a blast together." He began to sob. "She was the daughter I never had."

Jake straightened in his chair. "So you're not Jeanette's biological father?"

He shook his head sadly. "When Angie died, Jeanette was only fifteen. She got placed in a group home in Victoria, and I visited her about once a month. She knew I wasn't her father, and a couple of times she asked me who was. I told her I didn't know. I felt bad lying, but under the circumstances...

"She aged out of the group home and moved back here to Vancouver. Then a few months ago she started really hounding me about her father."

"Did you know about the DNA account?"

Bailey looked up. "She told me about it, and that she'd actually gotten a 'hit', not from her father, but from a sibling who wanted to connect. She was still a minor when she registered the account—I managed to convince the site to remove it. Jeanette and I had a big fight about it."

His lower lip trembled again as he spoke. "That was the last time I ever saw her."

"You say you lied to her. Why—what were you so worried about?"

Bailey didn't seem to hear. He continued. "I got really paranoid when she disappeared. I'd ratted out a couple of dealers back when I was on the street. I thought maybe it was a warning—that one of them was coming for me. I had money saved. I quit the gardening gig and decided to lay low for a while."

"The woman that came here," Jake said. "You're sure she was planning to kill you?"

Bailey's eyes went wide. "Are you kidding? She had a gun jammed under my chin. I was petrified. She had this wild look..."

This was taking too long. Jake imagined Evangeline, having eliminated Bailey as her target, now speeding somewhere to kill someone else.

"What did you tell Evangeline, the woman who was here?"

"She must have been really young when Esther was here, but I think she remembered her father well enough to know that I wasn't him. Anyway, I told her it wasn't possible."

"Why not?"

"'Cause as much I'd have liked to, I never made it with Esther Franklin."

"Well if you're not either Evangeline's or Jeanette's father, who is?"

Bailey sat like a beaten man, his hands by his sides on the couch and his head hanging. Jake tried to think of a way to speed things up, but Bailey seemed determined to go at his own pace. Again he looked like he was going to nod off.

Jake grabbed a shoulder and shook him. "Don't stop now," he said loudly.

Bailey blinked awake and looked up. He glanced at the gun still trained on his chest and flinched, as if he'd forgotten it was there.

"Come on," Jake said impatiently. "Why did you lie to Jeanette? Why did you have the account removed?"

Bailey shook his head and continued. "Angie told me she'd agreed not to reveal who Jeanette's father was. She said he never wanted a kid, but he couldn't convince her get rid of it. He gave her money..."

Bailey had to stop again, to collect himself. Jake was on the edge of his seat, praying for him to speed things up.

"The guy who paid Angie to keep quiet about Jeanette—who are you talking about? Who's Jeanette's biological father?"

"Who?" Bailey looked up, surprised. "My ex-boss—and bandmate, Tommy—Tommy Skylar."

"Shit," Jake said. "Is that what you told Evangeline?"

Bailey nodded.

"How long ago?"

Bailey shrugged. "I don't know—half an hour..."

"And she believed you?"

"I'm alive aren't I? I gave her Tommy's address—she looked in a hurry."

"She was driving?"

"I didn't get a good look—I was too busy slamming and locking the door behind her. Something fancy—a Porsche, I think."

Jake jumped up.

"I'm taking this," he said, holding up the gun.

"What if she comes back?" Bailey pleaded.

"She's not coming back here," Jake said.

He took off out the door.

XLI

A DESPERATE CHASE

Rule #37: Private Investigators are inevitably exposed to other people's lives. It's vital to maintain a professional distance from the subjects, and not become emotionally involved.
- Shadow Mac's Comprehensive Guide to Private Investigation

According to Bailey, Evangeline had at least half an hour's head start. Hopefully, she would have no idea he was after her. He could only hope she'd made a stop before heading off to Skylar's place. The Porsche should be easy to spot. Apparently, even her rentals were a statement of prestige.

He took off from Bailey's, blew past the strip mall, and took the on-ramp for Highway One, flying across the Second Narrows bridge and speeding along the Upper Levels highway. The forested hills above were a blur as he raced, weaving past car after car, keeping an eye out for cops, praying he wasn't too late.

With her head start, it might all be over by now. He didn't think she knew Vancouver. He dared to hope that even with a GPS somehow she'd get lost or delayed. He hammered the gas pedal on the EVO, blowing far past the 110 km/h speed limit, imagining how much faster she could move driving a high-powered sports car.

Traffic was light. In less than half an hour he was up into the hills, minutes from his destination. He spotted a cream-coloured Porsche 911 convertible about half a kilometer ahead, and accelerated. He passed by the green highway sign announcing the off-ramp for Taylor Way, the gateway to the British Properties.

Moving up closer to the Porsche, he confirmed that it was Evangeline, her blond hair billowing out behind her in the wind. He could also see why he'd been able to catch up. She was continually glancing at the GPS on the dash, and pressing buttons with her free hand.

She must have figured it out, because she soon swung onto the Taylor Way off-ramp. He followed at a safe distance. Somehow he had to stop her before she reached Skylar's place. He moved up closer, unconcerned whether she made him or not.

They reached a 'T' intersection and turned right. She was headed in the right direction, but she was still fiddling with the GPS, trying to both drive and navigate. He guessed that she hadn't set it up properly, and it wasn't giving her automatic directions. They were moving continually upward now, into the hills surrounding the looming North Shore mountains.

Jake pushed the EVO even harder. They were almost at the turnoff for Skylar's place, and if he didn't stop her by then, it might be too late. He couldn't catch up, but he let out a breath when she missed the turnoff and continued north. About five minutes later, what looked like some kind of Golf and Country Club came into view. Evangeline leaned over and accessed something on the dash, then swung the car suddenly into the driveway that led to the club parking area. It looked like she'd realized her mistake and wanted to turn around. It was Jake's chance.

He followed her into the lot. She turned and backed into a parking spot, with the idea of changing direction and heading back out. The rear of her car was blocked by the building behind her.

She was stopped, pressing more buttons on something on the dash, probably still fighting with the GPS. She hadn't spotted him. He gunned the EVO, and skidded to a stop directly in front and a fist's width away from her front bumper, blocking her exit.

She finally looked up and recognized him, her expression a blend of horror and anger. She grabbed the wheel as if to drive away, then realized she was pinned—she couldn't go anywhere.

Jake got out, and she glared at him as he approached and stood beside her passenger door.

"Move your car!" she yelled. "And leave me alone!"

He shook his head. "Not until you talk to me."

"Get lost!" she said.

"I think I know almost everything," he said, leaning on the door frame.

Suddenly, a gun appeared in her hand. "Move your car! Now!"

Jake flinched, but didn't change his position. He nodded at the patrons steadily entering and leaving the front doors. "If you shoot me, do you think you'll be able to get out, access my phone, unlock my car and move it, and drive away before the cops get here?"

She sneered at him, still holding the gun.

"You can't go anywhere," he said. "Might as well talk."

Indignantly, she pressed a button and he heard the passenger door unlock. He opened it and slid into the seat beside her. She sat scowling at him, with the gun lowered, but still in her hand.

"This isn't your affair," she snapped. "Move your car and let me finish what I started."

"I just came from Owen Bailey's place," he answered. "Thank God you didn't kill him."

She said nothing.

"I know what you're planning... Just talk to me for a few minutes— that's all I ask."

She set the gun in her lap, and sat staring out the windshield.

"Talk," he said, "or I'm not going anywhere. It's all about your mother, right?"

"None of your business," she said, staring straight ahead.

He didn't move. "I'm guessing that when you contacted Jeanette Mallory you said more than just 'let's be friends'."

Finally she spoke. "I warned her. In case she didn't know."

"About your father."

She closed her eyes and nodded. When she opened them again they were moist, and her features twisted in pain. "My mother said she'd taken me and left my father because he'd been abusive. She wouldn't tell me who he was, but she said he was violent and dangerous, and not to go looking for him."

She turned to him. "Now move your car!"

He shook his head. "I need more than that."

She sat motionless, again staring straight ahead. Jake felt like he could see the wheels turning in her mind.

Finally she continued. "I guess my mother was hoping I'd start a new life and forget about him. But her warning triggered my own memories, and they all came flooding back—at least enough to understand most of what really happened. And eventually I figured out the rest."

"What do you remember?"

Her face was deadpan as she spoke. "We were leaving town, leaving my father. I understood that much, though I didn't really understand why. On the way, we stopped at the place he used to work, to pick up some of her things. I asked if we'd be seeing him, but she said he wouldn't be there."

Again she turned to him. "Why can't you just leave me alone?"

Jake said nothing.

"When we got there," she continued, her hands shaking, "the front door was open, and we could hear shouting inside. My mother told me to stay where I was, and she snuck down the hall. But I followed her. We could see into the big room at the front. My father and another man were yelling at each other."

"Larry Karlsen," Jake said.

She nodded. "I used to call him Uncle Larry, but I didn't know who he was." She swallowed, and closed her eyes. "My father picked up a heavy statue from a table, and clubbed Uncle Larry with it. He went down, and my father kept hitting him. My mother turned for the door, and found me standing there. She took my hand and we rushed from the building.

"I don't think my father saw us, but my mother was never the same after that. She always seemed to be afraid. We moved far across the country, to Halifax, and she changed our names.

"Later, she got more and more paranoid." Evangeline said, her fists clenched in her lap. "We spent years just scraping by. Finally I couldn't take it anymore and moved out. When I found out how she died, I knew—I knew it was him... I vowed to make him pay for what he did to me and my mother."

Jake closed his eyes momentarily, thinking. He opened them again. "Owen Bailey told me the last thing he remembered was passing out in the bathroom of the studio. Your father must have dragged him into the lobby and dropped him beside Karlsen's body, then wiped his own fingerprints from the statue, and wrapped Bailey's hand around it. Owen spent twelve years in jail for something he didn't do."

"My father killed Uncle Larry, he killed my mother, and now he's killed my sister Jeanette, his own daughter," Evangeline said, her voice breaking.

Jake glanced to their left. There was a dining room attached to the golf club.

Jake nodded at it. "Let's go and talk this out. You're upset—you need to think about what you're doing. You say your mother wanted you to forget about it all and start a new life. Maybe that's what you should do. Nothing's going to bring her or Jeanette back. We can tell the cops about Karlsen, and your mother and Jeanette. Your father will pay for what he did."

She continued to stare out the windshield thinking, her hands shaking. She turned and stared at Jake. Finally, she nodded. She slid the gun into her purse, opened her door and got out, and Jake did the same.

"You'd better move that," she said, nodding at his car and smiling. "You'll get a ticket."

She pressed a button on the dash to pop the trunk. He looked at her.

"I need something from my bag," she said. He eyed her suspiciously, then stretched out his hand. "You better give me those," he said, nodding at the keys she was holding.

She glared at him, but complied, and he walked over and moved his car to the spot beside hers. When he returned and followed her to the back, she was bent over, looking at something in the trunk.

"Got it?" he said leaning over himself to look.

She rose from the trunk with a tire-iron in her right hand. Before Jake could react, she swung it at his head, and everything went black.

When he awoke, Jake was lying on the sidewalk. As his blurred vision gradually cleared, he could see a middle-aged woman with red hair bending over him, and a small crowd of people standing around.

"Thank God you're alright!" the woman said, placing a hand on his shoulder. "We thought you were dead. Did you slip or something?"

His fingers explored the rising bump on the back of his skull as he sat up. When he removed his hand, it was covered with blood.

He looked up. Evangeline's Porsche was gone.

"How long have I been out?" he asked.

"I don't know," the red-headed woman said. "We've been here about ten minutes. Don't move. An ambulance is on its way."

"Did you see the car that was here? The Porsche? With a girl?"

"Porsche? Girl?" the woman shook her head.

"Don't get up," the woman cautioned, as Jake rose shakily to his feet. "You've probably got a concussion!"

He checked his pockets. The keys to the Porsche were gone, but she'd left his cell phone—he could still drive the EVO. He headed toward his car.

"Wait!" the woman called after him. "You're injured!"

"I'll live," he said, as he accessed the app and opened the driver's door. He jumped in and sped away.

"Shit! Shit! Shit!" Jake shouted, hammering the steering wheel with his fist as he drove.

How could I have fallen for that?

His vision was still blurry and the lump on his head was throbbing as he flew back the way they'd come. He blinked and shook his head to clear it, praying he wasn't too late. With Evangeline's latest head start, it might all be over by now.

He retraced the route back to the turnoff that she had missed, and squealed into it, the EVO fishtailing as he entered. He pushed the car to its limit as he flew along the road headed west, toward Skylar's place.

This time he drove right up to the iron gate across the driveway. It was smashed open, with Evangeline's Porsche jammed halfway into it at a weird angle. He put his hand on the gun in his belt as he snuck through the lush terraced gardens surrounding Skylar's mansion. The gardener, Armando, was nowhere to be seen.

He made his way up the steps to the massive wooden door at the front. It was partly open, and he could hear voices talking inside. He snuck up to the opening and poked his head around.

Bailey, then Evangeline herself, had filled in the last pieces of the puzzle—Jeanette Mallory and Evangeline had different mothers, but the same father—Tommy Skylar. And Skylar was guilty of at least two murders.

"...now that's a name," he recognized Skylar's voice.

XLII

TOMMY SKYLAR

Rule #18: A Private Investigator may come into contact with individuals who become hostile, aggressive, or even violent. He must always be on his guard.
- Shadow Mac's Comprehensive Guide to Private Investigation

Jake pushed the door open and made his way into the front hallway. He glanced to his right and flinched at the sight of Mona, Skylar's assistant, lying in a pool of blood in a nearby alcove. He pulled the gun from his belt and held it in both hands as he climbed the set of stairs and stopped in the shadowed entryway to Skylar's incredible living space.

From Jake's current vantage point, Skylar appeared to be alone, sitting in an armchair, a cigarette in his hand, framed by the stunning view of the inlet below. On a small table beside him was a glass of amber liquid—probably Bruichladdich. Skylar looked a lot more beaten up than the last time they'd met—his past deeds were finally catching up with him. He was staring intently at something across the room, something, or someone, out of Jake's sight.

Evangeline stepped into view, holding a gun in her right hand. It was trained at Skylar's chest. Even after what Bailey had told him, until now, Jake hadn't believed she'd actually kill her own father. He thought of Mona's lifeless body lying a few meters away, and it became pretty clear that he'd been wrong.

Neither she nor Skylar had spotted him. He scanned the room. The handgun he'd seen under a magazine on his last visit was gone. But if Skylar had it he probably would have used it by now.

Skylar smiled at Evangeline. "Yeah, Esther was a pretty little thing. Well, I must say you are a sight for sore eyes." He was trying to sound confident and flippant, but the cigarette in his hand was shaking. He tapped an ash into an ashtray on the arm of the chair. "You've grown into a real hottie, just like your mother. I take it this isn't a social call."

"You know why I'm here," Evangeline said.

She stepped forward, and Jake backed further into the hallway. His foot bumped against a potted plant behind him. It tipped over and fell to the floor.

Skylar looked up and noticed him. He smiled. "I was wondering when you were going to show up."

Now that he'd been spotted, Jake stepped fully out into the open. Evangeline stared at him with pure horror.

"Don't do this," Jake said. "Let the police handle it."

"Didn't you think I'd work out who this *friend* was you were talking about before?" Skylar asked, smiling and studying Jake. "You should have stuck to playing piano, kid." He turned back to Evangeline. "And *you* should listen to your boyfriend, honey."

Evangeline glanced at Jake several times, careful to keep the gun trained on Skylar. Jake's arrival had rattled her. Finally she turned away and continued her conversation with her father.

"So you *do* remember what happened," Skylar said to her.

"I remember enough," she answered, the gun shaking in her hand. "My mother's murder filled in the blanks."

"Murder?" Skylar said. "You think that was me? I had nothing to do with your mother's death."

"You're lying!" Evangeline shouted.

"Your mother," Skylar said, tapping another ash into the ashtray, "was deranged. It was only a matter of time before she did something drastic. Anyway, why bother? Who would have believed anything she said?"

Evangeline stepped forward and primed the gun. "She would never have committed suicide. I knew her well enough to know that. It was *you. You* had her killed." She raised the gun and pointed it at his head.

"Look," Jake said to her, "he killed Larry Karlsen, he probably killed your mother and Jeanette Mallory. And it was probably him that tried to kill you and me. The cops in Halifax are having another look into your mother's case. That will be enough—"

"Shut up!" Evangeline shouted. "He's got to pay!"

"Poor old Larry," Skylar said, glancing at the magnificent view outside, where a giant cruise ship was just sailing into the inlet. "He wanted to squeeze me out of Stone Cold. But let's face it, he wasn't fit to be a partner in a world class business. Anyway, he's in a much better place now."

He turned back to Evangeline. "It's a touching story about your mother. But what proof have you got? The Coroner herself declared it was suicide."

"So you *did* find her," Evangeline said. "You found her in Halifax and had her killed."

"You're delusional," Skylar said, "like your mother. You don't even know that I'm your father."

"I remember—I was young, but I saw it all. The cops need proof—I don't."

She lowered the gun, pulled the trigger and fired, the bullet exploding the stuffing in the arm of the chair under the hand with the cigarette. Skylar jumped to his feet and dropped the cigarette on the floor. The blast reverberated through the room. The strings of the Fazioli vibrated for a few seconds, filling the air with a jarring chord.

There was now finally fear in Skylar's eyes. The cigarette continued to burn into the carpet, producing an acrid smell. Skylar held out his hands in placation. "Look, honey, you wouldn't kill your own father... I've done some bad things I know. I'm a hard driver, an alpha personality—you know, 'work hard, play hard'. You gotta be, in this business.

"But deep down I'm a good guy. You'll see. I can be a real laugh when I want to. It's great to finally meet you again after all these years—I mean that. My own flesh and blood... We can finally spend some quality time together. You can get to know your old dad. And I've got lots of money. Give me a day or so..."

"I don't want your money!" Evangeline shouted. "I want you to pay!" She aimed and fired another bullet between his open legs. It barely missed his crotch and tore another divot out of the chair behind him.

He jumped again. He took a step toward her. "Come on," he said. "Don't fly off the handle. You're a good kid. I can see that just looking at you. You've got your whole life ahead of you. Do you really want things to end this way?"

Skylar took a step closer. Evangeline stepped back and wrapped both hands around the gun, raising it to point at his head, both her hands now shaking.

"Give this up, Evangeline," Jake shouted. "Give it up before it's too late!"

Skylar extended his arms plaintively. "Come on, honey. You're my long-lost daughter—I love you."

As soon as he was close enough, he swung his left arm up under hers. She fired again, but the bullet drove itself into the ceiling.

He grabbed her wrist with one hand, and punched her hard in the stomach with the other. They wrestled for the gun. Jake tracked his weapon left and right searching for an opening, but they were too close together. He couldn't be sure of not hitting Evangeline.

Skylar twisted the gun out of Evangeline's hand and she staggered backward, gasping.

He turned toward Jake and without hesitation, before Jake could react, pointed her gun at him and fired. It was as if a concrete fist had been driven into Jake's stomach.

Evangeline screamed.

Jake dropped his own gun, which bounced toward the windows facing the inlet. He fell to his knees, pressing his hand against the bleeding wound, and fighting against the pain. For a moment Evangeline stood staring at him in disbelief.

Then she lunged at Skylar, her arms raised. Skylar turned to face her. Her body snapped back as he fired a shot into the center of her chest.

"No!" Jake screamed, staggering to his feet. His abdomen, and the carpet where he'd knelt, were soaked in blood.

Evangeline collapsed to the floor.

Skylar shoved the gun in his belt and moved past Jake, heading for the stairs and the front door. As if he'd just remembered something, he stopped and turned back.

"One thing you should know about me," he said, smiling. "I'm a guy who always finishes what he starts."

He reached for the gun in his belt. Jake knew if he didn't act right now he was dead. Calling on some force, some deep instinct for survival he never knew he had, he screamed in pain as he dove at Skylar and knocked him off his feet. Skylar was pushed along the entryway and part way down the stairs. His head bumped against the wall and he dropped his gun, which bounced all the way to the bottom and halfway down the entrance hall.

Momentarily stunned, Skylar shook his head to clear it. He glanced at the gun in the hallway, then his eyes settled on Jake's gun, which lay a few meters away, near the open door to the patio. Jake followed his gaze, and at almost the same moment they both jumped up to grab the weapon.

Jake was closer, but was injured, weak, and bleeding heavily now. He stumbled toward it, as Skylar clambered up the stairs and across the room. Jake suddenly felt light-headed and collapsed, but woke almost immediately, his hand touching the gun. Skylar had caught up, now almost within reach.

Jake found the butt and his blood-smeared hand shook as he tried to lift the weapon. Skylar arrived and stomped his foot down on Jake's fingers. Jake screamed. The gun went off and fell from his grip.

Skylar bent down, but was off balance as he leaned over Jake's body, frantically scrambling for the weapon. Fighting through the pain, Jake drove his shoulder upwards knocking Skylar back on his heels, then crawled forward and grabbed the gun with his good hand. He rose to his knees, but didn't have a chance to aim and fire before Skylar jumped him.

Jake's strength was ebbing with every breath. He dragged himself to his feet, still wrestling with Skylar. Together, they stumbled to the open door and out onto the stone patio. Jake almost blacked out again, but willed himself to remain conscious.

They fought for the gun, staggering to the edge of the patio. Skylar tried to punch him in the face, but Jake was able to twist away and avoid the worst of the blow. Jake tried to set his foot down and found nothing under it.

Glancing down, he realized he was standing with his back to the steps leading down to the pool. Skylar swung again. This time Jake was ready. He stepped aside and the punch hurtled past him, Skylar now off balance. Jake kicked at Skylar's back foot. His attacker staggered forward, stumbling halfway down the stone steps.

Jake turned to face him. The magnificent view of Burrard Inlet was weaving back and forth before his eyes as he swayed, teetering on the top step. He was again on the verge of unconsciousness. His vision was blurred, but he heard Skylar roar, and could make out a shape rushing back up the stairs.

Barely able to stand now, Jake swung the gun toward the amorphous blob of colour moving toward him, and fired. There was a deafening blast as the gun went off.

Skylar grunted, and Jake's vision cleared long enough to see the music producer's body driven back, toppling down the stone steps, stumbling, and finally landing with a splash, face-down in the mansion's swimming pool.

Sirens approached in the distance as Jake staggered back into the living room, leaving a trail of blood. Evangeline was lying where she'd fallen, a deep red stain expanding beneath her. She was moaning and her body was twitching. He knelt down beside her.

She opened her eyes and looked up at him. "Jake…"

He took her hand, collapsed and knew no more.

XLIII

LATER

Rule #26: Being safe on the job is something that should come naturally to a Private Investigator. Safety is an integral part of performing investigations properly
- **Shadow Mac's Comprehensive Guide to Private Investigation**

When Jake opened his eyes, he found himself staring at a white ceiling. A machine was making a steady beeping noise somewhere behind him.

He raised his head to survey the room, and cringed. Was he dreaming? Or in hell. Sitting at the end of the bed, a self-satisfied smirk on his face, was Bert McCluskey.

"Where the hell am I?" Jake croaked.

"You're in a hospital room at Vancouver General, recuperating," McCluskey said, smiling. "You've had a slight accident. In fact, for a while we thought you were a goner."

"Vancouver General?" Jake said.

He tried to sit up, and was met with an excruciating stab of pain in his midsection. He lay back down, but managed to lift his head far enough up to see a large bandage wrapped around his stomach, and a cast on his right hand. He lifted his good hand and felt another bandage wrapped around his head.

"Yeah," McCluskey said, "you're the walking wounded."

"How long have I been here?"

"You've been in and out of consciousness for almost a week. They called me yesterday to say you were finally exhibiting some signs of life, so I rushed over. Detective Harrow's here too. He's off somewhere, getting a coffee or something. Apparently, you lost a lot of blood, but the bullet didn't hit anything important. You're a lucky man..."

"Lucky," Jake said weakly. "Yeah, that's describes it perfectly. I'm lucky."

"Well, you could be dead," McCluskey argued.

"That might be an improvement," Jake said. "Have they got any nurses in this place? Or security? Who let you in here?"

McCluskey got up and pressed the button on a cord beside the bed. A nurse soon arrived. She gave Jake a pain-killer, fluffed up his pillow, and helped him into a more comfortable position.

Minutes later, the doctor walked in.

"Good to see you're finally awake," she said, smiling.

She verified the outputs of the machines, and checked Jake's bandages. "It will take a while," she said, "but you should make a full recovery. The bullet—"

"Didn't hit anything important," Jake interrupted her. "Yeah, I heard. I'm a lucky guy."

"Get some rest," the doctor said.

McCluskey moved up and put a hand on Jake's shoulder.

Jake closed his eyes as the horrific images came flooding back: Skylar face down in the swimming pool, Mona's lifeless eyes, Evangeline's body twitching in a pool of blood...

Suddenly, he felt light-headed. He lay back and whispered: "Did it all really happen?"

"I'm afraid so," McCluskey said, patting his shoulder.

The sensation passed, and Jake opened his eyes. "Evangeline?"

McCluskey shook his head slowly. "Sorry, kid—sorry for everything—I really am."

Jake clamped his eyes shut again as the image of Evangeline's last moments returned. It was as if a black well was opening up in his life— a well that threatened to swallow him.

"And Skylar?"

"Dead as a proverbial doornail," McCluskey said. "But I don't think you've got a problem on that score."

The image returned of Jake's finger pulling the trigger, and of Skylar's body driven backwards and down the steps to the pool. All the time he'd spent in the army and he'd never killed anyone. Now, back at his safe, quiet home... A wave of nausea rippled through his body.

"Mr. Sommers," Harrow said cheerfully, arriving with a coffee as McCluskey had claimed. "Looks like you survived—for a while there we were doubtful."

The detective sat in a nearby chair. "We'll want to interview you, but right now, just focus on getting better. While you were out of commission, we've continued our investigation. Are you up to hearing about it?"

"I figured out most of it," Jake said, "but maybe you could fill in the blanks."

Harrow took a sip of coffee. "We got the results back of the reopening of the case of Eleanor Rumford's death. Ironically, it looks like Skylar had nothing to do with it. Somehow he figured out that Elinor had witnessed the murder, but it took a while to find her, and when he finally did she was so far gone I guess he decided she was harmless.

"Halifax police finally caught the actual murderer and he eventually confessed—some low-life she'd surprised while he was trying to rob her place."

"So Evangeline's—Betty's whole motivation for all this was based on a delusion."

Jake shook his head. Even the most basic premise of this story was a lie.

Harrow nodded. "But the case led to us to investigate Eleanor's relationship with Skylar, and a forensic team managed to dredge up Betty's communication with Jeanette Mallory. That opened the floodgates. A truckload of stuff has been coming out about Skylar — including the deaths of Larry Karlsen and Jeanette Mallory.

"From what we've been able to piece together, when Betty found Jeanette on the DNA site, she introduced herself as her half-sister and asked if she knew who their father was. She also relayed her mother's warnings about him.

"Forensics also dug into Skylar's computer and found emails from Jeanette. After their fight, Bailey finally revealed that Skylar was her father. Putting that together with Betty's warning and Bailey's recollection of Karlsen's murder, she must have guessed the truth: that Skylar murdered Karlsen and pinned it on his stoned-out band-mate.

"She had no loyalty to Skylar, and considered Bailey her 'real' father. She confronted Skylar with her theory. That was her big mistake. Either Skylar did her himself or hired somebody to do it for him. He arranged to have all her social media accounts removed in case they contained anything incriminating."

Harrow smiled. "And we've got a small-time gangster in custody who confessed he was hired by Skylar to take out both of you."

Jake closed his eyes. It all seemed like a dream—or more properly, a nightmare. Another wave of nausea and fatigue seemed to wash over him.

"Thanks," he said to Harrow. "Thanks for coming. I'll be happy to answer your questions, but if it's okay, I think I'd like to be alone right now."

When Harrow, McCluskey, and the doctor were all gone, Jake lay back and again closed his eyes. His hands started to shake as the images again came flooding back. He fought to drive them away with extreme prejudice, but they continued, cycling through his thoughts like a never-ending line of swirling tornadoes. How could he go on like this?

He reached for the call button. The nurse came back and he asked for another sedative.

XLIV

A NEW DAY

Rule #1: How do you know if you're cut out to be a private detective? You have boundless curiosity. You are innovative and resourceful, and pay attention to detail. You can think out of the box and put together a case given a limited number of clues.

- Shadow Mac's Comprehensive Guide to Private Investigation

Five months had passed since the events at Tommy Skylar's. It was now late summer. The air was still warm, but the sun was beginning to hang lower in the sky, and the days were getting shorter. The last cruise ship of the season was about to sail away, and though the tourists still crowded the streets of Victoria, the numbers were beginning to fade.

There had been a major investigation into Evangeline's and Skylar's deaths, and the trail of death Skylar had left behind him over the years, but in the end, Jake had come out completely in the clear.

It had taken two months for his broken hand to heal, and another month of physio, which was still ongoing, to restore it to full operation. He'd been terrified that the break would affect, or even end, his musical career, but his playing chops were returning quickly.

Tonight, there was a healthy crowd at the Salty Dog, and they clapped loudly and shouted their approval as Jake finished his last set and stood up from the piano. He grabbed the ginger-ale resting on top and made his way, still limping slightly, to the bar. His new act was billed as 'Jake's Old-time Swing Party', and was actually developing a following.

"Looks like a little bit of you goes a long way," Max said to him, smiling. The manager clapped him on the shoulder. "The crowd loved it. And I gotta say, you sound better than ever. I guess the bullet didn't hit anything important."

"*Is* there actually anything that isn't important?" Jake answered him. "Anyway, I guess if you want to be an artist, you've got to suffer."

After the gig, Jake strolled back to the Wharf and to the *Rose*, and as always, stopped for a moment and marveled at the sight of his beautiful home. He had to admit he missed the buzz he used to get from alcohol, but the waking up the next day and feeling good part probably made quitting worthwhile.

His replacement was still the main attraction at the Salty Dog, but Jake had made an arrangement with Max to play one night a week, and play mainly Stride and the old-time music he loved. It was working out perfectly.

He couldn't spare the time for more gigs anyway—after all, he now had other work to do.

The next morning, when Jake opened his eyes, he felt full of life, with a renewed strength and energy. He jumped out of bed and climbed down the ladder from his loft.

A shaft of morning sunlight lit up the stained-glass ornament hanging by the window, bathing the interior with a rainbow of colour. He smiled as he surveyed the *Rose's* living space. It looked lived-in, but was clean and tidy, like he remembered from when he was a kid. He'd added a new set of shelving to hold items he'd previously had trouble finding a place for, and a small bookshelf beside his keyboard to hold his sheet music.

The picture of Fats Waller, which had originally been a page ripped out of a magazine, was now trimmed and framed, and retained its place of honour on the wall.

Satisfied with the results of all his work over the past few months, Jake stood by the door, facing the portrait of his great-aunt Deirdre. He placed his hands in prayer position, and bowed his head deferentially.

"Namaste, Auntie," he said. "And please forgive me for not taking better care of her."

He made himself a cup of coffee, and carried it out onto the aft deck. The *Honeysuckle Rose* had never looked better. He'd repaired the two bullet-holes in the roof, scraped and sanded the outer walls of the cabin and given them a fresh coat of stain. He'd had the deck sanded and refinished, and re-potted most of the plants. He'd kept all the knick-knacks, but cleaned them up and placed them properly.

He smiled and gazed up at the morning sky. It was a gorgeous, sunny autumn day. The leaves on the trees were turning yellow and red, and spiraling into the sky in the stiffening wind. On the Wharf, the late-season tourists were thick already, threading through the restaurants and along the docks, booking whale-watching trips, and crowding the mini-ferries to the Songhees.

A bevy of them were shouting, pointing, and rushing toward the end of the dock. Jake turned to find Gordon lying there contentedly in a patch of morning sun. The giant sea lion heard the commotion, lifted his head, and noticed the hoard approaching. He quickly slid off the dock into the water and disappeared. Jake stood drinking his coffee and admiring it all, giving thanks for getting a second chance in life.

His chest tightened as he pictured Evangeline, standing there in her red dress, smiling, or laying back on *Spinner* with the sun lighting up her face and the wind blowing through her hair as the vessel heeled in the wind.

Sadly, still loaded down with memories, he headed back inside, poured himself another cup of coffee, and sat in his nook. Why had he made the decision he had, after all the horror and pain of the past few months? Was it the excitement? The intrigue? The mystery? The pursuit of truth? Even Jake didn't know.

He'd only taken a single sip of coffee when there was knock on his front door.

He rose, stepped up, and opened it. A middle-aged woman with grey-streaked hair, wearing a business suit, was leaning over him.

"Mr. Sommers?" she asked.

"That's me," he answered, smiling at her. "Come on down."

He took her hand as she stepped down into his living space.

"I saw your ad on social media," she said, "the one saying you're a private detective. I'd like to hire you for some urgent work."

Jake swept a hand toward the Private Investigator's license now hanging framed on the wall beside them.

"Yes," he answered, "The ad is correct—I am a licensed PI. Now, how can I help you?"

AUTHOR REQUEST

My Kingdom for a Review!

Thank you for reading *The Houseboat Detective*! I hope you enjoyed it.

I know there are millions of books out there for you to choose from, and I'm honoured that you chose mine. It's a challenge for authors like myself to reach new readers, and this is where you can help.

If you enjoyed reading this book and think it would be of interest to other readers, please write a customer review on Amazon.com at: *http://www.amazon.com/dp/B0DQQ25M6Z*. A few words are all that's required. Positive reviews are the best way to attract new readers, and I'm grateful for each and every one I receive.

ABOUT THE AUTHOR

Jay Allan Storey has traveled the world, passing through many places in the news today, including Iraq, Iran, Afghanistan, and the Swat valley in Pakistan. He has worked at an amazing variety of jobs, from cab driver to land surveyor to accordion salesman to software developer.

Jay is the author of eight novels: **THE ARX**, the **BLACK HEART** series, **ELDORADO**, the **VITA AETERNA** series, and **THE HOUSEBOAT DETECTIVE**. He's also the author of a novella, **TUCKER VS. THE APOCALYPSE**, a number of short stories, and several screenplays. A new novel is currently in the works.

His stories always skirt close to the edge of believability (but hopefully never cross over). He is attracted to characters who are able to break out of their stereotypes and transform themselves.

He loves both reading and writing, both listening to and playing music, and working with animals. He's crazy for any activity relating to the water, including swimming, surfing, wind-surfing, sailing, snorkeling, and scuba diving.

Jay is married and lives in Vancouver, BC, Canada.

Contact Jay at:
    Website: *www.jayallanstorey.com*
    Email: *jayallanstorey@shaw.ca*
    Sign up for Jay Allan Storey's mailing list at:
www.eepurl.com/MH-Sv

THE ARX

Ex-Homicide Detective *Frank Langer* is a broken man - but he's all that stands in the way of a deadly conspiracy.

Since a mental breakdown put him on medical leave from the squad he was once hand-picked to lead, Frank spends his days drinking and chain-smoking, and his nights waking up screaming from a horrific recurring nightmare.

Until one day, by chance, he stumbles on a monstrous plot to kidnap children.

When the mother of one of the missing children commits suicide, Frank is driven to see justice done. But when he shows up at the squad with the wild story, his former colleagues pat him on the back and tell him to go home. Instead, he stamps down his demons and, together with the dead woman's sister Rebecca, plunges into the case.

One heart-pounding step ahead of the conspirators, he races to fit together the pieces of an intricate puzzle. When he finally unravels the mystery, the answer is more deadly than he ever imagined.

But can he stay alive long enough to find someone to buy his story?

What Readers Say About *The Arx*:

★★★★★ 'One of the best books I've read this year.'

★★★★★ 'Recommend it from beginning to end.'

★★★★★ 'Love this book. Kept me reading & wondering where it was all going.'

★★★★★ 'One of those "can't put it down" novels we hear others talk about but rarely find ourselves.'

★★★★★ 'The Arx by Jay Allan Storey is a TOP READ.'

THE BLACK HEART OF THE STATION
The BLACK HEART Series

How did we get here? Where are we going? Those are the questions *Josh Driscoll*, a teenager living in *The Station*, a city built one kilometer beneath the surface of a frozen, lifeless earth, is determined to answer. Josh comes to believe that the *Black Heart*, a computer complex buried in a sector critically damaged in a massive asteroid strike centuries ago, holds the answers to all his questions, and is vital to their future survival.

What Readers Say About *The Black Heart of the Station*:

★★★★★ 'It's a long time since I've stayed up until 2 o'clock in the morning to finish a book, but I honestly couldn't put it down.'

★★★★★ 'loved all of Storey's books so far, but this is definitely my favorite.'

★★★★★ 'This tops my favorite's list in this genre.'

★★★★★ 'I rarely give 5 Star rating but this book and author demanded it.'

★★★★★ 'One of the best I have read in a long time.'

VITA AETERNA
The VITA AETERNA Series

With the fate of the world in the balance, one outlier could tip the scales towards salvation or disaster.

Alex Barret lives in 'the Quarters', a set of broken-down slums surrounding a glittering walled-off city called the First Circle. Like all kids his age, on his sixteenth birthday Alex is scheduled for Appraisal, an unpredictable medical procedure with the potential to extend his lifespan. In a world where everything else costs, for some reason Appraisal is free.

But no Appraisal outcome he's ever heard of has prepared him for his own experience - abducted, imprisoned, and subjected to brutal medical experiments in a high-tech lab. He finally escapes and goes on the run, a heartbeat ahead of a ruthless army led by the most powerful man in the world. When he finally pieces together the clues behind his kidnapping, he uncovers a treacherous plot that only he can derail.

But to succeed, he must penetrate the First Circle, the forbidden abode of the ruling class.

What Readers Say About Vita Aeterna:

★★★★★ 'I absolutely loved this book.'
★★★★★ 'Never read anything quite like this, read it!'
★★★★★ 'One you have to read!'
★★★★★ 'Awesome plot. Unique! Thank you for writing it.'
★★★★★ 'An excellent dystopian novel with plenty of action.'
★★★★★ 'A must read for anyone who loves a good, original adventure/thriller!'

ELDORADO

Lost and alone in the desolate wasteland that was once Suburbia.

In an energy-starved future, *Richard Hampton's* world is blown apart when his younger brother Danny disappears and the police are too busy trying to keep a lid on a hungry, overcrowded city to search for him.

Richard has to make the transformation from bookish nerd to street-smart warrior to survive when he jumps the 'Food Train' for the disintegrating suburbs in a desperate search for Danny and his dog, Zonk.

Branded a criminal by a community of outcasts and condemned to death, Richard is rescued by streetwise Carrie, who joins in his search. As they trek across the remnants of the suburbia, facing criminal gangs, renegade militias, and the hardships of the road, their friendship evolves into something more.

The trail finally unwinds at a deserted complex in the remotest corner of the sprawling suburbs.

The incredible secret they uncover there will alter their lives and their world forever.

What Readers Say About *Eldorado*:

★★★★★ 'Amazing read of an amazing futuristic journey.'

★★★★★ 'An engaging and thrilling adventure.'

★★★★★ 'On the edge of my seat throughout the whole thing.'

★★★★★ 'I was hooked right from the get go.'

★★★★★ 'Can't wait for a sequel. Very believable, couldn't put it down.'

TUCKER VS. THE APOCALYPSE

A Good Dog Lost in a Bad World

Household pet dog **Tucker** is thrust into an apocalyptic world when not only his own 'master', but all of humanity, are stricken with a deadly plague. The disease is fatal in almost one hundred percent of cases, but affects only humans, leaving empty cities and towns that are quickly being repopulated with domestic animals and wildlife.

Tucker eventually connects with a group of other dogs, all former pets. Deprived of their human caretakers, and guided by the mysterious *Web of Life*, Tucker and his 'pack' must learn to fend for themselves, confronting cold and blinding snow, blistering heat, the threat of starvation, ferocious predators, and the violent remnants of humanity as they search for a new home.

What Readers Say About Tucker vs. the Apocalypse:

★★★★★ 'This was a timely beautiful gift. I read it all in one day ...it was lovely ...encouraging...beautiful. And it brought peace to my Spirit.

Thank you to the Author.'

★★★★★ 'Dogs? Apocalyptic story? That caught me right away, and wasn't disappointing.'

★★★★★ 'action, romance, sadness, camaraderie, great danger, success, failure. Everything you want in a book.'

★★★★★ 'I loved this book. Couldn't put it down. If you are an animal lover like me, this book is for you

www.ingramcontent.com/pod-product-compliance
Lightning Source LLC
Chambersburg PA
CBHW060407180626
46817CB00007B/2539